Praise for
FLOOD

"*Flood* is my favorite kind of novel—characters you care deeply about from the moment you meet them in a story of class, family, and love that is both timeless and of the moment. With a feminist twist, Melissa Scholes Young has given us a sparkling addition to literary works inspired by Mark Twain—a modern classic to be read again and again."

Andrea Jarrell, author of I'm the One Who Got Away

"Scholes Young's pursuit [in *Flood*] is classic and eternal: 'the human heart in conflict with itself,' in William Faulkner's mighty phrase. In Scholes Young's hands, the conflict is waged with fierce consummate compassion and, finally, apocalyptic and enigmatic grace."

—Ron Powers, Pulitzer Prize winning author of White Town Drowsing: Journeys to Hannibal, Dangerous Water: A Biography of the Boy Who Became Mark Twain, and Mark Twain: A Life

"Filled with pithy dialogue and cultural references, Young's writing ties Laura's journey of self-discovery squarely to Hannibal and its famous young troublemakers. As Laura reckons with her past, Young reckons with Twain's influence on the region. This debut is a wonderful story of home, hope, and the ties that bind us to family."

—Publishers Weekly

"Young will leave readers thinking about their own flood of memories in this debut novel."

Library Journal

"Hannibal, Missouri, o not only the setting for Mark Twain's hometown of Laura Brooks, who grew a [nurse] in Florida. But now Laura is iver is rising."

—Kirkus

"T. S. Eliot said of Mark Twain's writing of *Huckleberry Finn* that the book would give readers what each reader was capable of taking from it, and that Twain may have written a much better book than he realized. Eliot was not excusing Mark Twain: What Eliot wrote is what genuine wisdom looks like on the printed page. The same could be said of Melissa Young and *Flood*...*Flood* reflects America's rural-urban divide, racism, empty-headed faith, willful ignorance, wheel-spinning, and marveling at distracting fireworks instead of the vast universe looming behind them. It's more than a hillbilly elegy."

—Kevin Mac Donnell, Mark Twain Forum

"Melissa Scholes Young is immensely talented. Her eye is clear and her powers are on high. I read *Flood* with admiration and growing excitement. I so strongly recommend her. Read her, now!"

—Luis Alberto Urrea, author of
Into the Beautiful North and
The Water Museum

"Melissa Scholes Young's first novel delivers two unforgettable characters: the exhausted but not down-for-the-count Laura Brooks running back to her hometown of Hannibal, Missouri, and the Mississippi River—both looking to climb out of their confines and willing to become displaced in the process. Fans of Mark Twain's beloved work will recognize *Flood*'s conflicted characters and endearing contradictions. Like Twain, Laura Brooks tells the truth, mainly."

—Dr. Cindy Lovell, executive director, Mark Twain House & Museum

"*Flood* is a beautifully written novel that explores perennial questions of identity and belonging. I say 'perennial' not because the novel beats a well-worth path but because these questions are existential and urgent. Scholes Young is a thoughtful realist who creates a rich fictive dream without sacrificing character and voice. In *Flood*, she avoids the pitfalls of rural caricature by refusing the hyperbolic dialect and false cadences common in contemporary fiction that privileges place. Her characters come to life through patient accumulation, not grotesque gesture. The prose is sharp, full of momentum, and yet restrained. There is no false nostalgia here, only complexity."

—Stephanie Grant, author of
The Passion of Alice and *Map of Ireland*

"Melissa Scholes Young knows how to tell a story, one that captivates and charms. She also knows the land and the heart's attachment to it. *Flood* is a novel about coming home, which in this case is Hannibal, Missouri, on the banks of the Mississippi River, the land of Mark Twain and his unforgettable characters, Tom Sawyer and Huck Finn. This novel's take on the question of whether to 'light out for the territory' is a wonderful read, one that will make you think about what it means to call a place home."

—Lee Martin, author of *The Bright Forever*
and *Late One Night*

"Melissa Scholes Young's debut novel, *Flood*, bubbles up from the home ground of Mark Twain. Those storied banks of the Mississippi crest anew with all the humor and hunger of Hannibal's current haves and have-nots—and this time it's women in the leading roles, YAY! *Flood*'s pages will swell and rush over you with their deep yearnings. This is fertile ground indeed, and Scholes Young is brimming with Twain's loam and legacy."

—Marc Nieson, author of *Schoolhouse:*
Lessons on Love and Landscape

"*Flood* is character-driven fiction that appeals on both a gut and an emotional level. Melissa Scholes Young tackles difficult situations and never veers into cliché. Her endings are sublime. And her characters are as believable as anybody's friends and neighbors. I marvel at her poetic language, her accumulation of details, and her uncanny ability to key on exactly what it is that makes a story. She has admirable range and creates real people with depth, plus plot points that stick in the heart and mind."

—Richard Peabody, author of *The Richard Peabody Reader*,
editor and publisher of *Gargoyle Magazine* and Paycock Press

"A dazzling work as wide and turbulent as the Mississippi itself. *Flood* delivers a seductive sense of belonging and intimacy before ultimately breaking your heart. Young takes on big themes of identity, family, and the idea of home with a riveting mix of honesty and enchantment."

—Aline Ohanesian, author of *Orhan's Inheritance*

"Melissa Scholes Young's charming, energetic debut brings to life a town steeped in and hindered by its own rich history. Huck Finn and Becky Thatcher are still alive and well in modern-day Hannibal, Missouri, and the rising Mississippi River provides the mercurial backdrop for a young woman's quest to determine whether home is ultimately where she belongs."

—Susan Coll, author of *The Stager*

"*Flood* is an absolute delight. Melissa Sholes Young captures a time, place, and town with authenticity, humor, and an obvious love for her characters. A great debut by a wonderful new voice!"

—Rebecca Barry, bestselling author of *Later, at the Bar*

"*Flood* is a story of home and place, but it's also a story of class and difference, and at the same time it's a story of love: familial love, the love between friends, romantic love, and even the love of literature itself. That Melissa Scholes Young is able to so deftly weave these together—in evocative sentences and heartbreaking scenes—is testament to her remarkable ability."

—Rumaan Alam, author of *Rich and Pretty* and *That Kind of Mother*

"The Twain thread of the story is unique. The author has attempted an interesting feat, creating characters reminiscent of Twain's work, and even people drawn from Samuel Clemens's real life. One technique Young uses with great success is a series of chapters that purport to be excerpts from a book written by one of Laura's teachers, Ms. Bechtold. These sections weave in and out of Laura's story, providing historical information about Clemens and Hannibal, and dropping clues for astute readers."

—*Washington Independent Review of Books*

FLOOD

A Novel

MELISSA SCHOLES
YOUNG

CENTER
STREET

New York Nashville

This book is a work of fiction. Names, characters, places, and incidents are the product of the author's imagination or are used fictitiously. Any resemblance to actual events, locales, or persons, living or dead, is coincidental.

Copyright © 2017 by Melissa Scholes Young

Cover design by Jody Waldrup. Cover copyright © 2017 by Hachette Book Group, Inc.

Hachette Book Group supports the right to free expression and the value of copyright. The purpose of copyright is to encourage writers and artists to produce the creative works that enrich our culture.

The scanning, uploading, and distribution of this book without permission is a theft of the author's intellectual property. If you would like permission to use material from the book (other than for review purposes), please contact permissions@hbgusa.com. Thank you for your support of the author's rights.

Center Street
Hachette Book Group
1290 Avenue of the Americas, New York, NY 10104
centerstreet.com
twitter.com/centerstreet

First published in hardcover by Center Street in June 2017
First Trade Paperback Edition: May 2018

Center Street is a division of Hachette Book Group, Inc. The Center Street name and logo are trademarks of Hachette Book Group, Inc.

The publisher is not responsible for websites (or their content) that are not owned by the publisher.

The Hachette Speakers Bureau provides a wide range of authors for speaking events. To find out more, go to www.HachetteSpeakersBureau.com or call (866) 376-6591.

An excerpt from "Cardiff Hill" was originally published as "Holding Hands" in *Sliver of Stone Magazine*, 2012.

Library of Congress Cataloging-in-Publication Data has been applied for.

ISBNs: 978-1-4789-7077-4 (trade paperback), 978-1-4789-7076-7 (ebook)

Printed in the United States of America

LSC-C

10 9 8 7 6 5 4 3 2 1

For my parents,
who always let me roam
and welcomed me home

FLOOD

"You know, they straightened out the Mississippi River in places, to make room for houses and livable acreage. Occasionally the river floods these places. 'Floods' is the word they use, but in fact it is not flooding; it is remembering. Remembering where it used to be. All water has a perfect memory and is forever trying to get back to where it was."

—Toni Morrison

"When a man goes back to look at the house of his childhood, it has always shrunk: there is no instance of such a house being as big as the picture in memory and imagination call for. Shrunk how? Why, to its correct dimensions: the house hasn't altered; this is the first time it has been in focus."

—Mark Twain

CHAPTER ONE

Running Backward

NOTHING COULD HOLD back the Mississippi that summer. Our flood stage was sixteen feet and when the river crested at thirty, folks panicked with good reason.

Jackson's Island, which jutted out of the river as an overgrown sandbar, was completely submerged. The island, immortalized by Mark Twain, wasn't very big to begin with, though Huckleberry Finn and Jim found it to be plenty. The annual spring rains usually caused minor flooding, but the trees on the island reached up from the river like bushes floating on the muddy surface.

Water was what people talked about, worried over, and watched. Upstream and downstream, levees busted by force and by sabotage. Barges were stuck for months and the trains stopped running.

On land, we prayed to crumbling rock and gravel walls for protection and piled up more layers of sandbags to push back the pressure. If a levee broke on one side, there was temporary relief on the other. Some farmers walked their lines with shot-guns, threatening anyone who came near their sandbags.

The fight was fair at first. Until it wasn't. Until it came to sacrificing others to save yourself. Until those with power didn't want to protect those without. Maybe that's why I left. But by then, the Mississippi had taken more than six hundred miles and much of our lives in its wake. Ten years ago, even as I was falling for Sammy on that steamy July night parked at Lover's Leap, one of my feet was firmly planted on the ground, even as I hiked the other to welcome him.

The river's to blame. When you grow up on the banks in Hannibal, Missouri, you need an escape route. You never know when the water is going to rise and you have to run.

MAMA THINKS I'M HOME AGAIN for my ten-year high school reunion. I don't tell her much more when I park my Honda in the grass, scattering chickens, and come through the door about ten o'clock. I drove twenty-two hours straight from Jacksonville, Florida, alternating between the Dixie Chicks' first album and Shania Twain's latest, skipping over sad songs. My boots make my feet ache, but I keep them on for courage.

The house smells like Jiffy Pop and tomato soup: Mama's favorite. The tang and salt make my skin itch. I scratch at the rising bumps on my forearms, but there is no relief, only more allergy to this part of me.

Mama is dozing in her recliner, waiting for the late news to announce the flood stages and her Lotto numbers. When you can see the Mississippi out your windows, flood stages are your religion. And when you can't imagine how to dig yourself out of your hole, you put your faith in the Powerball.

On the screen, a retrospect from that summer shows houses flooded past their roofs, land stripped of crops, and schools ruined. *"The National Weather Service claims the Great Flood of Nineteen Ninety-Three was extraordinary. It's considered the most costly and devastating flood in modern U.S. history. The many record river levels, people displaced, crop and property damage, and its length exceeded all previous U.S. floods."* The voice is cheerful, as if it's a sunny weather forecast rather than the Mississippi's destruction.

The bumps on my arms swell to hives. I drag my bags in from the car, and the weight of them feels useful. If I just keep moving, I won't have to think. Just like Mama, I always kept the news on in the background of my apartment in Florida, just for the noise, to feel like I had people around me when I didn't.

As I lug in the last suitcase, a threadbare maroon one Aunt Betty bought me for my high school graduation, the zipper busts and a pathetic pile of dirty socks spills out. Mama opens her eyes, and we both stare at the socks. Then she sighs like this is exactly the kind of mess she expects from me. "Be careful with my girls out there, Laura," she says instead of hello. "Y'all haven't been properly introduced yet."

"Girls?"

"My girls. The chickens."

"Those yours?"

"Yep. Oh, they're sweet girls. Fresh eggs every morning. You'll see."

I nod at the prospect and go to my room. It's the second one on the left from the kitchen, down our trailer's narrow hall.

My veins buzz from too much coffee. Black paint chips flake off as I open and close dresser drawers and toss in my stuff. A pale pink peeks through the laminate. My best friend, Rose, and I painted the walls and furniture Charcoal Magic in ninth grade. We thought it sounded sophisticated.

Mama turns up the TV volume and follows me down the hall. "Take your shitkickers off in the house."

I hold up one of my boots to show her the spotless snakeskin. "They're clean."

She shakes her head but doesn't insist. "Looks like a long visit."

"Maybe." The last ten years of my life are these four suit-cases, my shrinking savings account, and the car that barely got me here. It doesn't look like much more than I took when I left. I've given myself until the Fourth of July to decide what's next.

Mama leans against the doorframe while I unpack. The Lotto tickets are tight in her right hand.

"You play the same numbers?" I ask. I know the answer, but I know she wants to tell me, too.

"Always."

"Which ones?"

"You and your brother's birthdays. Always."

"They lucky?"

Mama huffs. "Not yet." She chews the nicotine gum I sent her, like a cow working its cud. Her face is rounder since she quit smoking. Her creamy skin is healthier, and there is a flush to her cheeks. She smooths her purple striped blouse and black jeans to have something to do with her hands besides squeeze the tickets. I've come home unannounced and caught her wearing the clothes I sent, the ones she never thanked me for or acknowledged. Clearly, she didn't hate them.

"Just a few weeks. Maybe a month," I finally say, telling the truth, mainly. "That okay? I've got vacation time comin'. Thought I'd spend it here catchin' up." I slip back into Missouri talk so Mama won't call me out for being uppity. You can reach, Mama always says; just don't look like you're doing it.

"Catchin' up with who?" There it is. Mama's suspicious. She smells trouble. At least there's usually more on Trey, my older brother.

"It'd be nice to see Trey. Aunt Betty, of course. Rose and Bobby."

"And?" She wants me to say Sammy. I don't. Maybe she thinks I'm rooting around for Daddy, too. We haven't heard from him in years, but that never stopped me from scanning crowds and searching the eyes of every ER patient on my shift. Just in case.

"Haven't seen Rose in almost a year," I say, trying to distract her. Mama could mention that I haven't bothered to visit her or Trey or Aunt Betty in almost three years, but she doesn't. Sometimes she's merciful. Usually not, though. I hinted about the reunion on the phone last week, after everything that happened happened, but I didn't tell her directly that I was on my way home. I could hardly believe it myself.

"Rose? I seen her out and about. Her and her boy, Bobby."

"He's a good kid, ain't he?"

"I guess." She watches me unpack. "Rose's gettin' divorced is what I heard. Second time. Same guy."

"I heard that, too. Straight from Rose." I move aside a pile of yearbooks and unpack my underwear. "They both want custody of Bobby."

"Even I wasn't stupid enough to marry your daddy twice." She watches out the window and shakes her head. I hold my breath, hoping she'll keep talking and tell me something about Daddy she's trying to hold in. "I told you Rose was a wild thing. Don't know why you never listened."

"I listened, Mama. Best I could. You know how it is with Rose." I move two fat nursing textbooks from my nightstand. Nothing in this room has changed. I never bothered to take any of it with me, like I always knew I'd be back. Mama hasn't touched it either.

"Rose is saved is what I heard. Found Jesus at that slick new church downtown. You should see it."

"Do I need to?" It's an evangelical Christian getup with a rock band and indoor baptism pool. Rose says they even have a coffee bar with cappuccinos no one will drink. Kids love the bouncy house, too. Bobby apparently adores the place, but I have my doubts.

"Yep. She's got Jesus on the brain. Doesn't slow down none of her runnin'-around ways, though."

"Rose and Bobby came to visit me at the beach last summer. Did I tell you that?" I ask. "Drove all the way down. Bobby'd never seen the ocean." I picture Bobby on his first boogie board ride crashing into the waves and spitting out salt water. Rose and me in our rented beach chairs sipping piña coladas. "They just wanted to get out of town for a while. Florida's nice."

Mama fluffs a flattened pillow. Shreds of cotton stuffing

spill out. She pokes them back in and props the limp pillow up on its side. "Don't know why folks think they gotta leave. I've stayed. I'm just fine, ain't I?" The pillow tilts over again and she ignores it. "This place has always been good enough. For some of us, anyway."

I sink my weight into the twin bed, closer to her. She tucks in the quilt Aunt Betty made for my thirteenth birthday. Next to the bed on my nightstand are framed pictures covered in dust: Sammy and Rose and me at graduation, us in swimsuits posing before we dove into the muddy Mississippi, us laid out on Aunt Betty's quilt watching the fireworks. My favorite is the one where we'd parked Sammy's daddy's bass boat on Jackson's Island and grilled hot dogs and s'mores with Rose and Josh. Rose had finally lost her baby weight. She was awful proud of herself in that red, white, and blue bikini. There's also a tiny framed picture Sammy's mom gave me of him the year he won Tom Sawyer. He wore a straw hat with red suspenders and held a fishing pole, embracing his new town celebrity. Bobby's baby picture peeks out of the corner of a photo of me and Daddy— the only one I have.

Out the window facing the road, a motorcycle kicks up dirt and speeds off. I wonder if it's Trey. I didn't even let him know I was coming. I hope he's clean, but drugs are too easy to come by in a town with nothing else to do. If it's Trey on the bike, I can't see him; the glass is cloudy and needs to be scrubbed.

"I don't know why you never visited, Mama," I say. "I think you'd of been proud of me." I missed her more than I expected, even her complaining. She sighs again but doesn't answer, so I open the dirty window to let in some fresh air. A parade of dead flies rests belly-up on the sill, their legs reaching toward freedom.

"You know I had to work. You know I can't just get time off. Your brother always needs somethin'. It ain't easy keepin' him on the straight and narrow. Besides, you seemed just fine without us." She studies a picture on my bulletin board. It's the one of me in a tutu with Trey making bunny ears over my head. Mama says I wore that same hot pink tutu for almost a year, pulling it on over my jeans every morning. Aunt Betty sewed it for my fourth birthday. It had three scratchy tulle layers, but the silk band on my belly was soft. I stuck my fingers in the waistline and stroked it for comfort. The band turned dingy and brown from rubbing. I loved that tutu until Daddy ruined it. He wasn't home much, and when he was, Mama yelled at him about money. Sometimes he brought me a pack of Hubba Bubba and remembered that I liked the grape kind. On Saturdays I watched cartoons until my eyes burned, but one morning I found Daddy in front of the TV. The night before he and Mama had had a screaming match in the front yard and he'd left in a fit. But here he was flipping through the channels and sipping iced tea. A bottle of whiskey was jammed between his knees. I stared at the weatherman on the screen, wanting to watch Scooby Doo but not wanting to make a sound. He filled most of Mama's chair. His T-shirt was crumpled in a ball on the floor. His arms were brown branches against his fish-belly white stomach, and he had freckles, like me. "You like to fish?" he asked, stubbing out his cigarette and pulling on his shirt. "Get your boots. You can help with the traps."

The walk to the river was only a few blocks; he told me to

hurry up. I jumped over busted trash bags and dog poop. I ran through an empty lot, tripped on a tree root, and scraped my knee. He didn't stop. When we reached the riverbank, I grabbed the rope to the trap and pulled hard, but it didn't budge. Then he leaned over me, lacing his arms with mine, and we pulled together. The metal cage skidded along the rocks. Leaves and sludge from the mud at the bottom of the Mississippi camouflaged it.

The first trap was empty. Daddy baited it with a can of old cat food he'd poked holes in, and he weighted the trap down with a big rock. Then he tossed the cage back into the water. I pinched my nose to keep out the rotten tuna.

The second trap was heavier. "Hot damn!" he said. "I'm eatin' fish tonight." I wondered if he'd let me have a bite. When Mama cooked fish, she coated it in milky eggs and flour and fried it in a sizzling pan of oil. She made hush puppies and Trey and I dipped them in catsup. I hadn't had any breakfast that morning; my mouth watered against my tongue.

Daddy reached in the trap and pulled out a catfish the length of his arm. The fish jerked its tail around, splashing, and Daddy's T-shirt turned dark and stuck to his skin. "You wanta touch it?" he asked. The long whiskers shot out like tentacles. It smiled in a mean way. "Come on. It won't hurt. Just don't touch those or they'll sting ya."

I inched closer and strained my neck to look down its throat. His thumb was jammed in the bottom of the fish's mouth. The catfish was oily and silver with small black polka dots. Its whiskers teased the air. I reached out my hand to poke a greasy eyeball. Just as my finger met slime, Daddy tossed the fish on my tutu. I screamed, my hands flopping aimlessly. The fish fell to the dirt and flailed until its body was coated in dust and gravel. Its breathing slowed to a gasp. Daddy laughed so hard he choked. I stomped off, clutching my dirty tutu, and ran home without him.

"You smell nasty like river rot," Mama complained, tucking her nose in her own pit to keep from smelling me. She made me strip off my tutu and stuff it in the trash. When I reached down to rub the silk band, I found the worn-out elastic of my jeans instead, and I hated Daddy even more.

Mama traces her finger down the tutu picture and turns away.

I search around in my suitcase for my toothbrush. "I can stay, right?"

"Looks a little late to be askin'."

Then she shuffles down the hall trailing her hand on the flimsy wall, flips off the lights, and shuts her bedroom door for the night.

I'M HOME WITH MAMA TEN hours before I really get her going. Seven of those hours were sleeping. It's a new record. I'd only asked if the towels in the bathroom were clean. They smelled a little musty to me. "My towels are fine, Laura!" she yelled. "Things are just fine. We don't all need fixin', ya know." She dropped the skillet into the metal sink and I knew I'd lost my chance for her cheesy jalapeño scrambled eggs.

I wipe the fog off the bathroom mirror, and the deep creases on my pale forehead make me look older than twenty-eight.

Small lines creep from my hazel eyes. Sammy always saw specks of brown in them, too. He called them my river water. "You can't get rid of us," he told me, "no matter how far you run." My hair hangs in dry layers from the perm I've been growing out. I pull it back and think about cutting it all off, about starting over again. My face is puffy with the extra twenty pounds that lump around my bra and belly. Mama doesn't know yet that it's me that needs fixing. I didn't even know I wanted the baby until I found out it was growing inside me. I was three weeks late. I didn't tell anyone. Not Mama or Rose or Aunt Betty or the married doctor who was the daddy. I waited three weeks to be sure. By the time the pregnancy test was positive, I'd moved from panic to hope. I'd figured out a plan to do it on my own, to be someone's mama. Until the bleeding began. Until it all slipped away. I was hollow in a way that wasn't possible but was. I toss Mama's towels in with my dirty laundry and hang up fresh ones.

After my shower, I sit on the front porch and watch Mama's girls peck at the grass where she's spread their grain. "The big black one is Pamela," she tells me. "The three red ones are Copper, Scarlet, and Ruby. And the little brown one is Sugar." She's fenced off a patch of side yard with a small doghouse for nesting. Mama stands inside their pen with a basket of fresh eggs. She couldn't be prouder if she'd laid them herself.

Every morning, after two cups of Folgers decaf, she walks the tiny garden of hydrangeas and peace lilies, picking out dead leaves and misting the plants with a squirt bottle. At the base of the trailer's steps is a rolled-out ten-by-ten section of Astroturf surrounded by a white picket fence. A black rubber mat declares it a HOME SWEET HOME. Two red metal chairs sit beside the planters and an American flag sticks out of a bucket of sand. Every few weeks, Mama uproots and transplants her hostas in search of the perfect shade.

"You heard from anyone yet?" she says instead of good morning, joining me on the porch. I kick at the chain-link she's used to secure the chairs to each other. Mama worries that everything beyond the city limits is more dangerous than the petty crime in our neighborhood. The Jacobses' house on the corner was robbed three times last year. Their guns were taken, too. And if you leave your car unlocked, Trey says, your change tray is empty by morning, even the pennies. It could be him stealing it, though. "You got a plan?" she asks.

"I left a message for Rose," I lie, not ready to face her just yet. She'll know immediately what a mess I am. "Don't you want to know about Florida? About my job?" I'm pathetic for pushing, for wanting her approval so much. Ten years is a long time, but it's not long enough for Mama to forgive me for leaving in the first place. She always thought my future with Sammy looked better than my solo one.

"Seemed like you did fine. You didn't come back much anyway. Until now." A brown paper bag filled with corn sits between her legs. Another bag is empty beside it, waiting to catch the husks. She hands me an ear. "Make yourself useful. Aunt Betty brought these yesterday. Lord, that woman knows how to grow corn."

"She always told me the trick was to plant enough for the deer, too. At least you hear from her. Every time I call she tells me to just come home if I want to talk." That makes Mama grin. Her ornery sister always has. Loving Aunt Betty and worrying about Trey may be the only things Mama and I agree on.

"You could of called us more, ya know," Mama says, picking at the pale silk threads.

"I sent postcards. From Disney, remember? Rose and me took Bobby there. And you know I called at least once a month, even if you didn't call me back." I shuck her two to one, ripping off the outside green shell. "You could of written, too."

"I ain't gonna write to your fancy hospital or your fancy Florida with your fancy job. Figured you were too busy anyway." A breeze blows in and spills the husk bag. I kneel to collect it all and stuff it back in. Silk strands cover my arms and cling to my hair like spaghetti.

"I wasn't too busy. And I'm not too fancy. I worked hard." Maybe it's too much to expect a soft place to land in a place that was never soft to begin with.

"I know you did. Don't get all fussy," she says, as if it's me that cut her down instead of the other way around. "Besides, you ain't the only one workin' hard."

"Oh, yeah?"

"I'm up for a promotion. Down at the hardware store. Assistant general manager. Pay's good, too. I sure the hell earned it."

"That's real nice, Mama," I say and mean it. "When will you hear?"

"Couple of weeks. Definitely by the Fourth. You stayin' that long?"

"Plan to. That okay?"

"Since when do you ask me what you can and can't do?"

Her tone tells me I don't need to bother answering. She sniffs at the air. "Smells like rain. River's up again."

"River's always up." We both turn to watch Mrs. Parker in the tan double-wide across the holler limp out to pick up her morning paper. Mama waves hello.

"She's a nice gal. Just a little crazy."

"Not much has changed, has it?"

"Not much," she agrees, "except you."

"For the better, I hope." I'm fishing for a compliment. It's unlikely I'll get one.

Mrs. Parker tucks her paper under her arm and hitches up her skirt to scratch her leg. "She had both knees replaced last winter," Mama says. "Lord, she looks old."

"Street looks the same."

"Mostly. A couple of teenagers rented the trailer at the corner. A brother and a sister. They remind me of you and Trey at their age. Worse off, though. No parents. I heard they fell on hard times. Times are tough all around." Then she opens her own *Hannibal Courier Post* and scans the headlines. "Paper says flood."

"That paper always says flood." It's true. When you live in a floodplain, you're always wrestling water.

"Your brother's out sandbaggin'. Left a note on the kitchen table. I hope he ain't spendin' more time out at Digger's. Those boys are up to no good and everyone in town knows it."

I didn't hear Trey come in last night or leave this morning. "I thought he'd at least say hi to his little sis."

"What? You expect some royal welcome? Trey's probably expectin' you to find him."

"Where's he at?"

Mama flips the pages to the weather map. Her girls coo from the side porch and she clucks back at them. "Salvation Army, I imagine. There's a crew from the cement plant. That pricey floodwall don't reach the south side, ya know. Figures." That summer the newly installed cement-and-steel floodwall held back the Mississippi from the historic downtown. They saved Mark Twain's boyhood home, but the water seeped in all around and overtook the land where a three-quarter-mile gap in the wall let it in. The floodwall separates the haves and have-nots even more. If you got money, you move away from the Mississippi, out to one of the new subdivisions by Walmart. Money buys you safety from the river and the train tracks. If you're like Rose and me, you're stuck where the water always reaches you. Mama says it doesn't make us any less for living on this side. Our view is better. Who wants to watch a retention pond? It's a good story, anyway, even if it's only half a truth. "Sammy might be there, too. His daddy's gas station always gets it the worst."

"I know, Mama. I ain't been gone that long." We spent most of that flood summer covered in slime and stink from the river. It took a week just to clean the mud from the station's ceiling. Sometimes, even today, when I wash my hair, I still feel caked mud and smell rotting catfish.

"I'm just sayin' you should let folks like Sammy know you're in town. They're gonna hear about it anyway. He's one of your oldest friends. You don't want Rose or some other busybody breakin' the news." She waves at George, our postman, who has just filled our mailbox at the end of the street with bills.

"Unless that smart degree made you forget where you're from."
It's a common jab. But it's also a battle you can't win. If you try
to better yourself, you're acting like you're too good for the folks
who raised you. If you stay and don't, you're a loser who never
even tried.

"I know where I'm from," I say, but it sounds weak, even
to me. I carry the corn into the kitchen and let the screen door
slam. I don't catch it. Mama's been training me since I could
walk not to bang the door, but the sound is comforting. The
whap as the metal hits the plastic frame and the *whoosh* of wind
that flows through the worn-out screen. It pops out like a balloon from years of escapes.

"You're lettin' the damn bugs in!" Mama yells. She hunches
over in her chair, calls back at her girls, and swats flies with a
rolled-up *People*. Britney Spears's face is splattered with fly juice
and bug guts.

CHAPTER TWO

Taming Water

TREY BACKS HIS bike up to the house, under my bed-room window, and sends exhaust smoke in my direction as a way of announcing himself. His long black hair hangs limp in a ponytail; his green eyes are hidden under metallic sunglasses. He scratches at his neck like a dog. I sprint from my bed to catch him. He inches his bike forward to grow the distance between us, but I grab him in a bear hug from behind. "Sis," he says, patting my hand.

"You been hidin'?" I ask. My voice muffled into his back.

"Not from you I ain't. Maybe from Mama." He unpeels my arms and moves me away. I wasn't expecting a welcome wagon, but I'm starting to feel that if there was one, it would run over me. Trey keeps his sunglasses on and revs the gas more.

"Want to hang out?" I ask.

He shakes his head. "Can't now. Got someplace I need to be." He cocks his head to the side and watches the road. "What's your sentence, anyway? How long you in for?"

"A few weeks. Maybe a month. Definitely until the Fourth."

I kick one of the loose rocks in the driveway. I'm grateful it's too early for the neighbors to watch me chasing my brother in pajamas like a kid.

Trey raises his eyebrows in surprise. "Did ya lose your job or somethin'?"

"Maybe." It's the first time I've said it out loud. "Don't tell Mama, all right?"

"Hell, I lose my job all the time. Keeps findin' me, though."

"Still at the cement plant?"

"Sure. Mostly." I can never get a straight answer from Trey. I have to ask twice and still figure it out for myself. "I've got other things goin', too. I'm savin' up."

"Oh, yeah? For what?"

"My own place. I've almost got the down payment on a trailer down by the Salt River. Just a few miles from Aunt Betty's."

I imagine walking down the dirt road to her house for dinner. "Sounds nice." How come Trey, who's always been the mess-up, and I, who've always had a plan, have switched roles? "My reunion is comin' up, too," I mention. "My ten-year." Pamela, the big black hen, peeks her head around the corner and sizes us up. Trey gives it some gas and she runs back to safety.

"Uh-huh." He nods, seeing right through me. "Never known you for the reunion type, Laura."

"Well, maybe you don't know my type anymore." I'm still raw from Mama. Going to the reunion is definitely not on my list.

"Uh-huh." He nods again, picking at the cuts up and down his neck.

"Want me to clean those for you? Looks like you've been in a catfight." Across the street Mrs. Parker comes out to water her plants. We both turn to watch her fuss filling her watering can.

"I see how it's gonna be. Nurse Laura to the rescue, huh?" He rolls his bike forward a few more feet.

"I just meant I've got Band-Aids. I know how to clean wounds, Trey."

"Nah, I gotta go. Later, Sis." He salutes me and speeds off. From behind, he looks just like Daddy, but maybe it's because I only recognize Daddy when he's leaving. One night when I was eight, he snuck in rather than out. I was climbing into my bed and heard a noise from the corner. I turned around, and there he was, huddled on the floor of my bedroom under the open window. A breeze blew in and swung the bottom of the curtain into his face. "Hey, kid," he said. "It's your daddy. Shh." He put his finger to his lips. I wanted to scream but couldn't. The surprise stole my voice. Mama wasn't home anyway. It was her night to close the hardware store where she'd been a cashier for years. Trey was supposed to be watching me, but he was gone all day.

"Why you hidin'?" I asked.

He whispered, "I need your help. You wanta help your daddy, don't ya?" I nodded. Of course I did. "I left somethin' here. Your mama has it. I need you to help me get it back." I nodded again. A floorboard creaked and we both froze. I listened for a car door but didn't hear one. Daddy put his finger to his lips again. Then he grabbed me too hard by my skinny arm and leaned in close. He smelled like chewing tobacco and taffy. "Go get your mama's ring. It's mine, and I want it back. Go." He released my arm and it throbbed where he'd squeezed. I ran to the door before he could hurt me again.

Just as I grabbed the doorknob, I turned. "What if Mama wants to keep it?"

"She don't," he said, raising his voice. "It ain't hers to keep. Go." So I did. I ran down the hallway into Mama's room and rifled through her jewelry box. The ring was the only one she owned. I squeezed it tight in my palm and ran back to Daddy.

"Here," I said, dropping the ring into his outstretched hand.

He looked at the diamond. It looked small to me. "You did good, kid. Made your old man proud. We'll keep this our little secret, okay?" I nodded. He climbed back out my window and walked toward the river.

Mama blamed the missing ring on Trey, of course. I told him that I'd seen Daddy, that he'd taken the ring, but Trey would never squeal.

MAMA'S HOME ON HER BREAK at the kitchen table. I pour myself a cup of weak coffee and sit down next to her. She's making a grocery list.

"Will you get bananas, please?" I ask. She writes *bananas*. "And low-fat yogurt."

"What for?" She puts her pen down and sips her coffee. She winces and I don't know if it's the taste or the heat. It smells a lot like my dirty socks.

"For me. Can't I eat low-fat yogurt?"

"Yep," she says. I can imagine everything she means.

"You should get some *real* coffee. I'll pay for it." I mean kindness, but I know exactly how Mama will react.

"Well, aren't you a knight in shinin' armor? Tell you what. Why don't you get the groceries yourself? That way they'll all be up to your standards."

I could fight with Mama. She's itching for one. It might clear the air. But I didn't come home to fight. "Okay," I say, grabbing the list and giving her a side-hug. She flinches a little but doesn't pull away. "I will."

I pull on jeans that are too tight, thinking they'll motivate weight loss, and drive down to the Save-a-Lot on Oakwood and scan the parking lot for any cars I recognize. I call Aunt Betty but no one answers. I decide to drive out to her property later. Maybe I'll go looking for Trey on my way.

Inside the Save-a-Lot there are dimly lit rows of bloody meat covered in Saran Wrap. The aisles are tight and the produce is bruised and dry. This isn't the sanitized Publix in Florida with smiling cashiers and fruit misters. There are rows of locked cigarette cases with flyers taped to the glass advertising the Tom Sawyer Days schedule. One of them announces the Tom and Becky Contest, too, with pictures of past contestants. Most of the last names are families who have been in Hannibal as long as mine has.

At the checkout, a teenager in a navy sweatpant suit with a name badge that reads CRYSTAL asks if I found everything all right. "You guys carry fresh herbs?" I ask.

"Fresh what?" she says in a raspy voice. Then she starts dry-hacking.

"Never mind," I mumble and bag the food myself.

"Hey, ain't you Laura?" she asks, squinting at me. "I know your brother."

"Yep," I admit. "I'm Trey's little sister." It's been less than twenty-four hours and more people probably know me in this town than all of Jacksonville put together.

"Yeah. We rent the trailer at the end of your street. I know Trey. I'm Crystal. Crystal Wilkens."

I nod. "Nice to meet you." I don't recognize the name. And why is my brother hanging out with this kid? "Did you say you and your parents just moved in?"

"Awhile ago. Just me and my brother. Mama and Daddy are dead. You ain't home much, are you?" Crystal wipes down the conveyer belt with a rag. She scrubs hard at milk crusts and a smear of dried peanut butter.

"I live in Florida. I'm a nurse. A CNA, actually. Like a nurse's helper. Just home visiting. For a while."

"That's cool. I've heard Florida is cool. You go to the beach?"

"Sometimes."

"I'd go to the beach. I'd go anywhere but here." She coughs again. "What was it you were looking for?"

"Don't worry about it, Crystal," I say, ducking out the door. I want to tell her to have a doctor check her lungs, that she's too young to smoke, that there is a way out, but I'm busy trying to find a way back in. "I'll find it somewhere else. Take care."

I drop off the groceries at the house and grab a banana and a yogurt. I cross off the groceries from the list even though I know I bought everything. It feels like an accomplishment. I look around at Mama's clean front porch and wonder if she'd mind a few pots of basil and cilantro. Maybe some rosemary and dill.

I make a new list for my life, too:

✓ Fourth of July (enjoy)
✓ Get new job (asap)
✓ Get new life

On my way out, I toss some grain to the chickens and watch them peck gratefully. Sugar doesn't fight for the food like the others. She just nips at the air. I make her a separate pile and guard it with my feet while she gets her fill.

Then I walk down to the river. My feet just take me there. It's a left on Market and a short walk over the bridge to Kiwanis Park. The ground gradually gives way until it meets water. It's an easing-in that can go either way. The water can take more soil anytime it wants. Or a drought can cause retreat. No matter how long I'm gone, this walk, the mist from the fountain, the floating foam at the river's edge, feels familiar. The noisy current gets louder and pulls you in. When I hear it, I know I'm back in Hannibal. The Mississippi doesn't sound at all like the ocean. The ocean comes at you in crashes and the waves are a soothing lull. I read once that the tides do something to reset your body's rhythms. The river, though, runs fast and churns. It laps brown at the banks, greedy to take more. It's sneaky, even. I take off my shoes and dip my feet in. The chill shocks my system. I feel alive and alert. Out of the fog I was flailing in during my last days in Florida. The baby. My job. The current will pull you under if you aren't careful. It's easier to let the river take you than it is to swim against it.

With my feet in the muddy water, I dial Aunt Betty again but the phone just rings and rings. She doesn't have a cell phone and she's convinced that answering machines report stuff to the government. I'll take the long way out to the country and see if I can remember the unmarked turns to Digger's place.

Digger grew up in a little brick house with his mom and dad, who used to manage the strawberry patch for Sampson's Nursery. His name is Scott but everyone calls him Digger. Trey told me once it was because he was the biggest nose picker in kindergarten, but then Trey said a lot of things. Digger's mom and ours went to high school together and during picking season, Mama would drive us out to Mrs. Douglass's for strawberry shortcake. She made her own angel food in a Bundt pan and served it with a huge helping of Cool Whip. I've never tasted anything since that was either as weightless as that cake or as heavy as that cream and berries. We'd stuff ourselves and then run into the fields with baskets. Trey and I competed for the fattest strawberries. We'd come back with pink-stained mouths, and Mrs. Douglass teased that they should weigh us before we went in and when we came out to know how much to charge.

It doesn't look like the house I remember. All the windows are covered with foil. One side of the brick is crumbling and bags of trash are stacked by the pile. The front door is papered with BEWARE OF DOG signs, and two huge mutts come barking at my car. The driveway is littered with empty soda bottles and cigarette butts, like someone had a party and never cleaned up. Digger's folks were killed a few years back in a car accident, but still. I'd never expect him to let the place go like this. I roll down my window and a strong rotten-egg stink wafts in. Digger comes out on the front porch wearing overalls without a shirt. His feet are bare and his beard is long. He's balding under his baseball cap and his arms have huge scabs. "Hey, Digg," I call from my car window. "Seen Trey?"

"Who wants to know?" He squints at me.

"It's me. Laura. Laura Brooks. Trey's little sister." I start to open my car door but one of the dogs lunges and growls at me. I wait for Digger to call off his dogs but he doesn't.

"Who?" He sways a little and I wonder if he's drunk. Maybe he just can't see me good from the distance.

"It's me, Digger. Laura. I'm back in town."

"You shouldn't be here. Just go on down the road. Now."

It's not like this family to kick me out. "I'm lookin' for Trey. You seen him?"

"Ain't seen him. Get now." Someone screams or laughs from inside the house. Another door slams. One of the dogs has diarrhea at Digger's feet, but he doesn't notice, not even to move from the smell. His eyes are completely glazed.

I nod to Digger as I back slowly out of the driveway and head down the dirt road in the direction of Aunt Betty. She lives south of Hannibal on New London Gravel Road. That's its actual name. It's near the town of New London. The road is gravel. Aunt Betty lives in a cement blockhouse Grandpa built. He painted it bright blue. The house is white now, but where it's chipping, the original garish color seeps through. From the road, the house looks like a perfect square. The roof is tin, which makes the rain equally deafening and soothing. As I drive, I imagine her in her rocking chair on the porch, hand stitching a seam and sipping sweet tea. Everything is better after a dose of Aunt Betty. She's

Mama's older sister and I spent sick days on her couch watching *The Price Is Right* and praying for rain so that we could take a good long nap. Aunt Betty didn't have to answer to nobody or nothing. She lived alone in a house she owned and did as she pleased. And what pleased Aunt Betty was making quilts, gardening, and growing flowers. She took in odd jobs mending and patching to pay her bills. She had an entire room set up just for sewing, with an enormous table in the middle for cutting patterns. Nails jutted out of the wall to organize scissors, measuring tape, seam rippers, and such. A wooden sign with AUNT BETTY'S SEWING ROOM burned in black hung above her machine. She let me organize and stack her fabrics by color. Sometimes she'd knock them off the shelf into a big messy pile just to give me something to do. "Aunt Betty!" I'd squeal as red paisleys and green ginghams and blue stripes rained down around me.

"Make it nice," Aunt Betty'd say, her signature phrase. "You want some tea, sugar? I'll *make it nice*." She added enough sweetener to pucker your lips and lived on a steady diet of saltwater taffy. At Aunt Betty's, you could have as much as your four-year-old belly could hold.

I knock gently on the screen door before I open it. Lulubelle, Dog's replacement, another hound with tan-and-white markings, howls. The sweet smell of dough and cinnamon welcomes me. "Paws off!" Aunt Betty says, gently swatting at my hand as I reach for the oven. "They gotta bake two more minutes. You'll just have to hold your horses, little missy." I peck her on the cheek and she awkwardly pulls me into a hug. Her bones exhale against me, as if she's been holding her breath the whole time I was gone. Then she holds me out and looks me up and down. "You're here," she whispers over and over and pats me, as if she can't believe it's true. "Well," she finally says, "let's sit down so you can tell me everything. And what the hell are you doin' with your hair? We've gotta do somethin' 'bout that."

We sit on the front porch and I spill. I tell her I'm still kind of in shock that the life I built was pulled out from under me so fast.

"Well, you're still a nurse, ain't ya?"

"Nurse's assistant. Yes, but an unemployed one." I dunk a whole cookie in my milk and stuff it in my mouth. The salty sweet makes the news go down a little easier. The day after I got the news about the baby that wasn't, Jacksonville Memorial, where I'd been a CNA, certified nurse's aide, for six years, announced budget cuts—at the patient level, of course, not administrative—and so I had my job to mourn, too. I spent a few mornings walking the beach, watching families on vacation. Little girls in pigtails with polka-dot bikinis sagging over diapers. A father trying to teach his baby how to blow bubbles in the pool. The baby cooed and bobbed in her inflatable rainbow float as the daddy puffed his own exaggerated cheeks with air. Eventually, she laid her head on his bare arm and dozed off. Back in my apartment, I started sorting furniture to sell.

"So? It's just an opportunity for 'nother adventure. You'll land fine. I'm glad you came home." Aunt Betty's voice is softer. I picture Mama finding out about my job and making me feel like a loser, especially since she's feeling all high and mighty, up for a promotion.

"Don't tell Mama, okay?" I ask, taking two more cookies. I decide just to call them lunch. I wonder if I can convince Aunt

Betty to hop in the car with me and drive back to Florida. I doubt it. And what would I go back to, anyway?

"Ain't mine to tell. Now it's time to buck up." She leans over and pats my knee before taking the cookie plate back in for a refill. She means tough love; I get that, but I was hoping for just the love part. As she leaves, she calls back over her shoulder, "Funny thing is you always wanted a way out. Seems like now you're lookin' for a way in." It stings. I watch the road, and the crickets call to each other from the yard. The noises from Aunt Betty's porch never change.

I pretend to protest the second plate of cookies, but I'm not very convincing. As I reach for them, something shiny flashes. Aunt Betty's holding her best scissors. "Come on," she says. "I certainly can't make it much worse."

"I can afford a haircut. I ain't five years old." I see my reflection in the glass of one of her framed pictures of me as a kid. My hair looked better then.

"You're bellyachin' like you are. Besides, I went to cosmetology school. I still remember a thing or two. Come on. Sit down. Let Aunt Betty *make it nice*."

BACK IN MY ROOM, I watch a daddy longlegs crawl across my old desk. He knows exactly where he's going. He climbs up my windowsill and squeezes his whole body through a tiny crack. It's bad luck to kill spiders. Everyone knows that.

I sort through my drawers and find high school notes from Sammy and middle school flyers from past National Tom Sawyer Days. *Brent B. as Tom,* Rose scribbled with a halo of red hearts, and

Stacey T. is a BAD Becky!!!! There are yearbooks, school pictures, ticket stubs, and class notebooks from my senior year. Hannibal High, where everybody goes, is the only school, a three-story sprawling brick building without air-conditioning. Most of the teachers were once students; the same old ideas are just recycled. Except for when they bring in out-of-towners, like Ms. Bechtold, our English teacher. We called her Ms. B to her face and the Feminist behind her back, even though most folks didn't even know what that meant. Ms. B was proud of the fact that she hadn't married. She wanted her independence, and most men couldn't manage that. "That probably means she likes girls," Trey said. Even then, I knew my brother didn't know much about the world.

Ms. B considered herself an amateur local historian. She'd moved to Hannibal on some type of personal quest. "You are so lucky to grow up here!" she told us on her first day. "A place so rich with literary culture. You can just surround yourself with the genius of Samuel Clemens." She told stories about Jane Clemens and the letters she wrote to her son. "Jane was the real family writer," Ms. B said, "but women, especially women of color, never have the same choices as men." Ms. B loved to visit the local sights on the weekend and tell us their histories in class. She even wrote a pamphlet as a study guide for the seventh graders who wanted to be in the Tom and Becky Contest like Sammy. The contestants represent Hannibal, "America's Hometown," at tourist events and literary festivals throughout the year. They have to answer a lot of questions and stay in character, so they have to know the history. I was her classroom aide and helped proofread the passages. Then Ms. B nominated herself to judge the annual contest during the Fourth of July. She said judging it was one of her lifelong aspirations. When the Chamber of Commerce finally asked her, she broke in on our school's intercom and shouted the good news.

Ms. B was the best teacher I ever had, and it was Hannibal's loss when the principal decided not to renew her contract. I'd heard she'd mentioned in the teachers' lounge that her colleagues objected to *Adventures of Huckleberry Finn* because Huck's voice was more black than white.

Among my high school papers is the essay I wrote for Ms. B about how my own family history was shaped by the Mississippi. I researched my great-great-grandma, Eliza Brown. Aunt Betty is the one who told me about her. Sammy and I spent months combing through the local library, learning about the river we all love and fear.

The Wrong Direction

by Laura Brooks

In 1812 a series of earthquakes along the New Madrid Fault Line shook the earth so violently that the Mississippi River flowed backward for a few terrible hours. The water raced in the wrong direction, creating dams and waterfalls that lasted days and capsized twenty-eight boats. Witnesses heard cries of help from the captains and crews, but nothing could be done. All lives were lost. The very ground where Lewis and Clark slept and that Ulysses S. Grant later conquered with his Union troops turned on itself with a force greater than man. The mighty Mississippi proved once again that its power paralleled that of God.

Eliza Brown recounted the Mississippi running backward in a letter to the Methodist evangelical Lorenzo Dow. She woke up around 2 a.m. to a thunderous sound that sent everything around her into the raging waters. Animals and people smashed into each other in their panic. Dense, heavy dust from the destruction and the debris choked them. At first, Eliza wrote, the river sucked in all the water from its banks. Then it roared backward as a monstrous wave some fifteen to twenty feet in the air. At one point Eliza saw a mother clutching her children in a boat on top of the wave before it swallowed them whole. The wave captured everything in its path. Then, just as suddenly as it began, the wave sank, and the river went right again.

Eliza Brown's eyewitness account reports that the first earthquake happened on the 16th of December in 1811. This was the monumental shock that sent the Mississippi, in Eliza's word, "retrograde." The earth struck again in January and continued to churn through February. In her letter to Lorenzo Dow, she wrote, "The earth was in continual agitation, visibly waving as a gentle sea."

Often before a flood or earthquake, there is a drought. Months of thirst give way to weeks of drenching rain. The ground swallows in gratitude, and then chokes. Most, including Eliza, returned after the quakes and floods, despite their visions of falling houses. They assessed their spaces, accepted their risk, and reassured themselves that the ground beneath their feet would hold, as much as it ever had, as long as the Mississippi behaved.

Ms. B gave me the only A+ in the class. It still makes me proud, even if my path since feels like I'm running backward, too.

Her book is on my nightstand next to the baby picture of Bobby. I thumb through the book and scan the dog-eared pages. She loved this town that always felt too small for me.

It was Ms. B who put Sammy and me together for a group project our senior year. She assigned passages from Twain's lesser-known works. She gave Sammy and me *Life on the Mississippi*, and we spent hours on his farmhouse's front porch reading it out loud. Sammy leaned against the white railing and listened while I marked my favorite passage to memorize later:

If I had really known what I was about
to require of my faculties, I should not
have had the courage to begin. I supposed that all a pilot had to do was to
keep his boat in the river, and I did
not consider that that could be much of
a trick, since it was so wide.

It sounded simple. Just keep between the shores, but even I
knew how naive that was. The task was never that easy, especially when the banks were always shifting.

Our assignment was to "contemplate the impact of setting
on story," so Sammy took me on a lot of walks down by the
river. He called it research. In the book published in 1883, Clemens wrote about the river:

Ten thousand River Commissions...can-
not tame that lawless stream, cannot
curb it or confine it, cannot say to it,
"Go here," or "Go there," and make it
obey; cannot save a shore which it has
sentenced; cannot bar its path with an
obstruction which it will not tear down,
dance over, and laugh at.

I told Sammy it was good luck to have a partner with the
same name as the author. Maybe he could protect me from the
river if it decided to have a good laugh at our expense.

Sammy'd wanted an excuse to talk to me for months. One night we were leaning over a poster board, gluing on pictures from a magazine of river stuff, and he kissed me. It wasn't the first time I'd been kissed, but it was the first time I'd felt what I felt, starting in the small of my back where Sammy put his hand and pulled me in, my stomach pressed against his and running up my spine to my ringing ears. I was afraid he could see it in me, how much I liked it, and I didn't want that. Not really. Not then. My body said something else, though. "White town drowsing," I said, catching my breath. "The title, I mean, of our project. Ms. B will love it. White town drowsing. What he called Hannibal in chapter four."

"That works," Sammy agreed, kissing my neck. I studied a crack shaped like a wave in the ceiling and let him. Then I kissed him back.

The next day we walked up the hill to Lover's Leap where townies went to make out; it was a necessary field trip to declare our relationship status in town. From the top of the bluff you can see for miles. The water lapped the shore and raced downstream. In my ear, Sammy quoted the opening lines in a TV documentary voice, "The Mississippi is well worth reading about. It is not a commonplace river, but on the contrary is in all ways remarkable." I nestled into his neck. "So are you," he said. "Remarkable, I mean." It was cheesy. That's clear now. Using Twain's words as a come-on. But it worked. Probably still would. Sammy was always a little corny, but his sincerity made up for it. I felt safe with him. He was calm to my chaos. No matter the rages of Mama or the roller-coaster trouble of Trey or the daily shouting matches at home, Sammy was steady. But still, I was scared of getting stuck between narrow shores. I feared a future in Hannibal. Sammy never dreamed of anything bigger.

The Monday our group project was due, Sammy and I stood together in front of the whole class and shared Twain's adventures learning to pilot from St. Louis to New Orleans. Ms. B was beaming. She clapped and rose from her seat when we finished. "Bravo! Brava!" I knew our grade would be gold, but I was more grateful that the work had brought us together.

Then Ms. B passed out the new book she'd been writing for the Tom and Becky contestants, the one she'd had me work on. It was just paper folded in half and held together with staples. The cover was a pencil sketch of the famous fence Tom tricked his friends into whitewashing. Ms. B drew it herself. The book was titled *Painting Fences* by Melanie K. Bechtold. "This is a treat for me, Class. I've never shared this with anyone before, anyone except Laura." Her top lip was sweaty, and she'd applied fresh hot pink lip gloss. "We're going to read *my* book for the rest of this quarter. It's not published, of course. It's just for the Toms and Beckys, to help them with their studies. But still." Then she read from the first chapter, "Cardiff Hill."

Sammy said I was the only one, besides Ms. B, who enjoyed her book. After reading us passages, many of which I knew by heart, Ms. B would point to a sign she'd made and hung above her desk: REMEMBER, YOU CAN TRY TO TAME WATER, BUT YOU CAN'T STOP INDEPENDENCE.

Cardiff Hill

There is a bronze statue of Tom and Huck at the base of Cardiff Hill. It's on the north side of the historic district. If you come out of the Mark Twain Dinette, take a quick left, walk past the boyhood home and Tom's fence, and turn left again when you see a horse and buggy, you'll run into it. Then you can climb to the top, all 244 steps, to the lighthouse. If you make it all the way up and down, stop in at the gift shop for a certificate that says you accomplished the feat. Tom and Huck would, if they could, just for bragging rights.

The statue, made by Frederick Hibbard, was erected in 1925 and stands about seven feet tall on its four-and-a-half-foot base. Tom has a pole slung over his shoulder, and a knapsack hangs from it. He's barefoot, of course. Huck stands at his side with his arm across Tom's back. They both look like they've either spent the morning in mischief or are about to make some more.

Tom and Huck's friendship was always complicated. Tom wanted Huck's roaming rights; Huck coveted Tom's home life. To the outside eye, Huck was a corrupting influence. He was feral and couldn't amount to anything. He'd grown up without schooling and was beaten regularly by his drunk pappy. His worst sin of all, though, was befriending a runaway slave named Jim. That Huck saw beyond color and class was unforgivable. Society, meaning the well-intentioned Aunt Polly, saw Tom's sins as redeemable. His pranks were of the adorable boys-will-be-boys variety. But it really took Huck to reveal Tom's best and worst sides. Together, they were invincible, even when they were wrong.

CHAPTER THREE

ROSE MEETS ME in the driveway and we squeal like little girls. Then she squints at what's left of my hair after Aunt Betty "fixed" it. I spike it up on the sides with my fingers and grin. It feels weightless.

"It ain't just 'bout your hair, Laura," Rose says, sizing me up.

Bobby hangs back, watching, but then he lets me fold him up in my arms, too, and he burrows in a bit. "Got a surprise for you," he whispers. He leads me by the hand to the fridge where two beer magnets hold up a letter:

Dear Hannibal Area Chamber of Commerce Tom and Becky Program,

It is my pleasure to recommend seventh grader Bobby Haymaker to your committee as a nominee for Hannibal's Tom and Becky Program. Bobby is a student in my third-period English class at Hannibal Middle School.

He has shown great promise this year as a student and a citizen. I expect even more outstanding things in his future.

At the beginning of the year, Bobby was a quiet kid in the back of the class. His writing caught my eye, though, because of its expressiveness and talent. He's funny on the page and in person, and these are assets that will make him a great Tom. Bobby also loves to read. He may be the only contestant who has actually read *The Adventures of Tom Sawyer* and *Adventures of Huckleberry Finn*. Bobby is also a responsible student who completes assignments often before the due date and always in an exemplary fashion. In class discussions, his comments are often more insightful and surprising than the more gregarious students. It is my opinion that students like Bobby are often overlooked, and that's a shame in our school and in programs like yours. Bobby would be a wonderful ambassador for Hannibal because he is an authentic product of our hometown. He'll be a real Tom: smart, witty, and sincere. He may need more support than the other contestants but he certainly has as much potential.

Sincerely,
Peggy Keller

"Bobby, I'm so proud of you," I gush, which turns his neck and ears all pink.

"You said to be brave," he says, like this whole thing is my doing. Last week while I was packing my apartment, Bobby called, just to say hello. Usually, we email. I've been his online pen pal since a school assignment when he was in third grade. It's easier to say stuff on email. Bobby told me about Rose and Josh fighting all the time and how messed up his life was with the divorce. He always asked when I was coming home.

It doesn't matter how long I'm gone; Hannibal is home. And when you don't have another place to go, your roots run deeper.

To celebrate, I order a pizza from Cassano's, pineapple and ham, Rose's favorite. Bobby and I play checkers while we wait. He tells me more about his upcoming Tom interview. If he does well before the judges on the first round, he'll start working on his costume, which Bobby seems thrilled about.

"Wish that delivery boy was deliverin' more than pizza," Rose says, closing the front door, flushed from the heat. She mouths *hot* to me and fans herself dramatically.

I've known Rose since kindergarten, since our mamas dropped us off in Mrs. Burrow's class with quarters for our milk. Rose drank the strawberry kind. I was riding shotgun in her pickup our sophomore year when she met the Bastard, her soon-to-be ex. He was pumping gas at Sammy's daddy's station in the lane next to ours when Rose told him his jeans were too tight. So he dropped them in front of God and everybody. I didn't think it was funny. Sammy's daddy came out hollering up a storm and told him to get off his property. Rose was pregnant one month later. Nobody was that surprised, but our classmates treated her like a leper anyway. She was an outcast, and I was her ally. I took Rose to the hospital the first time Josh busted her lip. I stood beside her the summer after my first year of nursing school holding a bunch of daisies when she said yes, she'd be Josh's wife. Bobby was almost three years old.

After pizza and goodnights to Bobby, Rose and I sit on an old plaid couch on her back porch drinking beers. "To tell you the truth, I'm a little scared," I admit when Rose asks about what's next. "I've always had a plan and that plan didn't lead back here."

"How come you didn't just apply for another job? I thought nursing was easy to come by."

"I don't know. A lot of the other nurses' assistants who were laid off went into private practice. I like the pace of hospitals, though. I'm never bored."

"So, you gonna apply around here or back in Florida?" Rose peels the label on her beer bottle and makes a pile of the shreds.

I sigh. Rose's question is so obvious, but I can't answer it just yet. "There's more," I say.

"There's always more. A man?" she asks.

"Not exactly." I shake my head and study my hands. "At least not one that stuck around."

"Most of 'em don't."

"A baby, actually. But it's gone now."

She passes me another beer.

"For almost a month, I was pregnant." I drain half the bottle and it feels good going down. "I was terrified at first, but then I got used to the idea. Too used to it." I tried not to think about the baby, but when the pregnancy test came back positive, I couldn't help myself. It shocked me how much I suddenly wanted it. Then the nurse came in to confirm I'd lost it, and I had to act relieved.

"But you did want it, right?"

"I did." It chokes me to tell her. To relive the feelings and know I can't change the outcome, to know that deep down I actually do want to be someone's mama, to wonder if I already would be if things hadn't turned out the way they did with Sammy.

"Did you tell the daddy? About the miscarriage, I mean."

I shake my head. It wouldn't have helped. We were never really anything but passing time. It's not that I haven't had lovers since Sammy. It's that I'm always looking for the next one, even when a good-enough one is in my bed. Something else or someone else has to fit better. Except they don't. I spent three years sleeping with Ryan, an RN who worked on my floor at the hospital. He was safe because he didn't want much. I almost fell in love with Noah, my downstairs neighbor, but he left for Europe and said good-bye in a note. Coward. Sammy was my one big love. I can't go back. You can't undo what's been done.

"So, what are you gonna do now?"

"I don't know yet. Take it easy at Mama's for a while. See everyone. I'll stay for the Fourth."

"Good. Then you can help Bobby! Lord knows I don't got time."

"I'd love to, actually. It'll be fun. I'll bring over that book Ms. B wrote. Remember? I researched some of the historical passages." Helping Bobby would help me, too. Ms. B spent afternoons and weekends advising contestants, quizzing them, and training for the judging. I know how much work it is, and Bobby could actually win.

"I haven't thought about that book in years. She was so embarrassing with that thing. So serious. So were you!"

"Maybe. Maybe that's true," I admit, smiling at the eagerness of my high school self, how little I knew then, how much I still have to learn.

"And the reunion?" Rose is scheming already. "Bet Sammy'll be there," she teases. Rose has always had boys on the brain. She sounds just like Mama with the Sammy stuff. Maybe they like him more than me.

"Nah, haven't thought about it," I lie, "but I wouldn't complain all that much about a man." We clink beer bottles to toast our potential plotting.

"I saw Sammy at the gas station last week. He still looks good. Asked about you." Rose drains her beer and reaches for the leftover pizza crusts.

"Oh, yeah? What did you say?"

"Told him you were still single. Told him you were skinny and all the Florida boys were chasin' you."

"You did not, Rose. He probably didn't even ask."

"He's gettin' divorced, too." Rose watches me for a reaction. I chew on the inside of my mouth and gather up the trash.

"Divorced? Huh." I rest my chin on my hands like the whole topic bores me.

"I heard he wanted kids and she didn't. That's what I heard."

"Why wouldn't she want kids?" A girl staying in town and marrying into a family like Sammy's and not having kids is unheard of.

"Don't know. I heard he messed with her birth control pills to try to get her pregnant."

"He wouldn't do that. I know Sammy."

"You used to. Folks do crazy shit for love. Seems like everyone we went to high school with is splittin' up. Carrie and Sean. Justin and Kaye. You name it, they ain't together anymore. There's gonna be a lot of single folks in Hannibal soon."

"Includin' you?"

"Includin' me."

I switch topics before Rose gets too carried away. I grill her about what she's heard of Trey, but she doesn't know much more than Mama. He's running around with Digger's crowd and they go dirt-biking and hunting out in the country a lot.

"Trey's gonna do what he wants. I don't think you comin' home is gonna stop that, Laura."

"True," I admit, "but I'd like to try. He said he's saving up for some land of his own. Maybe with a trailer on it."

"Oh, yeah? That'll make him a catch." We bust out laughing at how true and how sad that sounds.

Then, just like we did as kids, we start making plans. Outrageous ones about how we'll buy the biggest house in Hannibal and a boat to float down the Mississippi. We'll be just like Tom Sawyer and Huckleberry Finn. "Let's go all the way down to New Orleans!" I say, and Rose agrees. Rose decides she'll run for mayor, and I agree to run her campaign. We're both getting tummy tucks and she wants a boob job. Soon it's dark and the neighbors are yelling for us to keep it down.

"You know what we need?" Rose asks. "More beer. You'll drive."

"We could walk. It's not that far."

Rose stares at me and my dumb idea. "People don't walk in Hannibal."

In the Save-a-Lot aisle, Rose complains about the Bastard and his latest antics. She talks loudly and people keep peering over the aisles to get a good look at the drama she's stirring up. Rose pretends she doesn't see any of them, like she doesn't enjoy a little scene. She picks up some hair dye, reads the label. She's been a bleached blonde since middle school. It suits her olive skin and makes her brown eyes wide like a doe's. Rose in her uniform of tight jeans and clingy mesh layers. She could still pull off Madonna if she wanted to.

"So," I say, lowering my voice and hoping she'll do the same. "How's Bobby handling the divorce?"

Rose doesn't like to talk about how bad all of this is for him. She always insists he's fine, just fine, but I don't think so. I know what it's like to grow up without a daddy around. It leaves a pit that nothing fills.

"What *about* Bobby?" Rose shrugs. "He wants one of those expensive costumes and the Bastard won't even help. You wouldn't believe the shit I have to do just to pay our bills. It's all the Bastard's fault. Hand me some gum, will you?"

I hand her a pack of Bubblicious, the strawberry kind.

"Bobby's a big boy. It's up to him. That's got nothin' to do with me."

"It's got nothin' to do with you? How can you say that?"

"Because it's true. It's up to Bobby. I birthed him and raised him. If he wants to go live with the Bastard now, I can't stop him." Rose reads the side of the Bubblicious as if she's more interested in the ingredients than in what I have to say.

"You've got to try. At least. You'd just let him go? This ain't just about you, Rose." I snatch the gum out of her hand and shove it back on the shelf. It's a small, petty move, but it's all I've got.

Rose looks from the package to me, crosses her arms over her chest to push her cleavage up even more. "Look, I told Bobby what he should do. Of course I want him with me. I have to trust that Jesus has a plan, though. I ain't gonna go over there and drag his butt home, am I? He'd only hate me. He's old enough to figure this out."

"He's barely twelve! And what if he makes a mistake? What if he chooses Josh and then finds out what a jerk he is and wants to come home. You going to hold that against him—"

"Why would I do that? Who do you think you're talkin' to? You ain't his mama, ya know." She walks the aisles for three full minutes, ignoring me. The newsman on the TV behind the counter announces the rising flood stages and warns of more thunderstorms. Then Rose comes back with her finger in my face. "Everyone's got problems, Laura. What makes you think you're so special, anyway?"

I don't answer. I don't think I'm special, but I did expect some sympathy from my best friend. Rose pays for my six-pack and holds open the door. It's not enough.

"I gotta go," I say. I swallow a yawn and blink my eyes

wide. I haven't slept well since I've been home. And I'm not a mama and probably never will be. I can't keep a man. Even the stray cat I've been feeding at Mama's house keeps running away.

"Come on, don't be that way," Rose says. She loops her arm through mine. "You know what I meant. You'll be a good mama. You just haven't found the right guy. Kids love you. Bobby's crazy about you. You're just giving up too easy."

Rose never gives up, even when she's doing wrong. The summer after third grade at the Tom Sawyer Days with a full bag of quarters, she refused to get off the Ferris wheel. Said the ride wasn't long enough and kept squeezing my knee hard to keep me in the bucket seat with her. "No. The ride ain't done," she said. "I paid good money and it was too short. That's a week of paper-route coin there. We're ridin' again!" The hot metal made my thighs itch, but Rose wouldn't let me move. "Stay," she pleaded. I tried to push up the seat bar holding us in. "Stay!" she yelled, like I was a dog.

"No, Rose. I'm gettin' out. The ride is over."

"Is there a problem, little ladies?" The slimy carny worker had slicked-back blond hair with stiff comb lines. A cigarette hung in his mouth and bobbed up and down when he talked, like Ponyboy in *The Outsiders*. He leaned over the seat into Rose's face and ash fell on her knee near the burn marks some-one else had given her. "Ride's over. Get out, girls."

"We ain't movin'. You said five minutes. It ain't been five minutes. We're gonna go again."

"Suit yourself," he said and pushed the lock back into place. "You can ride it all night for all I care. Hope you puke."

We rode it until the stars came out. I smelled popcorn each time we got close to the ground and thought of sticky, pink cotton candy. "I'm gonna have a funnel cake," Rose said. "When the ride is over." But we kept riding, looking down on the people as they got smaller and smaller and we got farther and farther away. Rose held my hand, her sweaty palm in mine for the whole ride.

Chomping on a wad of gum, Rose struts out of the store, climbs into the front seat, and steers the conversation back to her revenge list for Josh. "I'm gonna get a cat down at the shelter and let it piss all over the floors before Bobby and I move out. You can never get rid of that smell," she says and laughs. She keeps giggling, but none of it's all that funny to me anymore.

"When you movin' out?" I ask.

"Next month. After the trial. Unless I win. House is in his name only. He was supposed to add mine but lied. Now he's claiming premarital asset. Asset, my ass. The Bastard said he'd send the police if we don't get out. He had my Cadillac repossessed last week. Bobby and me stripped it clean: floor mats, windshield wipers, speakers, everything. Even took the damn battery. Anything I can get some money for and Lord knows I need money, especially with this Tom stuff. Told him to push the car to the street."

"What did Josh do?"

"He had to wait in the tow truck. Bobby and me were eatin' Froot Loops and laughin' our butts off, watchin' it all through the front window. And then there's his favorite grandfather clock."

"What? What did you do?"

"I took sandwich meat and rubbed it all over the edges. The dogs chewed it to pieces. An eye for an eye, I say."

"Jesus said to turn the other cheek, Rose."

"Don't talk about my Jesus, girl, unless you're ready to come to church with me and Bobby." I keep my mouth shut. It just isn't worth it.

I try to change the subject once in a while, try to distract Rose. She leans over me to trace a heart in the fog of the driver's seat window, not really listening.

"There's this one thing I may need your help with," she says. I shake my head no and hold up my hands like a traffic cop trying to stop cars. But I can't stop Rose. Never could.

"Whatever it is, Rose, I ain't doing it."

"I told Bobby not to poop in the house anymore. We've been using the RV's shitter instead. The tank's almost full. I'm gonna take the dump hose and fill the crawlspace with crap. Nice, huh?"

I stare at Rose. We're sitting at a red light.

"Nice? No. That's just wrong."

"Serves the Bastard right!" Rose slams her hand on my dashboard. "I just need help with the hose, to hold the other end, to get it all in the crawlspace while I operate the tank. I asked Bobby and he said no." Rose looks out the window and not at me.

"You asked Bobby? To do that?" My voice is calm, but revenge ain't worth jail.

"Yeah, so? What? He knows his dad's a jerk. He even calls him the Bastard!"

"But it's his dad. He's the jerk that's still Bobby's dad."

"Whose side are you on?" Rose yells.

I take the corner sharp; she slides over into my lap. I shove her back. I look out the window and wipe off what's left of Rose's fog heart.

Becoming Mark Twain

Jane Clemens worried that her son Sam was denying his clan. His success as a writer made him a bit too big for his britches. She didn't like his pen name either. One time when he wrote to his mama, he signed it, "Yrs aftly, Mark." Jane wrote back, "I've got no son named Mark." Sam didn't do it again. But he did model Aunt Polly after the things he loved most about Jane: her sense of humor and spunk, her resilience, her ability to be cheerful even when life wasn't so kind. In Sam's stories, it's Aunt Polly who tries to make Tom Sawyer a good boy. It's Widow Douglas who tries to civilize Huckleberry Finn. That's what mamas do, apparently. Neither succeeded. After all, Sam's mama had been the one to send him to a life of print. Before he'd even turned thirteen, Jane found him an apprenticeship with Joseph P. Ament, the editor of the *Missouri Courier*. Money in the Clemenses' home was sparse since her widowhood; placing Sam in someone else's care was the only way to feed him. Sam's wit caught Mr. Ament's notice. He happily provided meals, lodged him in the printing office, and gave him two suits of clothes in exchange for his work.

Sam did pay back his mama, though. Once he began selling books, he sent money home. One day Jane wrote to him and requested an increase in her allowance. "Sam I hear you are worth a million of dollars. If so I want to call for a larger sum. I will not say how much more…" She wanted him to remember, no matter how far away he roamed, where and from whom he came.

CHAPTER FOUR

I MAKE BURRITOS and serve them with a fresh salsa I chop up from Mama's tomato plants. She ignores the pots of herbs on her porch, but she praises the fresh cilantro flavor. She declares it better than Taco Bell. We're sitting at the kitchen table with the window open watching a storm roll in. Neighborhood dogs bark and birds dart back and forth, confused about which way is clear. The chickens huddle together under the steps for safety. The air is thick and wet; we certainly don't need any more rain, though.

There's an extra plate for Trey, just in case. He still hasn't come home except to shower and change conveniently when I'm not there. Mama says to stop pushing. "Why don't you worry about your own problems, Laura? I'm guessing you got a few." Mama's right, but it doesn't make me worry less about my brother. "Sammy's aunt came into the hardware store. Did I tell you that? I mentioned you were in town again. I told her you'd probably be at the reunion. She said you should ring him up. For old times' sake."

"Sammy's probably a little busy, Mama. What with the divorce and all." I watch how the news registers. "Rose told me." Sammy, the perfect man, apparently makes mistakes, too. "Besides, I ain't goin' to the reunion."

"Even more reason to call 'im. He's going through a tough time, too. I heard his wife strayed a bit. That's what I heard. Said she didn't want kids at all. Can you imagine? You could at least be friendly." Mama roots around in the fridge for sour cream.

After dinner, we watch *Wheel of Fortune* and she lets me hold the remote. We don't argue as much when we don't talk. Just as Pat Sajak asks Vanna White for an *E*, Mama clears her throat. "I guess now is as good time as any, Laura."

"For what, Mama?" The puzzle doesn't need an *E*. I'd try an *A*.

"You ain't answerin' my questions straight and there's somethin' I gotta say."

Vanna turns two middle squares: an *O* and another *O*. "What's that?" I ask, half listening.

"You know you can't stay here, right? Not for good, anyhow."

The word starts with an *F*. "Huh?"

"You act like you're fixin' to stay. Trey said so." She picks at her cuticles and ignores the TV.

"Flood!" I shout, two seconds before the contestant.

"Whatever the hell happened, you gotta go back and clean it up. Your life ain't here, Laura."

Pat congratulates the winner, which cues the theme music.

"What?" I ask. "You're kickin' me out? Now?" I've missed a few steps in this conversation.

"That's not what I'm sayin'. Don't get your panties all in a wad." Mama shakes her finger at me like I'm a naughty kid who won't pay attention. She smooths the wrinkles in her pants and takes a deep breath. "I'm just sayin' this ain't your place no more."

"And how do you know where my place is? I'm pretty sure you've wanted me out since I got here." It feels true, even if it isn't. Part of me wants to cry. Another is mad as hell that the one thing I need right now, a soft place to land, is the last thing my own mama offers.

"Look, I was tryin' to be nice, but I'm just gonna say it like it is. We've got lives of our own now, too, Laura."

"I know," I yell. "And now I don't! Does that make you happy?" I cross to the kitchen and start banging around the dirty dishes for good effect.

"If you're just gonna throw another hissy fit, you might as well just pack up and be on your way. I've been watching you pout for almost a week."

"Fine! Have it your way, Mama. You can wash your own damn dishes. Apparently, I've got bags to pack." I don't know what else to say. My own mama throwing me out on the street. Like I need this right now. I slam my bedroom door and start shoving things from drawers into my empty suitcase. I can't catch my breath and the tears I've been holding in finally come. I fall onto my bed and curl into a ball. Outside, the storm starts with thunder bursts, white glares of lightning, and a wild lashing of rain against the windowpanes. I think of the baby, my job, how I thought it would all turn out. Ten years ago, I couldn't get far enough away, but now, I'm hopelessly homesick for what I don't have anymore, for what I can't have again, and what I don't even want.

The screech of an emergency message interrupts my crying. Through the door, I hear Mama flip on the police scanner and tune in the weather band. A funnel cloud's been spotted over by Palmyra, and Hannibal residents are under a tornado warning. It's a few miles away but storms travel fast around these parts. Mama knocks on the door but I don't answer. "That ain't a watch, kiddo, it's a warning. You better get out here!"

The local sirens wail through the windows. A wind stirs open the screen door, and it *whaps* against the side of the trailer. I open my door and join Mama with Aunt Betty's quilt draped over my shoulders. My puffy eyes and pity party don't matter much now. The wind is so loud we both have to raise our voices to be heard. Mama's brought the chickens in and they're flapping around the kitchen pecking at nothing just for comfort.

"Want me to call Aunt Betty?" This flimsy mobile home is the worst place we could be during a storm; choices are easy when you don't have any, though. Bet those fancy houses by Walmart have basements built into the side of hills. A few years ago, after another bad storm, Trey tethered down the back of our trailer to steel posts he drove into the ground, but those anchors wouldn't hold in a tornado.

"I'm sure she knows by now. I just hope Trey has enough sense to come in if he hears the sirens." Mama tunes the scanner back to the police signal. There's report of damage at the VFW on Bates Road. Downed trees are blocking some roads.

An overturned car is stuck in a ditch. She switches back to weather. They're repeating the same tornado warning: *"This is an extremely dangerous and life-threatening situation. If you cannot get underground, go to a storm shelter or an interior room of a sturdy building now. Take cover now. Stay away from doors and windows."*

"I doubt they even had time to open the elementary school shelter." Mama shakes her head. She's right. We don't want to be caught in the car. Trey's probably at Digger's. That's not so safe either.

"We should go in the bathroom, Mama. Away from the windows."

"I know." She's always feared the spring storms. They roll up loud and dark. They dump their load on our levees. Sometimes we're under tornado watches every other day. Mama will forget to turn off the scanner and hears every single piece of bad news in town. It's exhausting to be so scared. I wish we had a basement. I wish Trey was home. I wish I was back in Florida far from this. At least with hurricanes, you know they're coming.

"It's going to be kind of tight in there," I say, holding open the bathroom door for Mama. She puts down the lid on the toilet and sits, holding Pamela in her lap. I pull back the curtain and climb into the plastic tub. Thunder roars outside and Mama shivers. Her shoulders are up by her ears, protecting them. I spent most storms of my childhood hunkered down with Trey and Mama in this tiny bathroom. Trey would bring in his guitar and play loud enough to drown out the thunder cracks. He could really only strum a C major chord over and over. It didn't help Mama's nerves.

The scanner buzzes again. The tornado warning is extended

another fifteen minutes. The Salvation Army's roof has a tree in it. The winds make the police sirens faint. This tight little time bubble smells like mildew and wet leaves. We watch each other in the mirror over the sink. In the map of Mama's face is what this life has done and what it could do to me. I look from the toilet to the sink to this bathtub. I have nowhere to go. Nowhere safe.

"Did you quit?" Mama blurts out. "You quit your job, didn't you? Didn't know you for a quitter."

"I didn't quit. Do we really have to do this now?" The door pops open from a draft, and I slam it shut.

"Fired? I'll bet you were fired." Her anxiety has turned back to anger. When you back Mama into a corner, she bites.

"I wasn't fired." I stretch out my arms the entire width of the bathroom. I can touch each wall. "Not exactly. Will you just drop it? Why can't I just come home? Why's that so bad?"

She strokes the nervous Pamela and pulls out tufts of black feathers. "It ain't. It just ain't true."

"I *thought* it might be a nice visit, but if you want me to leave, say the word."

"Don't go puttin' words in my mouth." The thunder cuts off the end of her sentence, but I know what she means.

"I'm not. I just don't feel all that welcome is all. At least around you." I nod toward her in the mirror, but Mama looks away.

"I'm just sayin' things have changed, Laura. Your brother, I know he's into trouble, he's always into trouble, but he's also savin' up for his own place. If I get that promotion, I might make a move, too."

"Sell this, you mean? Our house?"

"You haven't lived here in ten years! It's not exactly 'our' house anymore. It hasn't even occurred to you that I might want something of my own, too. Maybe even an empty nest, for once." Mama's right. It really hadn't occurred to me.

She huffs. "You better shit or get off the pot."

"Can't."

"You can. You just won't."

"Can't because you're on the pot, Mama." She looks down at the plastic seat. Her legs are twisted around the tan ceramic base, holding on tight. She might slap me but she busts out laughing instead. Her shoulders are pumping up and down, and she braces herself against the sink not to fall on the floor. I got her. I made her laugh. Dry-heave laugh. It's been years since I did that.

Outside, the rain pounds on our metal frame. The winds rock the trailer just a bit and the lights flicker. A car drives up and down the road. The radio screeches again: the tornado warning is downgraded to a thunderstorm warning. We're safe for now.

She wipes her eyes and clears her throat. "Here's the thing, Laura. You gotta decide what you want. Not just what you don't want."

Pamela flaps from Mama's lap and joins the other chickens in the kitchen. They nest around each other, burrowing into each other's fluff.

Safe Passage

Samuel Clemens was born in 1835, when Halley's Comet appeared in the Earth's sky as it orbited the Sun. He always predicted that he'd "go out with it," too. But first, he had a few dreams to fulfill. Like many boys who grow up on the riverbank, Sam wanted to be a steamboat pilot.

In *Life on the Mississippi*, published in 1883, Clemens wrote, "I was in Cincinnati…I packed my valise, and took passage on an ancient tub called the *Paul Jones* for New Orleans. For the sum of sixteen dollars I had the scarred and tarnished splendors of 'her' main saloon principally to myself, for she was not a creature to attract the eye of wiser travellers." Sam was supposed to be writing funny travel letters for the *Keokuk Post*, but he found the water more enticing. After drafting only five installments of his commission, he decided he'd rather steer than write. By the time Sam made it to New Orleans, he had convinced Captain Bixby to agree to an apprenticeship. In 1859, at the ripe age of twenty-three, Sam earned his official steamboat pilot's license. He happily traveled the Mississippi for three glorious years, fulfilling his boyhood dreams, until the spring of 1861, when the Civil War closed most of the water traffic. He briefly joined the war effort in a volunteer militia called the Marion Rangers, but they broke up after two weeks of playing soldier and drilling. Sam didn't have a choice but to pick up his pen and return to his former career.

Just as he said he would, Clemens died on Halley's Comet's return visit in 1910, once he knew the passage was safe.

CHAPTER FIVE

THE WALLS OF this trailer have always been too thin. Nothing is private when nothing but plywood separates you. "You made the mess and you'll clean it up!" Mama yells. Trey's boots stomp around. He's on his way out, but Mama must be standing in his way. I've been laying low since the tornado, watching *Dukes of Hazzard* reruns with Trey, just happy to have him home. During the commercials, I would submit job applications for openings across the river in Quincy. Nurses are leaving both sides of the water for more pay. Not many with experience are begging for entry-level work. Mama saw my marker trail in the newspaper. At least she didn't kick me out again.

"You ain't leavin' until you clean up after yourself and give me my money!" It's a standoff. She's the one who always said you can't stop a man from doing what he's going to do. She couldn't stop Daddy. I couldn't stop Sammy. We can't stop Trey.

"Money? Your money?" The chains on his leather jacket clink like he's crossing his arms.

"That's right. My money. I know you took it. It was right there in my purse. Two twenty-dollar bills. They're gone." It's my childhood again. Mama's anger. Fights with Trey. Never enough money to go around.

"So I took 'em, huh? I stole 'em? What makes you think I need your money?"

"Because you probably don't got much of your own. Unless it's drug money," she sneers. "I hear you been skippin' shifts again. You're gonna lose that job for good, boy."

"You don't know what the hell you're talkin' about!" Trey screams back. She hasn't said a word to me about Trey selling. He can't be. Jesus.

"You don't even pay the rent you're supposed to. Just look at you. Stealin' money from your own people. You turned out to be trash after all. Just like your daddy." I've covered Trey's part of the rent out of my savings. Mama knows that. She's just picking a fight for nothing. And Trey is nothing like Daddy.

"You don't know shit," Trey yells. The front door slams behind him. A porcelain figurine falls from a shelf and shatters, probably one of Mama's Precious Moments. I wait for her to start cussing again, but she doesn't. I tiptoe from the bathroom to my bedroom.

Trey knocks on my window from outside. I push aside the curtains and unlock the glass. Through the screen, Trey whispers, "Going down to the levee. Sandbaggin'. You wanta come?"

"Sure," I say. "Give me ten minutes."

We've snuck out on Mama plenty, especially when the Missouri summer heat was at its worst and the water was at its highest. One summer day, Trey took a couple of dollars from Mama's purse so we could go to the fireworks stand. "Come on, Laura," he said, grabbing my hand. "Mama said we could get sparklers."

The big tent was just over the bridge from the south side in an empty lot near the boat club. When it flooded, they moved the tent out to the highway, too far for us.

Trey and I walked on cracked sidewalks and made a game of jumping over the widest breaks. We passed trailers and houses bigger than ours but run down worse. Busted trampolines dotted the lawns. Chain-linked fences marked territory. We knew everybody on our street, but other lots were abandoned with bald lawns, moldy plastic ride-on toys, and cars with popped hoods long past running. Most had a dog cage. Trey made up names for the dogs as we walked. "What's that one called?" I asked.

"That one?" Trey said, nodding toward a black-spotted mutt, panting in the afternoon sun. "That's Red."

"He don't look like a Red."

"He is."

"What about that guy?" I pointed to a brownish-red beagle.

"Popcorn. He's Popcorn."

"He looks like a Red. That other dog must be Popcorn. Because of spots."

"Yep. That's right," said Trey just to shut me up.

A train blared, and I had to shout to be heard. "HOW ABOUT THAT ONE?"

"MUD," Trey yelled. "SHE'S ALL DIRTY. JUST LIKE THE MISSISSIPPI." A whistle called and I wondered if there was a caboose. Aunt Betty always promised ice cream if the caboose was blue.

We passed the downtown where folks were getting ready for Tom Sawyer Days, sweeping down the sidewalks, putting up traffic barriers, and filling the mud pits with hoses from fire hydrants. Some store owners were out washing their windows, and event schedules printed in red, white, and blue hung on every door. Workers pounded hammers constructing platforms and tents. The carnival rigs were parked, ready to be unloaded. The Fourth of July weekend was their economic boom for the year.

When we got to the big tent, a scruffy, bearded man in overalls pushed back the red-and-white-striped flap and said, "Don't come in if you can't pay."

"We got money," Trey said, pushing past him. I picked up a plastic shopping basket to show him we meant business. We marched up and down the grass aisles, shoving our hands into the wooden bins filled with smoke bombs, bottle rockets, and poppers. A plywood sign was propped up by the checkout: EVERYTHING ½ PRICE! The tent was stifling. The industrial fans in each corner didn't provide any relief from the heat; they just drowned out all the noise from the town.

Trey let me pick out my own green and gold sparklers. He chose a tiny rocket that launched out an army guy who parachuted to the ground. "When it's done, you got a new toy," he said. "We'll save a dollar for a root beer float, okay?"

But I didn't want to save a dollar. I wanted a rainbow fountain that sprayed fluorescent sparks. "It's stupid," Trey said. "It just sits there on the ground. Fountains are dumb." My bottom lip quivered. Then he picked up the fountain and tossed it hard into our basket.

The checkout guy stared us up and down. He wasn't local. He wore a collared shirt in the heat and spoke with an accent. Trey whispered he was probably Mexican. He didn't offer us the free lighting punks everyone gets at checkout; I grabbed too many anyway and stuffed them in our bag.

When we got home, Trey wouldn't light the fountain for me. He played with his parachute and pretended that the army guy was shooting my fountain.

I stole Mama's lighter and snuck down to an empty lot and figured out how to do it myself. As a spray of sparks shot up two feet and rained down in multicolored hues, I saw Trey peeking at me through the chain-link, making sure I didn't hurt myself.

Outside, Trey revs his engine. Mama's in the bathroom, so I slip out the front door hoping she won't catch me and pick a fight with me, too. I climb on the back of Trey's bike. He feels thinner to me, but his eyes are clear today. He has scratches on both cheeks like he wrestled with a rooster and lost and his face is all broken out with zits. He doesn't look healthy, but he doesn't look high either. He throttles the gas. Mama heard that. We ride off together. I feel like a traitor, but I shouldn't have to pick sides.

Trey and I spend the morning in a line of folks making sandbags down at the elementary school. It's a precautionary measure. The water isn't a threat yet but it might be soon. It won't be another '93, but the south side will probably flood. If it gets really high, the road to the caves will be blocked off, too. The levees usually hold, unless someone messes with them. Mr. Meyers, the janitor at our elementary school, is three guys down the line. He has a trailer on the south side a few streets from ours. He nods. "Good to have you home, Laura."

"Yes, sir," I answer, a little surprised he remembers me. "Good to see you, too."

"You stayin' outta trouble?"

"Best I can." I pull a St. Louis Cardinals cap I swiped from Trey's room down farther over my eyes, hoping for more anonymity.

Trey's boss has given anyone from the plant two hours off with pay to sandbag, which is why there are so many men here this morning. I hold the itchy burlap bag and Trey shovels in the sand. When it's a little more than half full, I tie it at the top. If you fill the bag too full, it's too heavy to move. If you tie the bag in the middle, the sand can't settle properly and mold itself to the dike. You learn these things when makeshift sandbag walls are the only things that will protect you.

While we work in the blinding sun, I catch him up. The heat on my face feels right, like Florida, and it makes me mellow.

"So about that big reunion?" Trey asks, as we walk to fill our cart with sand. "You goin', fancy pants?"

"I doubt it," I answer, shoveling in more sand. "Why would I?"

Trey shrugs. "You're here. You ain't fat. Might as well. You turned out better than most."

It may be the kindest thing my brother has ever said to me, and he said it at the moment when I needed it most.

"Hey, I went looking for you at Digger's place the other day," I mention.

Trey looks up and meets my eyes. "Can't you just trust me, Laura?" He shoots me the same look he did watching me light my firework fountain through the fence.

"Fine. I was just trying to find you," I say, like it doesn't matter after all.

Just as we're loading our bags onto the platform, Rose's soon-to-be-ex husband arrives. "You work with him?" I ask Trey, nodding toward Josh.

"Used to. He quit a few months ago," Trey answers.

"Why'd he quit?"

"Don't know. No sweat off anyone's back, though. These are good jobs. Guys are fightin' for 'em."

"Are you?"

Trey laughs and wrinkles up his brow. "I'm lucky they've kept me. I'm not exactly employee of the month."

"Rose thinks he quit so he wouldn't have income to pay future child support."

"That'd be pretty shitty."

"But not surprisin'."

"Not really. Daddy never gave Mama a penny, either. Kids

are a pretty convenient weapon when you're pissed, and I'm sure Rose is pretty pissed."

"That's an understatement." We fill the last of our bags and load them on the platform. Trey starts walking toward his bike and I follow.

"It's a mess with Rose. A mess I don't want," I say. "She's taking him to a judge."

"For what?"

"Custody of Bobby. Money. Revenge. Because she can, I guess." I climb on behind Trey and he kick-starts the engine.

Josh sees me and raises a hand to wave. I look past him and pretend I don't know him.

"Hey," Trey calls above the motor, ignoring Josh, too, "you wanta have some fun?" He doesn't really wait for my answer. I hold on to his belt loops, grateful for the wind our speed kicks up.

After a few miles, he turns down a narrow gravel road. Trees have overgrown the path and we have to duck not to get swatted by a branch. Trey weaves the bike around the broken branches left by the tornado. The shade cools us off, and it's a peaceful little ride. I don't ask where we're going and Trey doesn't stop to tell me. The road slopes toward a bank, which means water must be near. Then he cuts the engine and I hear the familiar trickling. The path runs out of gravel into a clearing. Trey parks the bike and we walk down the bank to a hidden creek. Birds dart away as we approach, but a big bullfrog somewhere in the brush stands his ground with an enormous burp.

"Where are we?" I ask. Trey holds back a low branch so it doesn't hit me.

"This is the land I want," he says with an emphasis on *land*. "It's been for sale for more than a year. They just dropped the price again."

"Can you afford this?"

"Almost. My plan is to put a trailer in the clearing there." Trey points back to the empty lot we passed. There's a single electrical pole waiting to be hooked up.

"It's a beautiful property, Trey. It'd be nice to wake up to the sound of the creek." The grasshoppers have already begun chirping, and the big daddy bullfrog is getting a response from someone down the bend.

We settle ourselves on a pair of boulders, and I take off my shoes to dip my feet in the chilly water. "Aunt Betty is just down the road, too. One day I walked Bear Creek a few miles and ended up at her house. Scared her something good."

"Was she pissed?"

"Sure. But she fed me anyway. You know Aunt Betty."

"Let me guess. She made it nice."

"That she did. Always." Trey picks up skipping stones and hands me a few. We stand, taking turns, and his rock beats mine in distance every time. "Remember when we'd walk the Salt River and go fishin' with her?"

"I remember one time you wouldn't give me no worms."

"When? That don't sound at all like your sweet big brother."

"Uh-huh. I was eight. You were mean." As we walked a similar worn path that day, Trey uncovered a rock and grabbed a handful of slimy, wriggling bait. "Keep it still," he'd said when I held my fishing pole out to him. "Stop movin'." I didn't flinch. "If you can't stop movin' around, I can't get you no bait."

Aunt Betty snatched the pole from me. She held it in the exact same position and Trey slid the hook through the worm's guts. "All you got is each other," she'd said. "You'd better find a way to get along."

Later, Aunt Betty let me stir the cornbread batter and sit on the kitchen floor watching it rise through the oven window. We dipped the fish in Hellman's mayo with our fingers and ate the pan of creamed corn bread with three spoons. After dinner Aunt Betty sent us to the garden to pick out a watermelon. Then we sat on the back stump spitting seeds at each other until our spit ran itself out.

"So, when are you going to buy it?" I ask, following Trey back to his bike.

"Soon. But I'm short." He hands me my helmet.

"How short?"

"Five hundred dollars. And I need it by tomorrow."

"Why the rush? If you're saving and close, can't you wait?"

"There's another buyer. A family. The Hansons. They want the property for a weekend campsite."

"Hanson? As in Heather Hanson?"

"Uh-huh." He sits down on the bike and waits for me to climb on.

I wait for him to ask for the money, but he doesn't. I can't stand the thought of that stuck-up Becky wasting good land like this on a hobby, especially when my brother is trying to make it something. "You want my help?"

"Wouldn't turn it down, if that's what you mean. A loan, of course. Just so I don't lose the land."

"Did you ask Mama?"

Trey nods. "She wouldn't cosign. Said she doesn't mix family and money."

In the distance, the bullfrog calls louder. "I'll help," I say. "If you need it, it's yours."

Trey gets off the bike and pulls me into the biggest hug he's ever given. "I'll pay you back, Sis. I will. Every penny."

"Of course you will." And if I can get back to work, I can help even more.

He walks back toward the water and stretches out his arms, a preacher leading his flock to baptism. "This will be mine, Sis!"

"It will," I say with a nod, happy for my brother.

He turns to face me, his eyes lit up like sparklers. "I know," he says. "I know exactly what we're gonna do." I nod again and vow to say yes to whatever is coming.

THE NEXT THING I KNOW, Trey and I are both laid out in matching, side-by-side chairs at Aunt Polly's Tattoo Parlor. Aunt Polly is actually a redhead named Ruth with gorgeous green dragons climbing up her arms. The parlor is in a room of a top-floor apartment above Scoville's Tavern. It smells like fried tenderloins and grease and the jukebox below plays Willie Nelson's "You Were Always on My Mind" through the floorboards. I cannot believe I've let my brother talk me into this, but at least the parlor is clean. Ruth must take hygiene seriously; I like that in my needles. That sun may have made me woozy. Or I might just be getting carried away home with

Trey again. It feels ornery and right. Mama is going to have a fit.

"How about a rainbow? Aunt Betty would like that," I suggest, flipping through the laminated books of Ruth's work. While I look, she wipes over each counter with Clorox. The bleach smell calms me.

"Too cheesy," Trey says.

"A wave? For the ocean."

"I can do that," Ruth offers, pulling up the back of her shirt to reveal the Mississippi. A catfish jumps above a brown wave against the blue sky of her plump torso.

"You don't live by the ocean anymore," Trey reminds me.

"A wave could definitely represent the river, too. Remember how the Mississippi ran backward? I could get that."

"Maybe. What do you think, Ruth?"

She shakes her head. "Not for you." She doesn't explain more. I get the impression that if she doesn't approve, I'm not getting a tattoo.

Out the window is a giant billboard looming over the Injun Joe Speedy Print Shop advertising the upcoming Tom Sawyer Days. Frog jumping. Mud volleyball. Fence painting. Tom and Becky Contest. Fireworks. A braided Becky Thatcher is holding up the schedule.

"I've got it," I say. "I know exactly what I want. A raft. To keep me afloat."

Trey follows my stare, squints his eyes, and looks back at me. "That ain't bad, Sis."

Ruth sketches out my raft. I make a few suggestions, but she ignores me, mostly. She stands back and studies my body and declares, "Shoulder blade."

"Does that hurt less?"

"You're a nurse, Laura. Ain't you used to needles?" Trey teases.

"I'm a nurse's assistant. I use needles on others," I say, "not myself." I pull off my shirt, relieved I layered with a cami, and take a deep breath. The first needle pierces and stings like stepping on wet Florida grass into a pile of a thousand fire ants. "Almost done?" I joke. Ruth doesn't think I'm funny.

Trey chooses another arrow for the tree on his back.

"Make it blue like the king in *Huck* when he's guessing the tattoo," I offer. I can still hear Ms. B quoting Huck: "I k'n tell you what's tattooed on his breast. It's jest a small, thin, blue arrow— that's what it is; and if you don't look clost, you can't see it."

"But doesn't the king guess wrong?" Ruth asks, wiping something on my back. The relief only lasts a second.

"True." I nod. She tells me not to move again. She gets back to work. Ruth is raking a hot fork over the worst sunburn of my life. Why am I doing this again?

"I know what I'll get," Trey says, picking up Ruth's pad and sketching it himself.

"What?" I'm about to chicken out, but then I think of the shock on Mama's face and decide it's worth it.

"An oar. To help you steer." There are tears in my eyes, but they aren't from the pulsing needles.

Trey's lips twitch into a grin. Ruth busts out laughing. The joke's on me.

BOBBY CALLS ME AT NOON the following Saturday. Something must be wrong. What did Rose do now? Then I remember that today is the Tom interview.

"So, are you the next Tom Sawyer?" I tease.

"Just come get me, okay?"

"Does your mama know where you are?"

"Yep. She said she'd try to get me a ride. I called her cell phone, but it must be off. Come on, come get me."

"I'll be there in a second." I balance the phone on my shoulder and pull on jeans and a T-shirt while we talk. "Meet me out front."

Bobby is sitting on the curb of the roundabout in front of the Hannibal Middle School with his backpack in his lap. I pull up, and he gets in and crouches down in the seat. He's wearing a rumpled polo shirt, the one I told him to tuck in, and jeans that are so long they pool around his white high-tops. His brown hair falls over one eye and makes him look even younger. He's thin like his daddy and freckles cover his face and arms. He'll make an adorable Tom. Sometimes when I look at him, I still picture Bobby as a baby, with his fists balled tight next to his ears.

"Hey, partner," I say. "Where to?"

"California. The beaches." He doesn't crack a smile. California is our dream. Everything must be better in California. We make fun of the commercials on TV advertising the white sands, the frothy drinks with umbrellas, and all those tanned people, but we believe every one of them. When I was Bobby's age, Florida was so foreign, but now that I've lived there, it's just another place to run away from. I need something else to reach for. California, it is.

"Really? You got a swimsuit in that backpack?" I ask.

"Yep," Bobby answers, patting his bag. "Hat, too."

"Well, all right, then. Let's go. Sunshine or bust. Anywhere but here, right?"

We go to the DQ for hot-fudge sundaes. I taught him how to get the ice cream, the fudge, and the peanuts all in the same bite. It's the only way to eat a DQ sundae. Bobby has them add caramel and whipped cream, and we take our sundaes and sit on the top of a picnic table in the grass. The bench is sticky from ice cream spills, and birds are pecking at leftover cones. In between bites he tells me how upset Rose has been, how she's always on the phone with the Bastard screaming or on the phone with the church ladies crying and praying. His face is gloomy, and he looks like he might cry, too. His compassion is one of the things I love about Bobby. Even as a little kid when I'd see him on my visits back to Hannibal he'd waddle up and look into my face and announce, "Aunt Laura is sad." I didn't know boys were ever like that. Bobby's curious about the world, too. He loves hearing my stories about nursing and my patients. Bobby says helping is brave, and that motivates me even more to get back to work, even if so far I've only received form-letter replies. Each time I've gotten one, I've sent out another application. I also emailed the faculty I knew at the Daruby School in St. Louis where I studied nursing. Maybe they'll have some leads. Aunt Betty says to keep knocking. Doors will open, eventually. Bobby thinks my life in St. Louis and Florida was exotic. He once told me in one of his emails that he wants to be a pilot when he grows up. I squeezed my eyes shut at the thought of Bobby flying away from us.

"You going to keep me in suspense, Tom?"

Bobby shrugs. "Wasn't a big deal. Just some dumb questions. Ms. Keller was there." A grin breaks across his face and I think I know why.

"Did you study hard?"

"I even made myself a study guide. Here, look."

He unfolds the official letter on Hannibal Chamber of Commerce stationery inviting him to apply to the annual Tom and Becky Program. On the back are study questions with Bobby's answers. He's taped the creases back together three times.

1. What was Mark Twain's real name?

Samuel Langhorne Clemens, with an "e" added to "horn."

2. Where was Mark Twain born?

Trick question. Hannibal is his boyhood home, but he was born in Florida, Missouri, on the Salt River in 1835. There's two creeks, Spencer and Peno, a few miles south of New London, which is a few miles south of Hannibal, that feed the Salt River, which meets back up with the Mississippi.

3. Where did Mark Twain get his pen name?

Working on a steamboat. He was a pilot. "Mark Twain" means there is enough water for boats to pass and not get stuck. It means there's safe passage. "Mark Twain" means to measure two fathoms. A fathom = 6 ft.

4. Hannibal is the setting for which famous novels by Mark Twain?

Easy. The Adventures of Tom Sawyer *and* Adventures of Huckleberry Finn. *I like* Huck Finn *better.*

5. When was Hannibal founded?

Boring. 1819 by Moses Bates and his slaves. It's all because of the Mississippi. That's why the train is there, too, right by the river.

Bobby has more Tom stuff next week. He's been assigned a Becky he practices with after school. He acts like it doesn't matter at all. I don't believe him on that count either.

"Did your mama ever tell you that I helped write a study guide for the Toms and Beckys?" I offer. "Maybe they don't still use it, but I'd be happy to bring you my copy."

"Really? Mom said you hate that stuff."

"Well, I wasn't a fan when we were kids. Most of the Toms and Beckys weren't kids your mama and I hung out with, but when I was in high school, we had this teacher, Ms. B, who loved all things Hannibal and Mark Twain. She wrote the book, and I helped a little. I'll bring it by the house later." Rose wants me to talk to him about the upcoming meeting with the judge over custody, so I change the subject. "So, what are you going to do when the judge asks?"

"I don't know. Tell him the truth, I guess." Bobby reaches over and steals a peanut out of my cup.

"Which is?" I stop eating and watch him.

"That it don't matter. It don't matter who I live with because they're still gonna fight all the time and I'm sick of listenin' to it." He kicks at the bench and birds scatter.

"That bad, huh?"

"If I'm with Dad, he yells about Mom and calls her names. If I'm with her, she cries and tells awful stories about him. She says he won't pay for nothin' and we gotta beg for money or worse. All she talks about is gettin' even. The Bastard and all. She's crazy. Nobody cares about me."

"Aw, Bobby. You know that's not true." I slide the rest of my sundae over to him. He scoops out a heaping spoon of vanilla. "You know I care."

"Do you know some of the stuff she wants me to do to him? She's crazy."

"This is a tough time for everybody. For you and your mama. But you don't have to do stuff just to please her, okay?" I put my hand on his knee but then pull it back. He told me last week not to call out the window when I pick him up at school and not to hold his hand when we're waiting in line at McDonald's. I'm trying to remember. "You gotta do for you, Bobby."

"Yeah, but then she says I don't love her and cries even more. I hear her prayin' that we'll have enough to pay the bills." Bobby scoots closer. He leans over and puts his head in my neck. He smells like sweat and dirty socks mixed with sugar. "Truth is, it'd be easier to live with Dad. Mom would kill me, though."

If I could, I would just drive away with Bobby. From all of this. From Hannibal and how quickly it feels that I never left. Anywhere but here. Sometimes being stuck is worse than staying put. What we need is a signal, a *mark twain*, to show us that the water is deep enough for us to get out.

When I pull up to drop Bobby off at Rose's, she's standing by the screen door, smoking. Bobby's asleep on my front seat, his head resting against the window. For too long I sit in the car and we watch each other, Rose and me, each waiting for the other to make a move. Then she walks out to the car and leans against the driver's door, facing away from me. I roll down my window. "I didn't forget him," she says. "That's what you're thinking. I had to meet with my lawyer. Saturday's the only day he's available. I knew Bobby had the Tom thing. Stop lookin' at me like that."

"Like what?"

"Like I'm a bad mom. I've got my own shit to deal with besides some stupid Tom-and-Becky thing that some rich kid is gonna win anyway." Bobby stirs and Rose lowers her voice.

"If you feel like that, then why are you puttin' him through this? Why let him try?" I whisper.

"He's puttin' himself through this. I ain't done a thing."

I bite my lip so I don't agree with her lack of effort. Taking down Rose right now won't help Bobby.

"And what the hell is that?" Rose asks, leaning into my car and grabbing at my sleeveless shirt. A corner of my raft must be peaking out. *"Oh my God, Laura, you got a tattoo!"*

"Shut up!" I shush her. "You'll wake him up!"

"Let me see it or I'll scream!" I pull down the strap on my shirt and let her peek. Rose squints and cocks her head to the side. "Ahh. It's pretty. Tiny but pretty."

"Trey talked me into it."

"Figures. Why a raft?"

"To float, I guess. I'm looking for a job. Maybe an apartment."

"You stayin', huh?"

"I've got to do somethin'. I need to work. There's too much time to think."

"You could do somethin' for me." Rose perks up, like it's a game.

"That doesn't sound good. What?"

"I need you to testify," she says, blowing smoke into the night air. Some of the smoke wafts into the car. "I need you to be a good liar for once."

"No way. I told you I ain't gettin' involved." I wave my hand to get the smoke out and pretend it bothers me more than it does.

"You're already involved. You don't have a choice. You need to say he hit me, that he hit Bobby—" She turns to face me. Her hair is stringy and needs a wash. Her face is pale without makeup. I wonder if I look as old and tired as Rose.

"He never hit Bobby," I say, looking up to meet her eyes.

She leans over and rests her elbows on the windowsill.

"You never *saw* him hit me either, but you'll *say* you did."

"I don't want any of this, Rose. It's not going to make anything better. You can't change the past." She stands up with her hands on her hips and blows more smoke into the air.

Then Rose explodes. "You're such a chickenshit! I'm not tryin' to change the past. But I'm not gonna spend the rest of my life feelin' sorry for myself. I'm gonna do somethin'. And that somethin' starts without the Bastard. You come home all high and mighty wantin' to save everybody from their shit. The first time I ask you to help me, you say no. That's just great, Laura."

I look at her through the window and wonder how we

ever got here. Everything looks so small when you're looking backward.

Bobby changes positions in the seat, opens his eyes, and looks up at me. I lean over and smooth the sweaty line of hair from his forehead. He blinks a few times and reaches for the passenger door handle.

"Let's go, Bobby," Rose says. "Dinner's ready. Fried chicken. Your favorite, Laura. Come on in and eat with us?"

It's an invitation: a peace offering to put everything back where it was. It's easier to sweep it all under the rug than to really deal. Bobby climbs out of the car and starts walking toward the house. Halfway there he leans over and picks up a few rocks. He starts skipping them down the road just like I taught him to.

"I'm not testifying, Rose," I say, keeping my eyes on Bobby. "I really can't."

Rose leans into the car and grabs my hand. Her grip is tight, and her hand is hot. Bones and knuckles and flesh squeeze and hold mine. I shake my head at Rose. "No," I say.

Rose waits with tears hanging heavy on her bottom lids. They are about to spill. "Please, Laura," she says, "for him."

"Let go," I say. "You don't even know what you're asking." And she doesn't. Only I know, and it would cost me Rose, maybe even Bobby, and that's too big of a price to pay.

Rose nods in Bobby's direction. "Remember when he was born? You stood there in the hospital holdin' him and said you'd do anything—"

"Don't do that. You know that ain't fair. Of course I'd do anything for Bobby."

"Then help me." Rose moves her hands to my face and makes me look at her. "Please," she whispers.

I pull her hands off and squeeze back before I release them. I wave at Bobby and watch him in the rearview mirror until he disappears.

Compromising

When John Marshall Clemens moved his family to Hannibal in 1839, Sam was only four years old. Missouri was still a young state, too, having joined the Union in 1821. John hoped that the river town would be more promising for his career. Missouri hoped it would balance free states, like Maine, which had joined the Union the year before, with slave states.

Mostly, it didn't work out. Compromise is hard and sometimes it doesn't go the way you plan. Sam's father was never that successful. The Clemens family didn't have much money. In 1847, when Sam was just twelve, his dad died, and Sam had to work to help the family financially. He struggled to stay in school.

In 1857, the Supreme Court decided that Dred Scott, a slave who had lived with his owner in a free state before moving to Missouri, was not allowed his due emancipation. The court claimed that no black, whether they were free or slave, could be a U.S. citizen. Without citizenship, they couldn't have freedom or petition the court. Tensions grew. The Civil War erupted four years later.

Sam's dad had one slave. His uncle had more. Sam grew up playing in the slave quarters, learning to tell stories, singing their songs, and wondering if words could change the way people compromised.

CHAPTER SIX

I PLAY THE voice mail twice. Just to be sure.

"Hello. I'm calling for Laura Brooks. This is Martha Tilden, Human Resources manager at Quincy Hospital. We're scheduling interviews. Can you come this afternoon? We've just had an opening for a night shift. It's on the maternity floor. Please call me at your convenience." Her voice is hurried, like the phone call is one of a hundred things she has to do.

I dial Martha back immediately. "I can be there in an hour," I say. Hanging up the phone, I'm already imagining how I'll get an apartment on the Illinois side with a view of the river. A two-bedroom so Bobby can stay when Rose and Josh are fighting. And a balcony so I can watch the water at night and have a beer or drink my coffee when I come home from my shift and the boats pass by. I run my finger over my raft tattoo for good luck.

Mr. Eggleston, my guidance counselor at Hannibal High School, gave me the idea of nursing school. "Your grades are good. You've got an A in biology. You could get out of here. If you want," he said. It was the beginning of my senior year, before snow blanketed us for months, before the spring rains that never seemed to stop, before the water started rising. There was still hope. "How about nursing? Everybody needs nurses. It's good money."

"Can't pay for school, Mr. Eggleston. I'm gonna need to work," I said. "Can you get me on at one of the plants? General Mills is hiring. My brother said he'd put in a good word for me." Rose wanted a plant job, too, but they wouldn't hire her. Nobody in town gives a break to a teen mom without reliable childcare. She'd be stuck at minimum wage for the long haul.

"Factory jobs will dry up. Folks need to adapt. You've got the grades. If you want to go to college, there are scholarships. Have you thought about it?" Mr. Eggleston slid a glossy brochure across the desk to me. On the cover was a thin young woman in pale pink scrubs with a stethoscope around her neck. Her teeth were straight and white. She folded her arms across her chest like she knew exactly what she was doing. "There's a nursing school in St. Louis that has a program with funding. The Daruby School. It's only a few hours away. You go to school and get your degree. Then they assign you to a hospital for a few years, and if you stay, you don't have to pay them back. It's a good deal. Demand is high. We've sent a few girls down there. You know Amber Mudd? She graduated two years ago. She went there and did real good. First got her CNA and then went back for her RN. She just got a job out in California. Megan Shields is in school there, too. She was in your brother's class."

"I'll think about," I said, not really meaning it.

"I talked to Ms. Bechtold. She thinks it's a great idea, too."

"Really?" That shifted everything. Mr. Eggleston knew my family situation enough to know what was possible. Mama had been laid off from the hardware store for most of my senior year. We were using WIC stamps just to feed ourselves and grateful for Aunt Betty's garden. I was waiting tables on the weekends at the Mark Twain Dinette so I could buy school lunch and clothes when I needed them. Rose certainly couldn't afford a babysitter, so I took care of Bobby in exchange for pizza when her sister, Daisy, wasn't available. Sammy drove me everywhere and refused to take gas money, even when I tried to pay. "My daddy owns the gas station. It's one of the perks," he insisted.

Mama saw the brochures, but she didn't think I'd get in. Mr. Eggleston called her a couple of times and tried to explain the program and the scholarships. "You think you're too good for us, Laura. Is that what you think?" she'd asked when the acceptance letter came in the mail. "You just gonna leave us high and dry like this?"

I looked out the window at the Mississippi creeping in and there was nothing high or dry for miles. All I saw was a chance to run for safety, to leave, and to save myself. "Do you even know what you're doing, Laura? What do we know about college or the likes?"

I opened the acceptance letter at the kitchen sink and read every word twice. It was a five-year contract with a heavy penalty if I didn't complete it. Of course I didn't know what I was doing, even when I was doing the right thing, but that never stopped me. Then I tossed it on the table in front of her and didn't answer. I knew better than to try to explain it to Mama.

AFTER A THIRTY-MINUTE DRIVE TO the interview, I'm sitting in a cramped office wondering if the dying ficus tree in the corner is a bad sign. Its wilting branches are brown on the ends. It's as dry as a broom, and I worry it might crackle and crumble if I tap it with my toe. "You clearly have the training, but there's a difference between books and life," Martha begins, glancing up from my CNA diploma and transcript. I wish she was looking at more. I wish I'd stayed in school longer.

"Absolutely." I nod. "I worked the ER for three full years. Another two in Obstetrics and Gyno. One in Pediatrics. There's not much I haven't seen." Martha is impressed with my ER experience. As a CNA my job is to assist with whatever needs doing and sometimes that means anticipating a doctor's needs; sometimes it means jumping in when an RN's hands are full. Mostly it means knowing a little about everything and being able to manage the environment without losing your cool.

"So you've assisted with newborns before?"

I picture Rose screaming at me in the delivery room. Her eyes bulged like a puppy caught in a cage. Bobby came early. Three weeks before his due date, days after the end of our sophomore year. He rushed partway out with the cord wrapped around his throat. The doctor told Rose not to move. Then she slid one hand under the cord and cut it with the other. Rose yelled "Get *it* out of me!" and just like that Bobby was born. I'll never forget how close that moment was between life and death, how purple his little face was next to his pale stomach. I held Bobby as the color rushed through him. Then Rose reached out her arms, and I laid him on her chest. We were just kids. We didn't have any business with a baby, and yet, there was Bobby. Suddenly, Rose was on another side that I couldn't reach, so I decided I didn't want to. Until a few months ago, that is. If I can't be someone's mama right now, I can surely help someone else become one.

"Yes," I say. "I also did a summer on a neonatal wing. And one full semester of my curriculum in school was maternity. It's just that those weren't the jobs that were available when I got out of school."

"You've seen the worst?" She cocks her eyebrows at me.

"I've seen the worst." I look her straight in the eye. She needs to know I'm tough. That I won't go crying in the corner when a mom loses it or a baby doesn't make it. It happens. You never forget it. Recovery isn't an option. You just keep going. Hospitals are places of joy and loss, but they are also places of order and rules. They drown you in paperwork and schedules. Numbers determine fate. If I learned anything in ten years of nursing and training, it's that we are supposed to follow doctor's orders. Even if a patient's diagnosis is uncertain, there is a plan for me to follow, and I do. The shifts are usually so busy you don't have time to think; you just do. There is a clear hierarchy, and you'll get along fine so long as you don't question it.

"You were at Jacksonville Memorial for how many years?"

"Six years. Budget cuts did them in. I wasn't fired or anything."

Martha smiles. "I wasn't thinking that. Your recommendations are excellent. I was just wondering why you came home. Salaries are surely better in Florida." She looks at me over her glasses and squints.

I study the remains of the ficus. "Guess I just needed a change," I mumble.

She makes me wait in the silence while she looks back over my papers. Then she shuffles them into a neat pile and puts them all back in a manila folder without a label. My name hasn't claimed it. I'm just another applicant begging for another job. "We'll let you know soon," Martha says, folding her hands under her chin and looking me up and down one more time.

I stand to go because there is nothing left to say. I thank her for her time and let myself out the door.

"I think I knew your daddy," Martha calls, almost in a whisper, to my back.

I turn around and face her, waiting for her next move.

"Yes. I've been trying to place it. It's the eyes. He had green eyes just like yours. Maybe the nose, too. We went to high school together. He wouldn't remember me, of course. He was a senior when I was a freshman. So handsome. One of those guys on the edge. Makes them more mysterious. How is he these days?"

"I couldn't tell you," I answer. "He left when I was little." It sounds pathetic, even if it's exactly the truth.

"Oh," Martha says, her mouth forming an O, as if Daddy's leaving was definitely my fault. She opens my folder and makes another note. "We'll call soon."

I leave the hospital, sorry to go, wanting to put my hands in the mess of nurses and patients and noise rushing past me, and walk back to the parking lot and sit in my car, in the heat that has collected, wishing I knew so much that I don't and so lonely for the not knowing.

"LET'S PRAY!" ROSE SAYS WHEN I call to tell her that I didn't get the job. "Pick us up. You're takin' us to church. It's at seven o'clock. We'll ask Jesus for help!" I assume Jesus already knows I need help but I don't mention it.

Bobby is waiting on the front stoop when I arrive. He's holding a picture that just came in the mail of him whitewashing the fence downtown. I suspect he has a crush on his Becky by the way he keeps talking about practicing the engagement scene from *The Adventures of Tom Sawyer*. The Tom and Becky pairs stroll through the tourists in the downtown and perform when anyone asks. "We're gettin' really good at it," Bobby tells me. When I ask his Becky's name, he turns bright red and can barely whisper *Shelly*. "Everyone is sayin' she's probably gonna win, too."

"Oh, yeah? And what are they sayin' 'bout you?" I ask.

Bobby shrugs. "The parents talk a lot, but Mom hasn't been able to make it to most things. That's why Ms. Keller sent the picture. So Mom could see. I'd like to win for her, though. It'd sure make her happy. Happier than she's been lately, anyway." I cringe a little. Maybe if I'd agree to testify, Rose wouldn't be so miserable, but I'm not sure it's worth the risk. "Don't worry," he says. "I've got somethin' else planned. It's gonna make her real happy and proud."

"Your mama is proud of you, Bobby, just the way you are. You're plenty good enough." Rose barrels out of the house in a cloud of perfume. She's wearing black sunglasses and jeans. I nod toward the car and add, "And don't let anyone tell you different, you hear? Lots of folks like to put each other down around here. They don't have anything better to do, but you're special, okay, kiddo?" Bobby shrugs again and climbs into the backseat, but he smiles in the rearview mirror.

The River Passage sits on Broadway near the Save-a-Lot. The parking lot out back is twice as big as the building and it's full of oversized shiny trucks and well-worn minivans. Everyone drives their own, making sure that everyone else sees it.

Directly behind the preacher, there is a fake brick wall that makes the stage look edgy and urban. A full rock band, complete with an electric guitar, a bass, and a full drum set, plays beside the pulpit. The singers wear jeans and flannel shirts. They're clean-cut and trim and don't look like they're from around here. The River Passage feels more like a concert than a church. There aren't any pews or kneelers. Just wooden benches and folding chairs. Folks in T-shirts and shorts and coming and going as they please up the aisles as strobe lights swing back and forth. The whole place smells like pine, like someone just took down their Christmas tree. Rose sways in a trance of pure joy. I've never seen her so calm. She's given herself over fully to the music. "I just love praisin' Jesus this way!" she screams into my ear as the drummer takes a solo.

"Uh-huh." I nod, bobbing my head like I feel it, too. "Where's Bobby?"

"With his youth group. Probably in the ball pit."

"The what?"

"Oh, they have a ball pit for the kids. And a coffee bar for the adults. It's very casual. Everyone is so friendly here." And they are. It's true. Every single person we've passed has thanked me for coming to their "campus." I understand why Rose feels welcome. "Isn't Pastor Jordan so great?" He doesn't look much older than Bobby and he says "dude" when he leads us in prayer.

"I'm gonna tell y'all something, dudes," he begins, "we've got a lot to be grateful for today!"

Everyone shouts, "Amen!"

"But we've got some concerns, too, dudes."

They also answer his transition with an *Amen!*

"Y'all need to turn your troubles over to Jesus!"

"Amen!" Rose screams beside me like she's the biggest fan and her favorite band just took the stage.

"Jesus is on our side!"

"Amen!"

"Now, dudes. I know y'all are worried about the water!"

"Amen!"

"I seen it comin' up, too. Now, I'm here to tell you that Jesus is gonna make it all okay, now, okay?"

"Amen!"

I lean over and shout in Rose's ear, "Did he just say not to worry about flooding?"

"Uh-huh! Isn't that great? We'll just pray!"

I think about that for a minute and then I ask, "Did you pray for a divorce, too?"

Rose's face goes blank. Then she reaches out her hands toward my neck like she's going to strangle me.

I hold up my hands in surrender. "Sorry!" I shout. "I'm just tryin' to figure out how this works."

Rose gives me a look that says *Bullshit*, but she probably doesn't want to cuss in here, even though I've heard her cuss plenty on the sidewalks outside.

"You ain't in charge as much as you think you are, Laura. You want that job? Jesus does that! I think it's time you did some prayin', sister. Maybe a little compromisin', too."

I don't have a good answer, so I just bow my head.

"Let's pray for our hometown Toms and Beckys, too!" Pastor Jordan shouts, and the crowd erupts.

"Praise Jesus!" Rose high-fives me for no reason.

"But what if he doesn't win?" I ask.

"Then it wasn't meant to be. We have to follow Jesus's path for our lives, Laura, not our own."

Like I lost my job and came back to Hannibal because it was meant to be. Like one minute there was a baby and the next there wasn't because of some plan. I'm about to object when Bobby comes sprinting up the aisle and waves as he passes us.

"What's he doin'?"

Rose's hand is clasped over her mouth in happy disbelief. "Oh, Bobby!" she shouts. "Oh, Laura! I'm so glad you're here for this! My baby!"

"What? What is it?"

"Can't you see? Bobby is givin' his life to Jesus today. He's up there near the pool!"

The fake brick wall hides a huge tub of water on the far

left side of the stage. The water is at stage level so it's hidden from our seats, but the camera projects the baptism pool on the megascreen above us. It's surreal. Bobby is standing at the top of the stairs with big eyes watching the water. For a second, he looks like he's changed his mind. I want to tell him, *It's okay. You'll figure it out. We all stumble. You don't have to have all the answers today.* Then he leans forward and trips down into the pool. He splashes water as he goes and reaches out his arms like he's trying to catch himself. Pastor Jordan grabs his open arms and dunks him real quick before Bobby can say a word. The crowd erupts with *Amen*s and *Praise Jesus*es. Rose looks like she might faint beside me. I put my arms around her waist and hold her up, but my eyes are on the screen watching Bobby. He shakes his head like a dog and water sprays in Pastor Jordan's face. It's the way Bobby watches the pastor watching him that worries me the most, like every move he makes is for approval, like pleasing others is the only thing that pleases him.

Rose rushes the stage and throws herself into the pool, too. Then she and Bobby climb back up the steps together, holding on to each other, dripping wet. Bobby is surveying Rose. Rose is smiling for the cameras. She leans over and whispers something in Bobby's ear, and he breaks out in a huge grin like he just took the biggest gamble of his life and won the whole jackpot.

After celebratory doughnuts and an hour of rewatching the baptism video, Rose finally tells me they're ready for a ride home. We're walking to the car and Bobby is rehashing all the details of his dunk when I see them. Two cops are in a car parked next to mine. As we get closer, one of them steps out of his car. "Rose Haymaker?" he calls across the lot.

"I'm a single woman now, gentlemen. You can just call me Rose," she says with her flirty smile.

What the hell has she done now? I'm praying this has nothing to do with Josh and her revenge plans. Maybe it's about the trial? Can't be. Cops wouldn't come looking for you about a divorce and custody settlement. And how did they know Rose was with me?

"We have some questions, ma'am. Is there a place we can talk?"

"Bobby, climb in that car with your Aunt Laura," Rose coos. "I'm gonna chat with these nice men for a minute." I unlock the door for Bobby and slide into the backseat with him. I reach between the front seats and turn on the radio for a distraction, but I still have my eye on Rose. She leans against the car with one leg bent and plays with the cross on her necklace. One of the cops says something that makes her laugh, and she swats playfully at his badge. Her hand lingers on his arm. A few minutes later, she slides on her black shades, takes the cop's business card, and gets in the car with us. I move up to the front with her.

"Just drive, okay?" she says, buckling into the passenger seat.

I do. Rose is shaking. Her little act didn't fool me a bit. I know her.

"Hey, Bobby. Listen. Those cops had the wrong person, okay? They weren't lookin' for me. Got that?"

"Who were they lookin' for?" he asks.

"How the hell should I know?" she snaps. Rose takes a deep breath and starts again. "What I mean is it was someone else with my name. It's not me. We don't need to say nothing about this to your daddy, ya hear?" Rose doesn't call him the Bastard. I'm about to keep pushing for an answer when a voice mail pops up on my phone. I pull over to the side of the road. It's Martha, telling me what I already know.

"The prayin' didn't work, Rose," I say, "unless Jesus really wants me unemployed."

Rose turns up the radio to hear the flood stages like they really matter to her.

Lover's Leap

Hannibal's Lover's Leap isn't the only one. There are at least eight other similar bluffs overlooking the mighty Mississippi with comparable legends. Young lovers are thwarted Romeo and Juliet–style and leap from the rocky limestone and shale to their deaths below. An Indian squaw refuses her father's choice for marriage and embraces death rather than a miserable life. Much of it isn't true. Truth is overrated anyway. One of the exaggerated stories about Hannibal's Lover's Leap is credited to a young newspaperman by the name of Orion Clemens, Samuel Clemens's older brother.

On October 22, 1844, a group of local Millerites, followers of the American Baptist preacher William Miller, gathered at the top of Hannibal's Lover's Leap to wait for the prophesied return of Jesus Christ. They dressed in white robes in honor of the coming. Christ didn't show up. Their disappointment didn't make them leap, but it was a long walk back down the mountain.

During National Tom Sawyer Days each year you can run the Hannibal Cannibal, a 5K that begins in the historic downtown and climbs all the way to the top of Lover's Leap. If you make it up the steep slope, you're met by the judge looking for the runner who most resembles roadkill. Rumor has it the judge sits under an umbrella enjoying the view with his granddaughter.

The park at the top of Lover's Leap offers a panoramic view of miles of lush Illinois farmland and a picturesque scene of downtown Hannibal as it snakes along the Mississippi. There's a high fence protecting the bluff now. Those who want to die for love have to scale the chain-link first.

CHAPTER SEVEN

ROSE IS THE one who wants to make sure we run into Sammy. Our high school reunion—the one Rose and I aren't going to—is next week. There's a pre-reunion get-together at the Gossip Grill on Main Street. "You won't recognize the place, Laura," Rose says with her hands in a mound of ground beef. We're trying out a new low-fat recipe. "Hannibal's downtown is fancy now. I heard some of the gays from St. Louis bought up the falling-down houses. Bless 'em. They made artists' studios and showed some locals how to make money," Rose tells me, rubbing the spices into the meat. "There's even wine and cheese. Not that I want it."

"If you don't want it, who does?"

"Probably those grown-up Beckys. The kind that wear pearls to church. They went off to college and come home to visit for the Fourth and wanta sit with their grown-up Toms and reminisce. The good ol' days that still seem like every day to most of us."

"Then why are we going?" I ask, sprinkling more paprika into the meatloaf mound. Something besides the fat has to give it flavor.

"Stop it! You'll make it look like it's still bleedin'." Rose moves the pan out of my reach and I sneak under her arm to shake in more. "To be seen, of course. Sammy'll probably be there. I saw his big brother, Lance, who's gettin' married soon, by the way, at work this mornin' and he said Sammy was takin' the divorce real hard. Don't I know it." It never takes Rose long to turn the conversation back to her misery.

"Will his wife be there?"

"Why would she be? The divorce is as good as done. She ain't from here. His soon-to-be-ex wife lives in Quincy. She won't come over on this side, I'll bet."

I get a Diet Pepsi from Rose's fridge and stand in front of her air conditioner. She only has one window unit for the whole two-story house. Bobby and she don't go upstairs during the summer at all.

"Stop hoggin' the air. I can smell your pits from here. Gross!" Rose grabs a soda, too, and takes off her apron. She's wearing a pink tube top and cut-off jean shorts. She looks like she's already lost ten pounds and is showing it off. The butterfly tattoo on her lower back isn't stretched so thin and the hot pink wings are wrinkling a bit. "Don't even act like you don't wanta bump into Sammy. I know you better. You may have left. You may be fancy with your degree and your Nurse Laura shit, but I know you, sister."

I drink the rest of my soda and don't say anything. There isn't much I can deny. Except that I've always thought of myself as more of a Huck than a Becky. "Besides, you need to get out.

You're too mopey about the job these days. It'll happen. Pouting about it won't help."

"I have not been pouting," I lie. "I'm just disappointed."

"Put that on a shelf tonight, girl. We're gonna have fun!" Rose slaps my butt.

We walk downtown when the sun sets, and a quick rain shower drops the temperature to a blessed seventy-six degrees. Once we cross over the bridge from the south side, weeds between the sidewalk cracks start disappearing. The smoky scent of barbecue is in the air. There aren't as many empty beer cans on the street. The fresh blacktop is still shiny and bouncy. Rose must be right; Hannibal is on its way up. I always thought folks who stayed didn't have another choice. Maybe it takes more courage to invest, dig in, and make it a home you want. "Let's walk on the levee," I say and pull Rose up the hill with me. The water is up again. It's summer, after all. Mama says it's going to flood. She says it could be as bad as '93. She can't be right, though. The weathermen said '93 was a five-hundred-year flood. The Mississippi River crested at 31.80 feet in Hannibal. The waters have to stop rising soon.

Rose and I stand on top of the grassy bank of the levee. "Walls are in," Rose says. We both look over to the cement-and-steel walls that block Broadway from the Mississippi. Built to hold back thirty-four feet of water, they're an eyesore, for sure, but they do their job. If Mark Twain wrote today, he'd have Tom and Huck scale the walls somehow to get to the river. Climbing over the grass levee would be easier, but where's the fun? Huck would have a rope and Tom would toss a grappling hook. It wouldn't have the same effect as lolling down to the banks and watching boats and barges from every street corner, but those same street corners and Mark Twain's boyhood home wouldn't exist without the walls. If they weren't holding back the water, we'd be swimming downtown.

Standing on the levee, watching the water churn, I have second thoughts. "Let's get french fries and root beers and sit up here and watch the stars," I say. "Forget the Gossip Grill. I don't want to see all those people. It doesn't sound like fun. It doesn't sound very churchlike either."

"Jesus loved a good time! Come on. You're going."

Bossy Rose. Nothing changes. She takes my hand and drags me back down the riverbank, just like she always has.

A month after Sammy and I started dating, Rose decided she was tired of sharing me. "I ain't seen you in forever, Ms. I'm-in-Love. This weekend we're going out. All of us. Double date. It'll be fun. Friday night. Josh'll be at Hardee's after he gets off work. Daisy said she could take Bobby." Rose had been missing a lot of school because of Bobby's ear infections. Our principal had warned her that she might not graduate if her attendance didn't improve. She didn't have a lot of options, and a night out meant a night of still being a high schooler and not a trapped teen mom.

The Hardee's parking lot was across the highway from the high school and filled with kids looking for something to do in a town with nothing to do. If you got a new car, you drove straight to Hardee's to show it off. If your cousin was visiting from out of town, they debuted with a Pepsi and a hot ham-and-cheese. On the opposite side of the drive-through was a NO LOITERING sign. We parked right under it.

Josh was already drinking by the time he pulled into the

parking lot. Rose kissed him before he even said hello. He stumbled, leaned on the door like he was cool, and said, "Hey, baby! There's my girl. Prettiest girl in the lot!" Then he flashed us a brown bag of fireworks with a bottle of Jim Beam in the bottom. I wondered how he could afford liquor and not antibiotics.

Josh, Rose, and I followed the crowd over to the football stands. On the field, Sammy stared down the defensive line, waiting for their moves and calling out to his guys how to protect the quarterback. You could see the team trusted him. He was steady. He didn't always make things happen, but he knew exactly how to react when they did. Josh, Rose, and I had filled our Pepsis with Jim Beam in the parking lot and snuck them in through the gates. It made the game a bit blurry but the cheerleading much funnier. When the most popular girl in school, Heather Hanson, missed her footing and fell on her face, Rose and I almost peed in our pants laughing. "Hey, wasn't she Sammy's Becky?" Rose asked after she caught her breath.

"What's a Becky?" Josh said and that was hysterical, too. How could he not know what it meant to be Tom and Becky? Half of the pairs ended up mated for life. Then they had kids and repeated the cycle and filled the football stands on Friday night with the younger versions of themselves. They were Hannibal's royalty, and I was dating one of them. Heather wasn't.

The Hannibal Pirates beat the Booneville Buccaneers that night 28–14. I waited for Sammy to come out of the locker room. There was still water in his hair from the shower because he was in a hurry to see me. Me.

After the game, we drove out to Sammy's farm to shoot bottle rockets off the levee. More FOR SALE signs dotted the ditches than before. Most families, like Sammy's, were just trying to hold on to their land. The drought and rains had already ruined the crops. The stunted cornstalks swayed as we drove past. On the levee, the fireworks screeched and popped like gunshots. They lit up the sky, revealing the layers of sandbags the family relied on to keep out the Mississippi. Water lapped at the lower rock bed. Sammy said it was okay to sit on the levee because it helped pack the bags together. "Just be careful," he warned us. "That's about all there is saving us these days." Then Josh decided to launch one of the bottle rockets from an empty beer bottle and it went too far into a brush of withered trees. Everyone laughed but Sammy told him not to do it again. He sipped on a soda, too, but he didn't add anything to his. "Nah, man," he said when Josh tried to pour Jim Beam in. "Someone's gotta drive y'all home. Besides, Coach would kill me." Josh called him something under his breath, but Sammy just shook his head like it was a big joke. My drink started tasting sour, too, and I just wanted to be somewhere alone with Sammy.

Rose and I turned up the music from Sammy's truck and two-stepped on top of the levee to Billy Ray Cyrus's "Achy Breaky Heart." Then another truck came around the corner and shined its brights at us. It was rusted and mud-caked so we knew it wasn't Corporate. Sammy'd told me that his dad and ten other local farmers had signed a pact not to sell to Corporate, not even if the only thing they owned was underwater. From the window, Sammy's brother, Lance, called out, "Dad says it's too dry to be shootin' fireworks."

Sammy didn't answer. He nodded, stomped out the lighting punk under his foot, and changed the music to Michael Jackson's "Remember the Time."

Josh called Lance a buzzkill. "Man, you guys are wimps! And you like nigger music." Then the passenger door on Lance's truck slammed and we all turned as Jerome Hadley stormed toward us. Rose and I stopped dancing. Sammy stepped in front of Jerome and put both his hands on the brown muscled arms bulging out of Jerome's T-top. Sammy walked him back, talking low in his ear the whole time. Jerome towered over Sammy's six feet. He was the biggest guy on the defensive line. He kept his eyes on Josh, who acted like it was all not a big deal and busied himself refilling his cup. Lance just laughed, probably at how easily Jerome could kick Josh's ass if he wanted to. Then Josh leaned into Sammy's cab and switched the boombox to "Black or White." I never knew if it was on purpose or not.

"Cool it, Josh," Sammy yelled.

"Come on! We can take 'em," Josh called back but he was already climbing into his truck, and Rose was sliding in beside him. I kept my distance and watched from the levee.

That's when Sammy lost it, finally. "I ain't fightin' over the likes of you. Way to pick 'em, Rose." I worried that maybe Sammy would lump me in with them. Then I realized Rose hadn't even held the door out for me.

Josh peeled out, spinning dirt and rocks in our direction. A rock landed on something hard and I hoped it wasn't a windshield. Jerome and Lance charged after them and Sammy reached out his hand to pull me down from the levee. "Do we have to go, too?" I asked.

"This ain't over," Sammy answered, but his face looked how I felt. He didn't want any part of the drama, either. We drove back to the Hardee's lot. Jerome and Josh were already circling each other and a crowd was growing around them. Josh got in the first punch, but Jerome knocked his feet out from under him and was getting ready to pound him when the cops pulled up. They didn't ask questions. They just handcuffed Jerome and took Josh, who was bleeding from the nose, to the side. "He didn't throw a punch!" Lance yelled in the cop's face. He pushed Lance back and pointed to the NO LOITERING sign.

"You've gotta be fuckin' kidding me!" Lance screamed.

"Watch your mouth, son. I know your daddy," the cop said, loading Jerome in the backseat and driving off.

That's when Sammy came over and slid his letterman's jacket over my shivering shoulders. It wasn't cold. Heather Hanson stood at the front of the crowd, still dressed in her cheerleading uniform. A letterman's jacket meant everything—who you belonged to, how serious you were, your entire high school status. Sammy had given me his in front of all the popular kids, and he didn't care one bit what they thought.

"Let's go get Jerome," Sammy whispered into my ear. It wasn't what I was expecting to hear, but I knew he was right. Jerome didn't deserve any of this. He was a good kid, on the honor roll, a star football player, going places. His parents were probably already at the station. It seemed to me the only thing harder in Hannibal's hierarchy than being poor and white was being respectable and black.

GOSSIP GRILL IS WHERE THE cool kids from high school hang out when they're back in town. Rose and I were never the cool kids, but Sammy was close. Football elevated your status. When I wore Sammy's letterman's jacket with his name across my back, people noticed me. I was a marked girl; I'd scored a football player, one of the beautiful ones, even if most of them spent the rest of their days carrying a twenty-pound beer gut to their La-Z-Boy chairs every night. When they got back together, it was all about the glory days of high school, the best years of their lives. It kind of makes me sad. I want everything good to be in front of me, not behind.

At Gossip Grill there are four pool tables in the back; they have local ale from St. Louis on tap next to the Bud Light and Michelob Ultra. The taverns for real drinkers are on the other end of Main Street with darkened windows and an army of pickup trucks out front by four o'clock. At Gossip Grill, there's a halfhearted sign hung above the bathrooms: WELCOME CLASS OF '93. HALF-PRICE DRAFTS! Rose and I order onion rings to split and two Miller Lites. We find a booth with a view of the front door. "There's Tara Gerber. Didn't she go to school with your brother? Lord, time hasn't been kind to her," Rose says. "There's Colby Strauss, too. He runs the bowling alley now. I made out with him a couple of times back when. Oh no she didn't. Look at Stella White. What is she thinking? We don't do it like that here." I nod my head, but I already want to leave. It feels like I'm meeting myself in a dark alley and I don't recognize me.

"Got somethin' to say about everyone else but yourself, don't ya, Rose?" a voice cuts in. Rose smirks at Daisy, who stands two inches taller than her baby sister. She's straightened her platinum-blond hair and has an orange glow from a tanning bed. We idolized Daisy when we were younger, pointing her out on the cheerleading squad to friends at football games. But then she got pregnant, and we swore we'd never be like her—until Rose turned out exactly like her.

"Hey, Sis," Rose answers. "Where'd you stash all those kids?"

"Figured their dad could watch 'em one night," Daisy says, looking out into the crowd, still ignoring me.

"Which dad?" Rose shoots back. Daisy ignores her. She already has the upper hand and knows it. Bobby spent so much time with her when we were in high school, he called Daisy Mama first. She's never let Rose forget it.

"Oh, hi, Laura. Didn't see you there. What are you doin' back in town?" Daisy's eyes glow white from the tanning goggles, but she's covered most of it with charcoal eyeliner.

"Just visitin,' really," I answer, shaking my head at Rose. I don't want to feed Daisy information. She'll just twist it, and whatever I say will be all over town by morning.

"Couldn't hack it away from home, huh?"

I pretend I can't hear her over the crowd. "Let's play pool," Rose says, shoving in the last onion ring, saving me the calories. She drains her beer and walks off before I can answer. Then she calls back over her shoulder, "At least I didn't have a whole brood like my sis." I stop at the bar and get us two more beers. In the mirror above the bar I check my hair and take out the dandelion Rose tucked behind my ear on our walk. I look tired, but I don't look as heavy as I thought I did. I'm wearing a black shirt that smooths everything out and a jean skirt with gold sandals. My legs are still tan from Florida and my cheeks are rosy from the heat.

Rose is playing pool with two guys I've never met. "Laura, this is Johnny and his cousin, Seth. They're from Palmyra. You're on my team. Get yourself a cue." The cousins nod, their Cardinal ball caps moving up and down. I grab a stick from the bank on the wall and chalk up like I know what I'm doing.

"Stripes or solids?" I ask.

"Stripes," the one named Johnny says, leaning on the edge of the table. "You're losin'."

"Thanks for the update," I say and take my shot. The white ball bounces off the far end and lands neatly in the corner pocket.

"Scratch." Johnny laughs. "Thought you said she would help your cause. Don't look that way."

"She's been out of town," Rose explains. "Think she forgot how to play."

"Oh, yeah?" Seth asks. "Where'd you escape to?"

Before I can answer, Lance, Sammy's brother, walks up the back deck stairs. He's wearing a cowboy hat and boots. I lean over the balcony to check if he's alone. There's another cowboy hat, but it's facing away from me. Rose comes over and takes my stick. "Geez. You're gonna strain yourself, kiddo."

"Let's go," I whisper. "I don't want to do this."

"Do what? Play pool?"

"We're grown-ups. Let's act that way, huh?"

"Yeah, right," Rose says, leaning over for her shot. She splits the green striped ball from the solid purple and it lands in a side pocket. She grabs me for a celebratory hug and the black ball follows into the pocket, too.

"You just won the game for them. Congratulations!" I hug her back, and Rose turns to confirm.

"Shit! That was fun!" she says. "Good game, guys. Nice meetin' y'all."

"Wait," Johnny says. "Don't you owe us beers, pretty lady?"

"Sure thing. I'll send 'em right over." Rose leads me away to the bar and the guys high-five. I know she won't be buying them beers, so I smile back and wave good-bye. I take a stool next to Rose and hear a familiar voice.

"Does your mama know you're here?" Trey leans over to kiss Rose on the cheek and smiles at me. His long hair is tied in a ponytail and his goatee looks freshly trimmed. He looks exhausted and fidgets on the bar stool. He pulls me into a side hug. "How's your tat healin'?"

"Still a little red," I say, pulling back my shoulder sleeve to show him, "but I like it."

"Looks good on her, don't it?" Trey asks Rose.

She slides her arms flirtatiously around his neck. I shake my head no. She's always had a crush on my brother, and he's played along. "You buyin'?"

Trey nods at the bartender and he brings us three drafts.

"This is it for me, Rose," I say, taking my first sip.

"What? We just got here. You gonna ruin my fun? I'll just have to have Trey here walk me home. You know the way to my house, don't ya?"

"I wish," Trey answers. "Yeah, I'll give you a ride. You like bikes? I just got mine back from the shop. How you gettin' home, Sis?"

I slide the rest of my beer toward Rose. "I feel like a walk. Fresh air sounds good."

"Lame ass," Rose whispers as she hugs me good-bye. "You're gonna miss all the fun."

"I'm good, Rose. Thanks for bringin' me out. Call you in the mornin'." I put a bill on the counter and half hug Trey. Cutting out has always been my strength. Staying away has mostly served me well. Until now. I recognize a few more faces as I'm heading out the door and walk faster.

ON CHRISTMAS DAY MY FIRST year away at nursing school, Sammy showed up. I hadn't seen him since the summer flood. I didn't go home for the break, even though it was only a two-hour drive up Highway 61 from St. Louis. My boss at Denny's said to take as many shifts as I wanted. I'd called Mama three times, standing at the payphone in my dorm lobby with a roll of quarters, but she never asked me to come. "You do what you have to do, Laura. Don't waste your gas money on me," she said. We weren't Christians, and the holiday usually just reminded us of how much we couldn't afford. "Your brother's taking me to Ole Planters on Christmas Eve. They only had a table for two anyway. Twelve dollars for ham. You imagine chargin' that? There better be all-you-can-eat rolls. And I ain't standin' for no watered-down iced tea."

It was only the cook, me, and two old men in Denny's. I'd turned the radio to country carols, thinking it would cheer me up, but it made me even lonelier. The cook sang along from the kitchen to Kenny Rogers and Dolly Parton's "Christmas without You." I'd served both the old men the Grand Slam special with runny eggs while they talked about the war, which one I wasn't sure. I was refilling their coffee cups when the little bell above the door rang. We all looked up. Sammy's sandy-blond hair was freshly buzzed, and he had on a charcoal-gray sweater with dark jeans. He was wearing the red-plaid scarf I gave him the Christmas before. He smiled his wide grin, and the tiny gap between his front teeth made him look so innocent. But I knew he wasn't.

When he came into Denny's, Sammy nodded at the old men, sat down in a booth in the corner, and opened up a menu. He waited for me, just like he said he would.

I filled Sammy's coffee cup even though he didn't drink coffee. I wanted to be close, to smell him and home. He stood almost a foot taller than me and his arms were strong from farmwork. It was his smell that I couldn't get rid of after I broke up with him and left. Dial soap and Adidas cologne mixed with mint toothpaste. My pillow, my favorite jean jacket, even my books seemed to hold him, but none of that was enough to hold me. "That's it?" he'd said, three days after a levee breach had flooded his neighbor's farm and temporarily saved Sammy's family's land. I hadn't returned his phone calls. I doubted he'd even slept.

The whole town was tense and exhausted from the battle with the flood. "You weren't even gonna say good-bye?" he'd asked, looking at my bags in the backseat. I stared at the screen door for a long time, waiting for Mama to come out and say good-bye. I went back inside to see what was keeping her, but she had the bathroom door locked and the shower on like she had to get ready for some other place to go. There were six $20 bills on the kitchen counter with a sticky note that said *Laura*. I couldn't imagine what it had taken for Mama to spare it for me. I took half the money and knocked on the bathroom door, but she didn't answer.

Finally, I kissed Sammy on the cheek, breathed in his shirt one last time, and left. If I'd had a phone back then, he would have called and called.

Sitting in the booth that Christmas, he closed his menu. "I'd like to order one of you." We both giggled. He must have been working on that line the whole two-hour drive. Sammy wasn't shy, but he was sincere. That Fourth of July when everything broke, he cried on the drive home, wiping his tears and snot on his Hannibal Pirates T-shirt. I scooted far away on the truck bench and held on to the metal door handle, ready to jump.

"You want that fried or over easy?" I asked.

"Never known anything easy about you," Sammy answered.

"I'll get you some eggs and bacon." I turned my back on him and walked to the counter.

"Milk, please," Sammy called after me.

When my shift ended, I took Sammy back to my dorm. It had started to snow and I was shivering in my uniform and sweater. We stopped at his truck on the way, and he grabbed a backpack and a present wrapped in silver paper. There was a red velvet bow on top; from the looks of it, he'd tied it himself. My heart skipped when I saw the present. It was Christmas, after all, and I was feeling mighty sorry for myself. Mama had mailed me a pair of gloves with the Walmart tag still attached. They were powder blue with big white snowflakes on the palms. The gloves smelled like smoke. There wasn't even a card, but at least it was something. Sammy sat on my bed and patted the space beside him. "Don't I even get a hello?"

"We broke up, Sammy. I'm not sayin' I ain't glad to see you, but we're not together anymore." I turned my desk chair around to face him and sat down, sure to keep my distance. If I got close, I knew what would happen. My loneliness made an awful pit in my stomach. Mama, Trey, Aunt Betty, Sammy, and Rose and Bobby—none of them were perfect, but I missed them something fierce. I made things work at school, but nobody there really knew me, not the way my people did.

"You broke up. I didn't agree to it." He smiled when he said it, like the joke was on me. "I even brought you a present. Open it." I eyed the silver package. It looked like a sweater. I hoped it wasn't. Out my dorm window, the snow was coming down hard. Nothing moved, and the white blanketed the whole parking lot.

"Maybe I want different things now," I said.

Sammy studied my face like he didn't recognize me. I wondered what he saw. I'd lived years in the months since I'd left Hannibal.

"Maybe I do, too," he said.

"Then why are you here?"

"Because I still love you. That part is easy. You didn't answer my letters, didn't return my calls. I just wanted to know how things were. Between us." He held out the silver package. "It's somethin' you always said you wanted."

I walked over to sit beside him on the bed. He smelled exactly the same as ever. The box was heavy and it definitely wasn't a sweater.

I undid the bow carefully and tore off the paper. Inside were two novels: *The Adventures of Tom Sawyer* and *Adventures of Huckleberry Finn*. They were both navy-blue hardback editions with black-and-white pictures, copies of E. W. Kemble's, the illustrations in the original publication. "Thought since you'd left you might like a piece of Hannibal," Sammy said. I flipped through the pages and settled on my favorite: Huck climbing out the window in "Huck Stealing Away."

I let him stay that night. The snow kept falling, but we were naked and warm. I broke up with him again the next morning. Gave him the same silent treatment I'd given him in August when I'd left.

"All right, Laura. Have it your way. But I won't wait forever," Sammy said, climbing into the front seat of his truck. He leaned out the window and kissed me on my cheek. They'd plowed the parking lot and the roads were clear.

I CUT THROUGH THE PARKING lot down Main Street near the Becky Thatcher Bookstore where Sammy probably bought my books. Of course the fictional St. Petersburg was only a portrait of this place, but it's a myth that has lasted; it's the picture of Hannibal, of "America's Hometown," that we've built a tourist industry around. Some of the myth serves us well. Tourists come for the story and soak up the charm. We all know the tales: Tom and Huck on the river, Tom and Becky in the cave, Huck and Jim on the run. As kids we ran in the cemetery and played a game called Muff Potter tag as we raced each other to the top of Cardiff Hill. In the bookstore window, a Tom Sawyer

Days schedule is displayed next to boxes of Huck Finn's wooden whistles, bags of glass marbles, and Becky Thatcher paper dolls. On the second floor are the original rooms where Laura Hawkins, Samuel Clemens's first love, who helped him imagine Becky, grew up. For a quarter, you can listen to a recording that illustrates how Laura spent her days reading, practicing piano, and helping her mother make a home. Mannequins wear bonnets and calico dresses inside the staged rooms, and their lips are perpetually pink. A brick courtyard separates the bookstore from the Mark Twain Boyhood Home. You can imagine a young Sam running between the houses, trying to get a glimpse of Laura. A replica of the very fence he wrote about whitewashing waits with a bucket and brush and a plaque:

HERE STOOD THE BOARD FENCE WHICH TOM SAWYER PERSUADED HIS GANG TO PAY HIM FOR THE PRIVILEGE OF WHITEWASHING. TOM SAT BY AND SAW THAT IT WAS DONE WELL.

In the first-floor museum window is a group photo of the Tom and Becky contestants. I search the faces for Bobby. He's off to the side, not leaning in like the rest, caught mid-laugh.

I cross the street and walk under the lights coming from the Java Jive coffeehouse next door to Ayers Pottery. The night air is humid, but it feels less sticky than the stale bar smoke. In the window are handmade dishes and bowls. They've hung up a BUY LOCAL sign and crossed out the word *Walmart*. Maybe I'll get Mama her very own piece of Hannibal pottery for her birthday. She'd love something pretty to put in the center of the kitchen table now that the ashtray is gone. Downtown used to be dark after 5 p.m. The store owners didn't stay open late once the tourists went to dinner and back to their hotels. Jazz music trickles out from a new store, the Wine Stoppe, where twinkling white lights frame well-dressed couples inside, sipping glasses of summer whites. Families fill the benches outside Becky's Old Fashioned Ice Cream Parlor and Emporium. Folks are lined up pretending to paint Tom's fence and taking pictures of our quaint little way of life. Most of it's true and some of it isn't. Huck would fit in even less now. He was never this civilized, never behaved the way the town wanted him to. His poverty and neglect were embarrassing, so they shamed and banished him to the outskirts of town where the visitors never visit. Jim doesn't have a place at all. Not yet, anyway. If Hannibal had a slave history, you wouldn't know it by these streets.

I make my way back toward the water and climb the river-bank, stumbling a bit from my buzz. To my right is the bluff overlooking Lover's Leap and to my left is the lighthouse on Cardiff Hill. Lights are shining from both out over the muddy water. Sitting down on the grass, I lean over the ledge of the levee and stretch my arm down as far as I can to feel the frigid water. A bloated catfish tangled in a mess of branches floats by and I pull my hand back and wipe the wetness on my skirt.

"Rose thought you'd be here." It's Sammy. Of course it's him. For a second I consider just sinking into the water and letting the current carry me. But knowing him, he'd jump in, even if he thought I was a stranger.

"Sammy McGuire," I say, looking over my shoulder. He looks the same, maybe just a bit thicker, which looks good on him. He takes off his cowboy hat, and his hair is indented from it. He sits down a few feet from me on the riverbank and puts his hat in the space between us. I want him to scoot closer, and I hate that I want him to scoot closer, that I have sudden goose bumps. He's wearing a short-sleeve plaid shirt that's tight on his chest, and jeans. His work boots are surprisingly clean. "It's good to see you."

"We aren't supposed to be up here. They asked folks to stop walkin' on the levee. Makes the rock bed underneath break down. They can't keep the tourists off so they said locals should. Are you a tourist or a local?"

"Not sure," I answer, picking up his hat, playing with the brim, touching the faint sweat of Sammy. I put on the hat, which is too big, of course, but feels familiar. "Downtown sure looks different," I say, forcing small talk.

Sammy stands up and looks over the side of the river. He picks up a rock and throws it hard into the water, but the roar drowns the sound. "Yeah. Those fancy folks from St. Louis came in and spruced the place up, huh? Then the Chamber got involved. Looks good now. Brought in the business."

"I'm surprised they let them in."

"Money talks, don't it? There's more to like here than you think."

"I hardly recognized the place. Except for across the tracks, that is." A couple walks past while their two kids race ahead. The mom warns them not to get too close to the water. She shouts, "It's dangerous!" and she's right.

"Heard you were home for good. That true?"

I sigh and pull the hat down farther, hiding my face. "News still travels fast, huh?"

Sammy leans over me, pulls up the front of the hat, and looks straight into my eyes, like he wants to watch me answer. "You happy to be home?"

I nod my head and lie. "Mostly. Still feels a little weird to be back." He keeps watching me, and it's unnerving.

"This is home. Why's it weird? Or is it just hard to come back since you left?"

"Life was simpler in Florida. Lonely, sometimes, but not so much drama."

"Sounds like you've been spendin' time with Rose." He smiles, like we both know where all drama is born. "Good ol' Rose."

"She brings plenty, but it's more than Rose."

"She told me you got inked." He smirks.

"Damn it, Rose."

"Come on. Show me."

I pull the hat back down over my eyes. Then I slip out of my sleeve and let him peek at the raft. The redness has faded and the colors are glowing.

"Huh," Sammy says, not displeased. "And I thought I knew every inch of you."

Heat is on my cheeks, up my back, between my legs. Rose always says it doesn't add another number to your count if you sleep with someone you've already slept with.

Sammy asks everything about Florida. I'd forgotten what a good listener he is. I tell him about the beaches, my apartment, how much I liked my work. I tell him about Bobby and Rose visiting.

"So, why'd you leave then? You make it sound perfect, and all you ever wanted to do was leave home. And me."

I let the "me" part pass. I don't know how to separate Sammy from Hannibal. In my mind, you can't leave one without the other. "Turns out it was complicated there, too. I got laid off. It felt like a rug got pulled out from under me."

"Guess it depends on how you look at it, Laura. Maybe it's just a chance to try something new, start over again."

"You sound like Aunt Betty."

"Yep. She's good people." He makes it sound so simple. Good people. Good-enough life. I wish it was. Or I wish it was enough for me.

"I've thought about going back to school," I say, trying the idea out loud for the first time. I could always tell Sammy this stuff. He never once laughed at my reaching. "Just recently thought about it. To get my RN. There's more jobs for RNs and the pay is better."

"That'd be great, Laura. School was always your thing." It all sounds possible when Sammy says it.

"Speaking of good people, Bobby is running for Tom. I'm going to help him get ready." Now I'm just gushing information and ideas and can't stop.

"No kidding! That's great news. He'll be lucky to have you, especially with all the stuff you know."

I blush a little with pride. "I worry, though. You know how that stuff can be."

"Bobby'll be great. I can help, too, if you want. I do know a thing or two about bein' Tom."

I don't say yes and I don't say no. "How about you? How's the farm?" I ask. A merciful breeze stirs up. Could be a storm coming in. I hold out the hat to Sammy, but he plops it back on my head, and we both smile like it belonged there all along. Then he pulls it back over my eyes in case I want to keep hiding, but I look up instead.

"Levee's holdin', but we're surrounded. Should be okay this year, though. Not like '93."

"Nothin's like '93." That night flashes in my mind: the fireworks, Sammy's hands on me, the water rushing toward us both.

"True," Sammy says. He doesn't move any closer. He doesn't offer his hand to help me to my feet. He leaves me to scramble up on my own. We walk the bank together, and he tells me about the new crops. He's putting in soybeans this year. Market's up and the state subsidizes. He tells me Lance is mostly running the farm and getting married in a few weeks to a girl from St. Louis that he met online. Sammy's doing the books for the gas station. He's surprised that he's good with the numbers and likes running the business side.

I don't know how to bring it up so I just blurt out, "I heard about your divorce. I'm sorry."

Sammy picks up another rock, a bigger one this time, and tries to skip it again. It makes a faint plop in the dark. "Me, too."

"You wanta tell me about it?"

"In this town, you probably already know plenty."

I do. "Tell me something I don't know then."

His eyes close slowly, like he's trying to find the words. "She didn't keep our baby." He crosses his arms over his chest, then rubs his face like he's washing it with his bare hands. "She didn't want it. Ever. That's what ended us."

I don't know what to say, so I put my hand on his shoulder. I would have had my baby, but I never would have kept the father around. Sammy should have kids of his own by now. Maybe it was just bad timing. He tucks my hand in the crook of his arm, like old friends, and we walk by the water where it's easier to say things. We both look down and not at each other. Then I look up and start counting the stars.

Caves

Underneath the bluffs of Lover's Leap there are miles of interconnected caves. Mark Twain wrote about them in five of his books. In *The Adventures of Tom Sawyer*, Twain described them as "a labyrinth of crooked aisles that ran into each other and out again and led nowhere." Tom and Becky got lost in the caves. Injun Joe starved to death at the north entrance. If Becky had known that the caves are always a cool fifty-two degrees, she'd have brought a sweater.

Jack Simms and his dog were out hunting one day in the winter of 1819 when they stumbled upon the entrance to what would become the famous Mark Twain Cave. It was too late in the day for safe exploring, so he blocked the entrance and came back later with his brothers. It took another fifty years or so for the caves to be opened to the public. The Mark Twain Cave became Missouri's first show cave in 1886, ten years after the world had met Tom and Huck on the page.

In *The Autobiography of Mark Twain* edited by Charles Neider, Twain writes that the caves were "an uncanny place" because the cool temperature created a reasonable climate for embalming. He recalls that Dr. McDowell of St. Louis put his own daughter's decaying body in a glass case surrounded by copper and filled with alcohol. Local boys, such as himself, could reach their hands into the container and lift the dead girl by her hair. When they released it, she'd float back down like a ghost in a dunking booth. Twain thought the caves were much too lonely for a girl, even a dead one.

Locals swear that Samuel Clemens must have signed his name somewhere in the caves. He lived in Hannibal less than a mile from the cave entrance from the age of four until seventeen, ripe ages for underground investigations. Beneath a rock ledge, over a low-hanging stalactite, under a bridge. It's there. People still search for it. Just because it hasn't been discovered doesn't mean it doesn't exist.

In 1967, more than one hundred years after Twain's own Hannibal days, three boys went exploring in the caves just as they did most weekends. Their names were Joe Hoag, Bill Hoag, and Craig Dowell. They'd told their parents about a new cave they'd discovered, but they didn't say exactly where they were going that afternoon. When it got dark, the boys didn't come home. The parents filed a missing-persons report at the Hannibal Police Department. A rescue party was formed and a makeshift operation was set up at the YMCA. The caves were searched more than one hundred times. Despite being the biggest underground search-and-rescue mission in our country's history, not a trace of the boys was ever found.

CHAPTER EIGHT

THE NEXT MORNING I swing by Rose and Bobby's house. He's sitting on the couch watching *Transformers* when I come through the door. He says it's lame, but his eyes don't leave the screen. I put the straw hat I've brought onto his head and pull the brim down to block the TV. He laughs and swats at my hands in the air.

"Your mama awake?" I ask.

Bobby shakes his head no.

"Did you eat breakfast?"

The hat says no, too.

I flip the coffeepot on, and the water hisses as it heats. In the bedroom, Rose is tangled up in the sheets. She's wearing her bra and underwear, like she peeled off her clothes as she fell onto the bed. The comforter has been kicked to the floor. I get some Tylenol from her purse and put it on the nightstand with a glass of water.

"I ain't hung over if that's what you think," Rose says, pulling a pillow over her head.

"Sure you ain't," I answer. "No one said you were. Drink this."

"I know what you're thinkin', Ms. Too-Good-for-Hannibal."

"No, you don't."

"Yes, I do. You're thinkin' I shouldn't be out enjoyin' myself right before the trial. Like I'm supposed to stay home and be some goddamned perfect mother."

"I didn't say a word, Rose."

"Oh, please. Like you don't have your own drama and secrets." She peeks around the pillow. "Sammy find you?"

I hesitate. It's hard to keep stuff from Rose. Sammy walked me home. He stood on Mama's front porch and waved good-bye. That was it. Two old friends catching up, even if I was flirting a little.

"Just thought I'd check on Bobby," I answer, "and see if he needs help with the costume and stuff."

"He's been readin' that Tom and Becky manual you brought over. Out loud. To me."

"Sorry." Ms. B would be proud. I'm glad someone is still reading her work.

"Don't be. I didn't know most of that stuff about Hannibal."

"I promised I'd take him to the caves. He says he's never been. It's one of his required Tom assignments. Want to come?" I ask.

"Why the hell would I wanta climb around underneath Hannibal? It's scary enough above ground."

I open Rose's curtains and let the sun in. She winces and I

hand her the Tylenol and water. Rose gulps them down. Then she takes a big whiff of the coffee brewing and sits up.

"Cramps," Rose says.

"Uh-huh," I answer.

"Bobby's got some Tom meetin' this afternoon. Can you take him?"

"Sure. I'm makin' breakfast. It'll be ready when you get out of the shower. I even brought doughnuts."

"Strawberry-glazed with sprinkles?" Her face lights up like a little kid.

"Of course." Like I'd forget my best friend's favorite doughnut.

While I scramble eggs and fry the bacon, Bobby tells me he thinks the fishing pole part of his Tom costume will be the easiest. "Remember the one you gave me when I was five? It's still in the garage." I remember it. I shopped for hours to find the right one. It's a Zebco 33 with a cork handle. He'll dig it out and take off the hook, he figures. Some of the kids put on a plastic fish, but Bobby thinks it looks fake. If the pole is too fancy, he'll just get a long stick and tie a line to it. That's what Huck and Jim used when they were floatin' their raft down the Mississippi by night and fishin' and sleepin' by day. If it was good enough for a runaway slave and the village pariah, it will work for Bobby, too.

"So, you've got a pole. What else you need?" I ask. Rose plops herself down at the kitchen table. Her hair is wrapped in a towel and she's wearing a long T-shirt. She looks young and fresh again, despite the bags under her eyes. Bobby pours her a cup of coffee and she inhales it.

"There's a meetin' at the Chamber next Saturday. You're supposed to be there, too, Mom." Rose rubs her temples. The Tylenol and caffeine are starting to perk her up.

"You know I have to work on Saturdays. Did you ask your dad? He's not workin' much these days. That's what I heard. He's certainly not sendin' extra money over for a Tom costume."

"I've got a plaid shirt. Don't know if it still fits but it might."

"What else?" Rose asks. I join them at the table and spoon out eggs and bacon onto each plate. Rose takes two doughnuts, but she just sniffs them like she's not sure her stomach can handle it yet. Bobby takes one, licks out the filling first, and then stuffs the whole doughnut into his mouth and chews. I stick to eggs but allow myself one slice of crispy, delicious bacon. At least Rose has good taste in a strong coffee brew. That's something I can appreciate.

"Pants and suspenders. Aunt Laura brought over Trey's straw hat."

"It suits him," I add.

"Can't you wear jeans? We can get suspenders at Walmart. Don't think they'll look old timey, though." Rose clears the plates and throws the empty box of doughnuts into the trash.

"Ms. Keller said they didn't have jeans. We're supposed to have short pants. Like brown ones."

Bobby tells us about the Norman Rockwell illustrations Ms. Keller shared. Tom is in short pants with a bowler hat. Becky stands behind him in a frilly dress, wearing a bonnet.

"At least you're not a Becky," Rose says. "I heard those moms spend a fortune. Some of 'em even sew the dresses a year in advance."

"If you just give me the money, I'll have Aunt Laura take me, Mom."

Rose tosses her silverware into the sink. Bobby cringes and I brace myself for what is coming. "I'm tryin' to help, Bobby. You think she'd make a better mom?"

"That's not what he said, Rose. Lay off." But she won't lay off. Rose is on the attack now. She probably doesn't have the money, and she hates being reminded of it.

"You think your daddy is gonna come in and save the day? He wasn't even there when you were born." Her voice is angry, tired.

Bobby puts his head down on the table and rests his cheek on the plastic surface. Then he arranges the salt and pepper shakers into a neat row.

It's quiet for a minute, like we're all trying to figure out our next move. I don't want to piss Rose off even more. Sometimes she just needs a minute to breathe. We all do.

Rose turns away from us and draws a sink of hot, soapy water. "I wanted to be a Becky, too. Did I ever tell you that, Bobby?" She plunges her hands beneath the suds. "We all wanted to be a Tom or Becky. It's not surprisin' when you grow up with pictures of 'em all around. Like they're some kind of superheroes."

"Did you try?" Bobby asks. He seems a little afraid of the answer.

"Girls like me don't try. You know that." Rose runs more hot water. The steam rises from the sink toward her.

"It's different now," he says bravely.

"I doubt that."

"Maybe it is," I offer. But then I remember we don't have the same contest for Huck or even Jim.

"Ms. Keller says it is. She said anybody can be Tom or Becky if they work hard enough." It's a good idea, even if it's not completely true. You're still born into a place, into a class, a gender, and a race. People still want you to stay there. "Did you try, Aunt Laura?"

I start to answer but Rose interrupts. "I remember you took the form home. It was a big deal. We had to go to the front office after school and ask for one. Probably so the secretary could give us dirty looks. We almost missed the bus because the line of girls was so long. I remember we asked this one girl, Heather Hanson, if we could cut. She lived by the country club and could walk home. If we missed the bus, it was a long walk to the dirt road."

"Did she let you?" Bobby asks.

Rose shakes her head. "Do you remember, Laura? You reached over Heather's shoulder and grabbed one anyway. Then we ran."

Rose remembers me as the brave one. I learned how to make things happen the hard way. Like Bobby, I figured there wasn't anybody that was going to do it for me. Rose stacks the coffee cups neatly in the strainer and drains the dirty water. She wipes her hands on her jeans, walks over to Bobby's chair, and hugs him. The tenderness makes me look away. No matter her troubles, Rose is a mama. She belongs to someone and always will.

"You'd of made a good Becky, Mom." Bobby pats her arm. She sighs and her face turns hard again.

"I'm proud of you, son. It's not that I ain't. It's just this damn trial. The Bastard has to make this hard. I'm so tired of worryin' about money," Rose says, slumping down into a metal kitchen chair. "But here's the thing: you can help me. I need you both to testify. Will y'all do that for me?"

"Seriously, Rose. Not now. Don't drag Bobby into this."

"He's already into this. It's about him. I'm doin' this all for him. Desperate times call for desperate measures." I hope she's not referring to whatever the police asked her about. "You know I'm doin' this all for you, Bobby, right?" Bobby doesn't say anything.

"Let's talk about this later, Rose. Please," I beg.

Bobby pours out some of the salt into a pile. At the same time, we both reach for a pinch and toss it over our shoulders. When Bobby was little, Rose told me, they used to pretend their kitchen was a diner with the checked cushions and black Formica top. Rose would call, "Order up!" as she flipped Aunt Jemima mix pancakes. Bobby learned to pour the syrup into a small cup and dip it rather than waste it by letting it pool around his pancake.

"You're throwin' away that damn salt, you two. Like I can afford for y'all to just toss stuff on the floor."

"Sorry," Bobby whispers, but he smirks at me.

"Wanta say a prayer together?" Rose says, her voice softening. "Maybe Jesus'll help us."

"Sure," he mumbles.

She takes his hand and mine and closes her eyes. "Dear Jesus, please help us with Bobby's Tom costume. We need your guidance. Bobby really wants to be Tom. If that's what you want, too, help us any way you can. In your name, we pray. Amen."

Bobby opens an eye and peeks. I haven't closed mine. Rose's face is calm and her smile is angelic.

BOBBY AND I PULL UP to the Mark Twain Cave mid-morning. The summer sun is already brutal, but I grab my jacket from the backseat before we go in. The caves are cool year-round. Bobby insisted on wearing short sleeves, and I didn't fight him on it. Not having to is one of the benefits of being Aunt Laura. We buy our tickets in the gift store and Bobby sorts through a huge bin of rocks. "Are all of these rocks inside the cave?" he asks. I plunge my hand into the pile, too. The rocks are purple, orange, red, and silver. They're solid and comforting. Most of the rocks are smooth, polished, and clearly painted, but some of them are rough like the caves with sparkly edges. I pull out a metallic one, and Bobby and I smile into it and make faces at our reflections.

"I don't think so. These don't look like cave rocks. They're fun, though, aren't they?"

Bobby slides his hands to the bottom of the rock bin so that he's up to his elbows in the rocks. "Yep," he says.

"I'll get you a bag before we leave," I promise. "For five bucks you can have as many rocks as you can stuff in the bag."

"Really? Cool."

I let Bobby lead on our tour. He wants to be close to the guide so he can ask questions. He also wants to hurry ahead to find things for himself. I hand him the flashlight, and he shines it on the ceiling above and we watch the bats sleep. Rows and rows of furry brown balls cling to the jagged rock. They must feel safer if they stick together. I hold out the lantern to guide our step as we walk along the path.

Graffiti covers part of the cave walls and ceilings, mostly cursive signatures with dates and other hometowns: Maryville, Cairo, Louisiana. On an overhang: *The Hawkinses were here.* "You know about Becky Thatcher?" I ask Bobby. "Did you know her real name was Hawkins? That's probably her family right there." I point to a signature done in fancy loops.

"Really? You think so?" Bobby rubs the goose bumps covering his arms.

"Maybe." I hold up my lantern and read more names.

"If you picked up the application, how come you didn't return it? Didn't you wanta be Becky, Aunt Laura?"

"I wasn't exactly Becky material."

"Why not?" Bobby pulls on the velvet ropes that keep us up on the path, and the guide shakes his head in warning.

"Well, those girls didn't like me and your mama much. That girl Heather that your mama mentioned, she started growing her hair long in fourth grade just so she'd have Becky braids by middle school. She said her mom made her. Heather was definite Becky material. And she won, too." *But she never won Sammy,* I think, with a little smirk.

"I don't think it's the same with Tom, is it?"

"Some of it is, I'm sure. You got to have someone cart you all over town, fill out your forms, and buy your costume and stuff. My mama was always workin' and Daddy left. Aunt Betty would of helped but she didn't always know how. I just learned to do for myself."

"Hey, I wonder if Mark Twain signed his name in here. As

a kid. I'm goin' to find it!" Bobby sprints off to examine the signatures on a far wall.

I follow close behind, read the names, and imagine what their lives must have been like, these people who left their marks so we could find them. Then a signature stops me; it's Daddy's name: *Ben Brooks*. It can't be him, but Mama said he grew up here same as me. As a kid he could have played in here. It could be him. I shiver thinking of all our paths that might have crossed. It's hard not to know your own people. Makes you always wonder what part of you is missing. I don't show it to Bobby. The guide mentions Jesse James's hideout and Bobby runs ahead so he can hear the tale.

I stumble a few times on the rocky path and reach for Bobby, but he's doing just fine without me. The cave walls are cold to the touch, mostly orange-and-gray limestone. When Bobby's not looking, I put my cheek to an overhang to feel the smooth stone. It's damp and cold. Water trickles all around us. Smaller caverns have been eroded on each side. Water always finds a way out.

We make our way down narrow paths single file. A woman in front of us snaps pictures with her flash, lighting up the pressed layers of limestone. "Excuse me," she says to the guide. "Our hotel clerk said the water was up again. Will there be another flood?" She seems almost excited at the prospect. Clearly, she didn't grow up in a floodplain.

"Maybe. Hannibal floods almost every year because of our proximity to the Mississippi. It's a way of life for us. The levee walls are in downtown so that'll keep the water back." It'll keep the water out of the tourist areas, he means. Poor folks and farmers are always at risk. I look back up at the cave walls and away from the tourist's pleased face.

There are more signatures burned into the walls with the smoke from candle flames. *Lampton 1842*. The newer ones are etched in cursive with marker. *Margaret 1908*. A scrawling *Jennifer 04-09-88*.

Bobby makes like he's going to write his name, too, with a pen from his pocket, and I shake my head. "Just kiddin'," he says. "Tom would of done it." He reaches up to touch the low ceiling and his hand comes back wet.

"You ain't Tom yet." I link my arm through his, and he doesn't pull away. "But you will be." Bobby grins. The tour guide announces that we'll be stopping for a picture break.

"Let's look for more signatures," Bobby says, pulling on me.

The tour takes us almost an hour and then Bobby races back to the gift shop and stuffs as many rocks as he can into the $5 velvet bag. He declares the caves awesome, but he likes the gift shop even better. He can't get enough of the plastic frogs, rubber snakes, and corncob pipes. We pose together in a painted scene of Tom and Becky with the heads cut out. Bobby decides to be Becky, and that leaves me to duck inside the headless Tom. We make goofy faces for the picture, and then Bobby says, "Switch! You should be Becky now!"

In the car, he unpacks his rocks into his lap. He fingers each rock and holds it up to the window for examination. He's rubbing together two silver stones when he says, "Dad told me you won't testify in court. How come?"

"It's not my business. It's between them." I know Josh never hit Bobby, and I know he did hit Rose. I know she hit Josh, too.

"He says you've got too much to lose. What's that mean, anyway?" Bobby is absorbed in the rocks and doesn't see the rosy shame on my face. Divorce makes people ugly. I've been gone a long time, but revenge is the same.

I want to help my friend, but I can't. If I testified against him, I'd lose. Rose says I'm a terrible liar. The problem is, I'm actually not. I've been lying to my best friend for years. Josh would tell how feeling so bad about me made me almost hurt her in the worst way.

"I don't want to get involved, Bobby. I told your mama that."

"Yeah, but she said it would help her. That you can but you won't help her."

"Did Rose tell you to say that?" I ask. It's true, I guess. Maybe if I testify it would help. Maybe not. Either way, I don't want Bobby to grow up without a dad. Josh may be a jerk but at least he's trying, at least he hasn't left.

"No. Not exactly. But I know it's what she wants."

"It's complicated, honey. It's an adult problem. You shouldn't have to worry about it." But I know he does have to worry about it. Sometimes he seems more okay than all of the adults around him.

"Laura, if Dad won't pay for me and Mom just yells, can I live with you?"

"Absolutely. You going to bring all those rocks?" I ask.

Bobby nods and slides his finger on the edge of a sharp silver rock.

IF BOBBY CAN MAKE THINGS happen, so can I. Rather than staring at my phone and checking email every few minutes,

I drive back over to Quincy Hospital and ask to see Martha. She's surprised it's me but not that surprised after all.

"You have that same look," she tells me after welcoming me back into her office. "The one your daddy had, wandering around school like a caged animal, clawing for a way out, or in." The ficus tree in the corner is dead. Brown leaves huddle at the plant's base too late for rescue. Martha clearly doesn't water often. "But you may be in luck, after all. I fired two CNAs yesterday. They argued in a patient's room. Can you imagine? I have no time for catfights here."

"I'll take it."

"It's hourly. Starting is barely above minimum wage."

"I'm grateful, and I can start right away."

"Night shift. Sometimes double shifts. Pulmonary or Labor and Delivery?"

Asthma, lungs, bronchitis. Or blood and babies. I prefer the action. Nursing school was a perfect fit once I got going in the hospital. That first semester was mostly science classes: psychology, biology, nutrition, and anatomy. They told us we'd have to know it all for the state license test. Maslow's five basic needs for survival, ethics, rules for recording, interpersonal-relationship communication, plans of care. It was all just vocabulary to me then. Learning it all in a book was all right, but it was the patient part that made me feel good, like I could help make someone's path just a little less painful. Clinicals were my favorite. When I walked through the sliding glass doors, stepped onto the clean white floor, heard the beeping of machines, and felt the rushing all around me, it was a different world. I could be anybody I wanted. No one knew me there. It made me feel important when a patient smiled. The head RN, Mrs. Jenkins, said I had a knack for making folks feel comfortable. "Make 'em laugh a little," she said. "Humor helps." Blood doesn't bother me. Veins were easy the first time. I worked hard and made A's. Didn't do much but study and wait tables at Denny's, but I felt necessary.

"Never mind," Martha said. "You don't get to choose. I'll bet you clean well. I need that on Labor and Delivery."

I almost object. I almost decide babies are too soon. But I don't. Nursing makes me feel like a superhero, and I didn't grow up with much power. "I'll take anything. Anything at all."

I spend the rest of the afternoon in Human Resources doing paperwork and watching videos about hospital hygiene and stress management. I text Mama and Rose the good news: "I'm employed!"

Rose congratulates me. She suggests we celebrate by letting me buy her and Bobby pizza again. I don't hear anything from Mama, but when I get home, a new pair of blue scrubs with a Mickey Mouse print is folded up on my bed. They're the wrong size, but it doesn't matter. I throw them in the wash so they'll be fresh for tomorrow.

The RN I am assigned the next day welcomes me once she realizes I know what I'm doing. They give me the easy stuff first: vital signs, changing diapers, sanitizing bathrooms. There aren't any moms delivering on my first shift, but several are getting ready. I help one new mom get dressed and pack up her things to go home. She has me hold the baby while she showers. He's a little boy named Shane, snuggly and wrinkly with milky, new-baby smell.

I pull double shifts at the hospital for the next two days.

Three delivery assists, one C-section, one circumcision, a lot of diaper changes, and I feed a baby girl a bottle. Her eyes are barely open and she wraps her whole hand around my pinky and squeezes while she sucks. Then she falls asleep, and I just rock her, content to study the teddy bear wallpaper in peace and feel useful again.

One of the RNs, Vicky, is pretty bossy. She's been there the longest, and all the doctors favor her. Most of the nurses are from Quincy or other small towns in Illinois. On my break Vicky tells me I clean good. "Where you from?" she asks.

"Here. Basically," I say. "I was gone awhile. Now, I'm back."

"Well, you ain't new to this, that's for sure." I've been keeping my head down, but now I look up and there is a bit of kindness in Vicky. "You can do the charts, too, if you think you're ready."

Twelve miles across the river to Quincy is enough distance for me. I have the thirty-minute drive to myself every day. Jimmy Buffett sings "Margaritaville," and I pretend I'm back on the beach. Midwestern summers are just as hot and humid as Florida's, but the Mississippi isn't as predictable as the Atlantic.

MAMA AND I WATCH THE soaps together in the afternoons. She loves *General Hospital.* I point out the inaccuracies between what's on the screen and my job. "We don't actually get a lot of SARS. It's mostly been contained," I explain; and "Comas aren't that common really. Sometimes a doctor will induce a coma in a patient for their own good, but these poor people on these shows fall down a lot and lose their memories."

Mama tells me to stop, though. "I don't watch it 'cuz it's real. I got plenty of real around here." Yesterday she made a pie. From scratch. The house smelled like fresh cinnamon and apples for days.

I'm eating the leftover pie right out of the tin for breakfast when Mama comes in for coffee. "You could use a plate," she says, pouring her Folgers.

"It was too good to wait for a plate. And I'm finishing every last crumb," I tell her, licking the back of the jellied spoon.

"I'll have time to bake a lot more pies now."

"How come?"

She cocks her head to the side, like she's been patiently waiting for this moment to deliver this news. She takes another deep, dramatic breath and exhales. "I didn't get that promotion, after all."

"Aw, Mama. I'm sorry. I know you were countin' on it. Here I am going on and on about my new job."

"It's just as well. I couldn't be more tickled, to tell you the truth. When Don told me I wasn't being promoted, I told him to go to hell. He was a skirt chaser anyway." I'm holding the fork midair. Did Mama just say she was being harassed at work? And quit? "Yeah, your old mama told him a thing or two. But that's just fine. I know how to land. I've got it all figured out."

"You are not playin' Lotto, if that's what you mean. I told you no one wins that thing."

Mama laughs at my suggestion.

"I've bought myself a business. Well, a share in a business. I'm gonna make real money this time. And it starts with this."

She holds out a purple pill. It's about an inch long with a *J* inscribed on it. "Go on. Take it. I'll get you a glass of milk to wash that pie and pill down."

"What is it?"

"Jalaxy! It's completely all natural. There are pills and powders for drinks. It detoxes toxins you've been carryin' for years. Resets all your gut bacteria so your body can start doin' its thing again. And you'll lose weight. A lot of weight. Probably by the end of the week. Go ahead. Swallow it."

"Wait. You quit your job, and you're going into a pyramid scheme?"

"Bite your tongue, missy. This is an all-natural supplement. Jalaxy! is the next biggest thing. I got six orders this morning already. You'll see. If you don't wanta be skinny and healthy, fine. I was offering it to you for free. It's twenty-seven dollars for everyone else."

"And you want me to just take it? Can I read the package insert first?"

"Only if you don't trust your mama."

I swallow the pill. "You're looking healthier already," she says, hugging me for the first time since I've been home.

Later, Mama wants to pick up some stuff at Walmart and asks if I'll come along, as if we're friends. Going to town and a trip to Walmart is an event. Half of your social life happens in the parking lot. You see at least a cousin, a long-lost friend, and a lot of high school acquaintances on every visit. There are only three degrees of separation between you and every other customer, sometimes fewer. Hannibal didn't always have a Walmart. There used to be just two places in town to get what you needed: Huck Finn Shopping Center and Steamboat Bend Plaza. One of them had a JCPenney where everyone bought their winter coats and school shoes. The other had a movie theater where I once saw the Muppets. Stores came and went until Walmart moved in and put everyone else out of business for good. Folks love to hate on Walmart, but the place is always packed.

The first person we meet when the double doors swing open in front of us is Uncle Ronnie. He's not really my uncle but that's what everyone calls him. He may be loosely related to a great-aunt of mine on my daddy's side. Either way, Uncle Ronnie and I share a last name common to many in Hannibal, Brooks.

"You old coot," Mama says, slapping Uncle Ronnie on the back. "Let me give you a hand." Mama helps him settle into one of those motorized shopping scooters and balances his cane in the front basket.

"Who's the pretty lady?" Uncle Ronnie asks, nodding toward me. His beard is so long it sits in his lap. He's wearing overalls over a white muscle shirt, but he's all withered up and there isn't much muscle to show. When he smiles at me, all four of his front teeth pop over his bottom lip, which is stuffed with chewing tobacco.

"You know my daughter," Mama calls loudly into Uncle Ronnie's good ear. "She ain't been home in a while. This is Laura. My youngest. She's been off to college becomin' a nurse."

"Actually, I'm a nursing assistant. A CNA."

"College? A nurse? Well, that's handy," he says, looking me up and down like I've got a sales price tag somewhere. "Where you at now?"

"I was in Florida for years," I tell him. "Now I'm here. Workin' over in Quincy."

"Came back home, huh? Well, most of 'em do eventually."

"Not really," I try to explain. "Just until I get back on my feet—"

"Oh, leave her alone, will ya? Laura's doin' just fine," Mama breaks in.

Uncle Ronnie just stares, like he doesn't understand, like it's perfectly fine to tease me now that I'm one of them again. Then he zooms away, knocking over half of a pudding-pack display on his way.

Mama watches him go, but she doesn't look at me.

I hold my shoulders back to stand a little taller. Maybe I'll take all the little purple pills she wants me to.

After I get milk and new stockings for Mama, I run into Rose in the checkout line looking at the tabloids. "You avoidin' me?" she says, bumping her cart into mine. She's got four six-packs of Miller Lite, three bottles of Boone's Strawberry Hill, and two watermelons. Her fresh face of makeup looks like she's ready for a party. I'm glad to see her. I haven't been quick to return her calls. I don't want to testify. But I did leave her a message with the good news of my job. Bobby and I went out for ice cream yesterday, but Rose was at work. I'm walking a tightrope, and it's taking all of my balance not to fall.

"Nope. Been workin'. Mama needed somethin' from the store," I say, helping Rose unload her cart onto the conveyor belt. "Did Bobby tell you about the caves?"

"He's been playin' with those rocks for days. He sleeps with the bag by his pillow and packs them all away at night. It's all he's talked about." Rose turns to wait for me. "Makes him wanta be Tom Sawyer even more and show all the tourists the cool Hannibal stuff."

"He's such a sweet boy. Don't know how he turned out that way with you for a mama." Rose cracks a smile.

"You gonna go to the Y tomorrow?" she asks. "We could both probably use the exercise."

"I'm scheduled to work. Can't."

"Well, doesn't that sound nice? You enjoyin' it?"

"I am. More than I thought I would." Rose peels a $100 bill off of a wad of cash and hands it to the checkout clerk. "Whoa. Where'd you get all that?"

"Girl's gotta do what a girl's gotta do," she says, but I don't like what she means. "Hey, we're barbecuin' tonight. Folks are comin' into town for the reunion. We'll toast your new job! You know the Reed boys. They used to live out on Route O. They're both in from Hallsville for the pre-reunion stuff. They work in the cement plant over there. Their sister and me work together down at Deter's. Come on by. We won't bust your diet. Promise. You're lookin' skinnier these days, by the way."

I've lost six pounds. Working and not eating is apparently the only diet I need.

"Will Bobby be home?"

"'Course Bobby'll be home. Where else is he gonna go? I'm not even lettin' Josh see him until he catches up the money he owes." We walk together to the front of the store and wait for Mama by the shopping carts.

"It'll be a lot better when you tell the judge what an asshole

Josh is. Trial's next Tuesday at two. You ask off from work?" Rose leads the way to a bench, and we sit down together.

"I told you I can't be there, Rose. I'm not gettin' involved."

"Bobby said you'd probably change your mind, especially since it concerns him."

"Don't do that. That's not fair."

"Who said anything about fair?"

Rose's face turns back into her five-year-old self. She is about to throw a tantrum.

"I'll come by later. I have the night off. Want me to bring somethin'?" Mama comes out of the store, and I wave her over.

"Just your pretty self," Rose says, reaching in for a hug. It's the second time today someone's called me pretty. It's my second hug. Maybe Walmart's not so bad after all.

LANCE'S TRUCK IS PARKED IN Rose's driveway. She didn't tell me Sammy or his brother would be here. Bobby runs out the door to meet me. The screen door flaps shut behind him and Rose yells about the flies.

I hug Bobby too tight and he pretends to punch me in the gut so I'll let him go. *Charmed* blares on the living room TV and everyone ignores it. Then there's Sammy leaning against the doorframe with a Miller Lite in his hand. He raises it to his lips and I think about how wet that bottle must be.

"Sammy," I say, walking past him into the kitchen. "Good to see you again." I put my Jell-O salad on the island next to an assortment of cheese logs and Ritz. It's Bobby's favorite:

lime green with a can of pears in it. Rose has made homemade french fries in her deep fryer. They're crispy and drenched in salt.

"Have some fries," she says, holding out the tray to me.

Rose turns around from the kitchen sink and looks over my shoulder at Sammy, who is now on the back porch talking to the guys.

"Nice work, Rose," I whisper, grabbing a longneck from the kitchen sink she's filled with ice. "You could of mentioned that Sammy would be here."

Rose smirks like she's proud of her scheming. I fish out a can of root beer and open it for Bobby.

"There's more in the cooler out back. Burgers are on." The phone rings on the wall, but Rose ignores it.

"Aren't you going to get that?" I ask.

"Nope. It's just Josh. He pranks us like an immature brat. If I answer, he hangs up. Just ignore it." The phone rings again. Rose picks up the receiver and slams it down without speaking.

"Aunt Laura, wanta see my new Game Boy?" Bobby asks. I follow him to the couch and look over his shoulder as he chatters on about Pokémon. "Dad got it for me at Walmart."

Rose watches us from the kitchen. "The Bastard," she says, plunging the knife into the watermelon. "He's got money for a Game Boy but none for shoes."

"Need some help with that?" I ask, taking the knife from Rose's hand. "Bobby can hear you."

"Bobby should hear me!" she shouts. Bobby doesn't look up from the tiny screen. "The Bastard takes my car and won't help with the bills. Unless somebody stands up for us, he'll get the house, too. And by somebody I mean you."

"Do we have to do this now? Really?" I nod toward the back porch. "Thought you wanted to have fun."

"Screw it all," Rose says and cranks up "Friends in Low Places" on the CD player. She walks out through the living room singing and leaves me to cut up the watermelon. A few minutes later Sammy comes into the kitchen again. He stands at the counter watching me.

"Rose said you could use some help," Sammy says.

"Of course she did." I slice hard through the heart of the watermelon, and Sammy leans over to catch one of the falling lobes.

"You okay?" he asks, putting his hand on my shoulder.

Sammy's touch sends a shiver up my back and down my thighs. I roll my neck in a circle and take a deep breath. "I'm fine. And you?" I cut the fruit into triangles and flick out the seeds. Red juice runs down my elbow, and I imagine Sammy licking it off me.

Sammy arranges the pieces on a tray Rose left on the counter. He overlaps each rind so they're in neat rows ready to be served. There's one left over that won't fit his pattern so he eats the whole piece in one bite down to the rind. I watch his teeth, his tongue, and the ripe flesh. "That's delicious," he says. "I'm good now." I stare too long and remember what it felt like to have his weight on me. Rose's air conditioner doesn't seem to be working at all.

We sit around the picnic tables on the back porch talking until the stars come out. The brothers and Lance take turns playing cornhole in the backyard with Bobby. Rose makes spiked lemonade and serves it with Duncan Hines brownies. My hands are still sticky from the watermelon juice, so I wipe them on my sweating bottle of beer. The conversation turns to the reunion and Rose insists we aren't going, which makes the Reed brothers, Dwayne and Darren, and their wives, Chelsea and Lisa, complain that we aren't fun anymore.

"What's the point?" Rose asks. "Everyone I wanta see is right here right on this porch."

"You don't go to see people," Lisa says, "you go to be seen."

"I prefer hidin'," I admit. "It's easier."

"But you're back for good, yeah? Rose tells us you're workin' over in Quincy. How do you like it?" Chelsea asks.

"Good so far. The nurses are nice. So are the doctors. I'm on Labor and Delivery. That keeps me busy."

"Of course she's back for good," Rose interrupts. "She's been a big help, too, with Bobby. What with the divorce and trial, I can't keep everything straight." She pats my knee and gets me another beer. "How's the levee at the farm, Sammy? Y'all aren't desperate yet, are ya?"

"Holdin'. But not for long," Sammy says. "Might be yet another Fourth of July sandbaggin' and bulldozin'. 'Least we can watch the fireworks from the farm. My ex hated that, missin' the fun every year." His face is drawn like the waters are already wearing him out.

Rose squints at me to see if I care that Sammy mentioned his ex. I peel the label on my beer bottle. I never minded the hard work of sandbagging and bulldozing, either, but I do like to watch the fireworks.

"My sister says it just kills the businesses downtown when

they don't get the crowds," Lisa adds. Her sister's a waitress at Ole Planters, the oldest family business in town. "She can kiss her tips good-bye, that's for sure."

"Happens every year. It's just a matter of how bad and when," Chelsea says.

"Unless someone does somethin' about it, that is. Remember all those levees sabotaged in '93?" Darren says, popping the top on another longneck. Inside the house, the phone keeps ringing but we're all learning to ignore it better.

"That was some crazy shit," Dwayne adds, shoving two brownies into his mouth. "It just ain't right to bust up someone else's levee to save your own. You gotta fight fair." Nothing was fair that summer. We were robbed of all the glory of our senior year when all the celebrations fizzled into the rising waters. Maybe that's why this reunion looms so large.

"Your brother still at the cement plant, Laura?"

"On and off," I say. "Mostly on. I hope." They know Trey. Jobs are hard to come by when you've burned bridges. There's only so many times that Mama can apologize for my brother. "He's buyin' some land out on Route O. Savin' up some."

"Heard part of the plant's flooded," Dwayne says. He shakes his head at the loss. "'Least we get steady shifts in Hallsville. China hasn't stolen our jobs yet, and there ain't no water around to lay us off."

"Not much any of us can do to hold back the river," Sammy says, draining his beer. "Mississippi's gonna do whatever the hell it wants to." I watch him to see if he believes what he just said.

"Hey," says Lisa, "heard you got a little Tom on your hands, Rose!"

Rose nods her head and purses her lips like she's so proud she might cry. "Bobby has been workin' so hard. You wouldn't believe how much he's studyin'. Tell 'em, Laura."

"It's true. He's doin' great."

"You must be so proud!"

"As long as the waters don't get too high, this is gonna be the best Fourth of July ever. I can't wait for Bobby to be up on that stage!" Rose says. "Flood won't stop the reunion either. Not that I'm gonna go."

"I'll go," Sammy says. "It's good to catch up, to see old friends." That's the Sammy I used to know. Always looking on the bright side. I watch him closely and wonder if I could forgive him. "What about you, Laura? You wanta go with me to the reunion?" The guys hoot and holler like it's third grade and someone just got caught passing a note.

"She'd love to," Rose answers. "What time should I have her ready?"

My cheeks are burning red but I meet Sammy's eyes. "I would. Love to go that is." My words trip. "With you, I mean."

Dwayne high-fives Sammy and Rose flips open the lid on the cooler and offers everyone a celebratory round.

BOBBY'S ASLEEP ON THE COUCH with his Game Boy beeping beside him. It's sitting on top of Ms. B's Tom and Becky manual; the cover is so worn that the *g* is faded and it now reads *Paintin Fences*, which is probably how folks would say it anyway. I turn off the Game Boy and tuck a light blanket around Bobby. I crank the air conditioner and stand in front of the coughing breeze.

Out the front window, a truck is shining its brights on the house. Whoever is inside is laying on the horn and won't stop. Bobby stirs but falls back asleep. Dwayne and Darren come running through the house and out the front door in a rush just as the truck peels away. Sammy and Lance trail them and they all climb in Lance's truck and follow the truck like they're in an episode of the *Dukes of Hazzard*. Chelsea, Lisa, and Rose stand on the front porch watching the drama. "Bastard! What an asshole!" Rose yells at the empty road. It must have been Josh harassing Rose's little party. Looks like he's getting exactly what he wants. A high school car chase, a fight in a parking lot somewhere, drama that says nothing has changed at all.

The girls and I sit on the front porch talking and waiting for the guys to return. The conversation moves easily from Jesus to Jalaxy! "I heard your mama's selling it, Laura. That true? I've been thinkin' 'bout tryin' it."

"It's true. I'm her little guinea pig, too."

"Well, you look amazin'!" Lisa says, leaning over to look at my backside.

"I feel good, too, but I can't say that it's just the supplement. I'm eatin' better, too." No one is interested in my nutrition, though.

"I'm gonna call her up tomorrow, that's for sure," Chelsea agrees.

"My boss's wife took it and said her diabetes is completely gone," Rose adds.

I frown at Rose. "I highly doubt that." I'm about to launch into a medical explanation of diabetes and nutritional supplements, but Lance's truck comes around the corner and the guys are hooting and hollering from the cab. "You totally would of kicked his ass!" Darren yells, slapping Dwayne on the back. They didn't catch up with Josh after all, but it doesn't matter. It's all about the chase, the effort, how you look.

I slip out a side door and walk the dark alley to my car. I open the car door, sink into the driver's seat, and close my eyes. Rose is right. I do hide a lot when I'm in Hannibal. Something pulls me back here every time, but it strangles me just the same. I wipe the sweat off my face and turn on the key. The engine clicks five times before it stalls.

"Starter's out. Or it's your battery," a voice says from the dark. It's Dwayne. "Pop the hood." He walks around the car, unlatches the hood, and looks inside.

After a few seconds, he calls, "You ain't goin' nowhere. Battery's almost dead. Just wait. I'll jump you. Unless, 'course, you'd rather Sammy do it." Dwayne acts like he's falling over laughing at his own joke.

"You're hilarious, Dwayne," I say. "You got cables? Mine were stolen."

"Stolen?"

"You don't want to know. I was tryin' to help a guy in Florida. On the side of the road. He was broke down. He stole my cables and my purse."

"Huh," Dwayne says, like I'm speaking a foreign language. When someone breaks down on the side of the road, you help them. You probably even know them. He hands me his beer. "Hold that."

Dwayne walks over to the bushes and pees. Must be why he came out in the first place. Then he gets the cables out of his pickup and hooks us up. "Try it again," he yells. My car starts on the first turn. He unhooks us and walks back to the driver's side for his beer.

"Thanks," I call to his back. He toasts his beer in the air over his head and walks off in the dark.

Main Street

Tourists love to stroll South Main Street and see the grand hotel at the corner of Church and Main. It wasn't the first hotel in Hannibal. The Park Hotel, built in 1879, was on the corner of Center and Fourth Streets on the northwest side. Famous musicians and actors came to Hannibal to perform at the Park Theatre. They needed a fancy place to rest their heads. But the Park Hotel was destroyed by a fire in 1899.

By 1905, Hannibal was booming and needed a new hotel for businessmen who visited and considered investing in the growing town. The Mark Twain Hotel was built that year, where it still stands today.

For the centennial of Mark Twain's birth, in 1935, the hotel made a celebratory menu. Visitors could enjoy the "Special Mark Twain Sandwich" for just forty cents. It was a good deal, even then. While they ate, tourists perused descriptions of local attractions, also featured on their menu. Distances to nearby cities were included and paved roads were distinguished.

Many famous people, like Franklin Delano Roosevelt, Herbert Hoover, and Amelia Earhart, stayed at the Mark Twain Hotel. Norman Rockwell stayed there at least three different times when he came to town to soak up the culture he needed to illustrate the pages of Twain's most famous books. "The longer I worked at the task," Rockwell wrote, "the more in love with the different personalities I became."

CHAPTER NINE

ON THE DAY of the reunion, Sammy picks me up at five. He's called every day, just to make sure I haven't changed my mind. I haven't. Work has been a good distraction from the past.

Mama is waiting in one of the metal chairs out front. Her Miller Lite has a puddle underneath. She's fanning herself with an old *People* magazine and complaining about the heat. The seven astronauts who died in the *Columbia* space shuttle are staring back at Mama. She's set out a trap to catch the raccoon that keeps visiting her geraniums at night. She's terrified they'll try to take one of her girls. Every few minutes, she checks the trap. I don't know what she's going to do with a raccoon if she catches one. Or a skunk, for that matter. But I'll bet she'll hold an all-night vigil until she does. "Sammy!" she yells when he pulls into the driveway.

"Mrs. Brooks," he says, with equal enthusiasm. They make small talk while I pretend I'm still getting ready.

"How's the farm?"

"Basement's flooded. The well water is bad. Looks like '93 again." That summer is the last thing I want to think about tonight.

"Heard the rain might hold out a few more days."

"Well, that's somethin', I suppose. Lance and I worked on the levee today. Did what we could. Somethin's gotta give."

"How's your dad?"

"Tired."

"Don't I know that feelin'."

I look at myself in the hall mirror. Rose brought me a purple sleeveless sundress that is more revealing than I'm used to. All the redness has faded from my tattoo and it's done peeling. Now it's a smooth little blue-and-black raft that's fierce. Mama put what's grown out of my pixie cut in rollers at noon, but the curls are already starting to wilt in the heat. I oiled my cowgirl boots, and the green snakeskin details gleam. Vicky let me borrow some fake diamond earrings. The dress fits in all the right places and, for once, makes me love my hips. Jalaxy! may not work, but I do look good. Mama is thrilled that I'm taking it. She brags about me all over town now, Aunt Betty said. Rose called it my "gettin' lucky" dress, which might be true.

When I open the screen door to Sammy, his mouth forms an O. He blinks and shakes his head like he's trying to wake up from a dream. He's wearing a crisp white button-down shirt and black slacks. His hair is combed straight; he's left his cowboy hat in the car. Nothing fancy. Just simple and clean and right. I want to freeze him exactly like this.

"You're gonna catch some flies if you keep gawkin', boy." Mama laughs. "She cleans up pretty good, huh?"

Sammy nods. He reaches out his hand for mine. It's our prom night all over again. He picked me up on this very porch. I wore a red sequined dress with two ruffles at the bottom. Aunt Betty made it and told me when she zipped it up to keep it that way. I followed her advice. On prom night, anyway. Sammy rented a black tuxedo and matched his cummerbund to my dyed shoes. He brought me white roses and Mama put them in an empty tea pitcher in the kitchen. Tonight it's gardenias, and they make the porch smell fresh, like honey. I take Sammy's hand and thank him for the flowers. Mama offers to put them in water. The screen door slaps shut behind us, but, for once, she just grins.

THE REUNION IS ON THE first floor of the old Mark Twain Hotel, a three-story building that sprawls over an entire downtown block. Bobby told me that Clemens himself once stood smoking a cigar on the spiral staircase that leads to the second-floor landing. It's closed off now by a velvet rope and a sign that declares PRIVATE RESIDENCE, which really just means that the senior citizens who live in the renovated apartments above wouldn't like you to bust in on their nightly *Jeopardy!*. The hotel is rented out for events. The ceilings are high and the lights are dim, which hides the shabbiness and makes the hotel lobby almost glamorous again. The furniture has been pushed against the walls, so you can't see the fabric peeling from the back. A dusty grand piano sits in one corner, but no one's playing it. The entire room smells like a fake air freshener, maybe Ocean Breeze. A DJ puts on "Little Miss Can't Be Wrong" by the Spin Doctors. A small circle of girls dance with each other, holding bottles of beer in their free hands. Red and black helium balloons float up from the center of the tables and a life-sized cardboard cutout of a pirate waves his sword in the air. People are sticking their heads through the empty pirate face and taking pictures. We're proud Hannibal Pirates.

Sammy and I stop at the front table for name tags.

"I know you!" one of the girls behind the table exclaims. Her makeup is heavy; the foundation is several shades darker than her neck. She's clearly taken a few trips to the tanning bed. The aroma of hair spray stings my eyes. "You sat behind me in Mr. Stone's class. Economics. Our junior year. You don't remember? I hardly recognized you! Laura, right? Laura Brooks?"

I hug her hello. She doesn't give me much of a choice.

Sammy leans over and whispers, "Amy."

"Amy!" I say. "You haven't changed a bit!"

"Heard you were comin' with Sammy," Amy says. "Don't y'all look cute together! Tryin' to remember who told me." She holds up a finger like she's thinking. Then she leans over and nudges another girl at the table. "Jessica, who told us about Sammy and Laura? Remember? It was last week. We were in line at Walmart."

Jessica shrugs, looks me up and down, and turns back to her reunion list and the all-important job of checking off names.

"Where's Charlie hidin'?" Sammy asks, leaning over to kiss Amy's cheek.

"Didn't you hear? Levee broke this mornin'. He's movin' his mom's stuff into our basement. First one to go, I heard."

"Y'all need anythin'?"

"Not right now. We're fine. Thanks for askin'. At least it'll save your butt, huh?" Sammy's family farm is downstream. One levee busted is a relief to the rest.

"Let's get a drink," Sammy says to me.

"Oh!" Amy interrupts. "Here's your drink ticket. Just one, okay? Be good now. Jesus is watching!"

Sammy takes the ticket and looks at her a moment longer.

She might be teasing but I suspect she isn't. Rose said a bunch of the girls from high school found Jesus, too, and were going all over town evangelizing. Doesn't sound like all that much has changed in ten years except the reason that most of us were never good enough.

"Good to see you again, Amy," Sammy says, giving her a sideways hug. "Say hi to Charlie for me. Tell him my dad's got a free 'dozer if y'all need it. Happy to help."

"Will do," Amy answers. "Enjoy the reunion! I swear, Laura Brooks, I hardly recognized you." I still don't remember her, but now I wish I did. "Oh, don't forget to check out the yearbook table," she calls after us. "Jessica made us this adorable trivia game. It's more fun than alcohol, I promise. You'll love it!"

Sammy trades in our drink tickets for two Bud Lights. We stand at the bar and watch people pass. We whisper back and forth naming people we used to know, and he fills me in on what I've missed in a decade of being gone. Everyone who passes shakes Sammy's hand and slaps him on the back. A few hug me, too. My class-outsider status seems cemented, but standing next to Sammy has privileges.

Amy comes into the crowd and steers people out of the bar

and toward the yearbook table. It's just a matter of minutes until she realizes we haven't followed her instructions and shoos us over. She nods at us as she passes, but then she tells a girl in jeans loudly to leave. "I don't care if your brother's here, you are not a guest on the list for the class of '93! This is a private event! Now, go!" Amy's actually kicking someone out of the reunion. What makes her get to decide who belongs?

"Let it go," Sammy says, watching me watch the scene Amy's making. "Some people feel better puttin' other folks down. Nothin' you can do about it, Laura." He steers me away from the bar and toward the yearbook table in a far corner of the hotel lobby. Pictures have been blown up to poster size with GUESS WHO? tags where you write in your answer. Sammy picks up a trivia card.

"Who was the governor of Missouri in 1993?" Sammy asks, sipping while I think.

"Carnahan," I answer. "He stopped in to eat at Denny's my first semester at nursing school. He tipped well."

"Name the marching-band teacher."

"How the heck would I know?"

"Mr. Yardley. He was always fightin' with Coach for the football field," Sammy answers. "He wore cut-off jean shorts and a mesh tank top. Can't make stuff like that up."

"Let me ask one," I say, taking the trivia card from him. "What was the most popular song our senior year?"

"That's easy. 'I Will Always Love You' by Whitney Houston. Spent a lot of time nursin' a broken heart that year, remember?"

"You're such a sap," I say, punching Sammy's arm. I recall

him singing that song in my ear often while his hands were occupied elsewhere on my body.

"Guess the official Tom and Becky." Ten eight-by-ten pictures of our class's contestants from seventh grade are framed. All wholesome white faces. Most from the same neighborhood. You'd think there weren't any people of color in all of Hannibal. Most of those same faces are holding court over by the bar.

"That one is too easy." Sammy smirks and strikes the same pose as his Tom picture. He really was an adorable Tom. I'll give him that.

"Name the student that was suspended for making a realistic Renaissance condom."

"Caleb Houstead," we both say together. We laugh and then both look around to see if anyone heard us. It's a strange reaction. Caleb was probably the friendliest guy in our class. He never said a bad word about anybody. He shot a three-pointer that won districts our senior year. The whole town was at that game. The team lifted him onto their shoulders and carried him through the crowd like a king. He was killed in a car accident a year after we graduated. Just on the verge of everything.

"Refill?" Sammy asks. I lead the way back to the bar.

It's crowded when we return. Maybe stragglers like me who couldn't decide to come or not made last-minute decisions. Maybe they want to be seen, too. Or maybe they were in the parking lot building up their liquid courage.

I scan the bar and soak up the nerves, the small talk, the fake smiles, and some genuine hugs. Amy and Jessica circulate through the crowd checking tickets and name tags. Amy points toward the door and a couple of guys slouch off. Even now, ten years after high school, some people still don't belong. The reunion organizers keep our carefully drawn lines clear. Jessica starts her way through the bar making sure that people are using their one drink ticket and no more. It was Jessica who threw up on her graduation robe the morning of our senior picture. A bonfire party the night before the picture went all night, and Jessica and her friends showed up drunk the next morning. Apparently, her partying ways are a thing of the past.

Sammy keeps his hand on my elbow. A mustached man in the corner sips the foam head off a beer, and I know him instantly.

"Mr. Eggleston!" I say, too loud. "It's so good to see you."

"Well, well. Look who's here. Nurse Laura, huh?"

"Nurse Assistant Laura. I owe it all to you," I say, hugging him. "I've wanted to thank you for years."

"Me? It was you that went to nursing school and left us for good." Mr. Eggleston shakes Sammy's hand and leans in to give me a side hug. His eyebrows wiggle in their own conversation. The whiskers of his mustache have whitened.

"Where you at now?" he asks.

"I was in Florida. Now I'm home for a bit. Who knows? I'm workin' over in Quincy right now."

"Illinois? Well, honey, you're on the wrong side of the river," he teases. "When are you going back to school to finish your degree? CNA is pretty good, but don't you want to be an LPN or RN?"

"Maybe. Don't know yet. Seemed like the right time to come home."

"I'll bet you're sure glad she did," Mr. E says, nudging Sammy.

"Doesn't feel like a decade, that's for sure," Sammy answers. He puts his arm around my waist and pulls me a little closer. He rubs the small of my back with his palm, and I curl into him like a cat. Then we all turn toward the door.

Rose walks through it just as the music stops and the house-lights pop on. Or at least I think it's Rose. The lights spotlight her electric-blue sequined gown. The sparkles reflect directly into my eyes. Mr. Eggleston shades his view with his hand. Sammy belly laughs at my back.

Rose's dress is slit halfway up her thigh and the neckline plunges almost to her waist. She's either wearing a Jennifer Aniston wig or she's paid a small fortune for extensions. She looks like a movie star. She's leaning heavily on one of the guys from the pool game. He doesn't look much older than Bobby. He's wearing a brown suit and bolo tie. His goatee's hardly filled in and his long hair curls around his collar. A part of me is cheering her on. Another part needs to get to her quick before she does something Rose-like.

Rose and her guy hit the dance floor and start gyrating to the house music. She cups both of her partner's butt cheeks and pulls him toward her. She's even had fake nails put on and painted them Hooker Red. Aunt Betty would be proud. Rose doesn't notice that the DJ is on break.

"You wanta get your friend 'fore she makes a fool of her-self," a voice slurs in my ear. I turn around and see Josh, who's holding hands with Kayla Brothers. She's wearing a white sun-dress that shows off her tattoo sleeves. Her hair is bleached in the back and extensions shoot out above her ears. Josh is wear-ing jeans and a buzz cut. He looks so much like Bobby, and I hate it. He shouldn't be here. He's not even from Hannibal, but Kayla and I had gym class together for four years. We hid in the locker room together every chance we could. I nod at Kayla and scowl at Josh. He leans over and sticks his tongue in her ear. She pushes him away and giggles.

"I ain't her keeper," I say. Josh glares at me, and I look away.

"That's for sure," Kayla agrees. "Though she looks like she needs one." Josh and she snort a laugh together and clink their watery glasses. He scoops out an ice cube and tries to toss it down her cleavage. Then he gestures toward me, asking if I want one, too.

Sammy asks me to dance, and I nod yes just to get some distance. We join Rose and her boy toy on the dance floor. They're dancing to "Baby Got Back" like we're eighteen again.

"Laura!" Rose screams, falling into my arms like we haven't seen each other in years. She's probably already tipsy. The mixture of Aqua Net and White Diamonds catches in my throat.

"What are you pullin', Rose?" I ask, taking her beer and handing it to Sammy. "Simmer down now."

"Me? I'm just dancin'," she says. Rose dips her hip to mine and bumps me. Suddenly we're in seventh grade again, tickling each other in her basement and dancing to "Footloose." "Come on, sister. Don't you remember how to party? You ain't too good for us now, are ya?"

"Nah," Sammy says, "she's just right for us now."

The DJ returns to his table and shouts, "How about some 'Electric Slide,' folks?" People flock to the dance floor; Rose and I are arm in arm, caught up in the synchronized moves.

Out of the corner of my eye, I see Josh and Kayla inching toward us. Rose doesn't notice. She snatches back her beer from Sammy and finishes it. Sammy stays at my side, following my lead. It's a party, and I'm not thinking anymore. I have Rose—crazy, outrageous, lovable Rose—beside me and Sammy next to me. It's enough.

"My dress!" Kayla shouts. "You spilled beer on my dress, you bitch!" At first I think she's talking to me.

Sammy takes the bottle from Rose's hand. "Don't think so. This bottle's empty. Keep dancin', folks," Sammy calls. He steers our party forward, away from Josh and Kayla.

"She did too!" Kayla yells, pointing a fake fingernail at Rose. "I sure the hell didn't spill it on myself!" People stop dancing and stand in a circle around Rose and me. Rose puts her hands on her hips in a ready stance.

"Maybe you pissed yourself!" Rose shouts back. She reaches over and flicks Kayla's hair. Kayla grabs her by the shoulders and tries to push her down.

Someone yells, "Catfight!" as they both trip and fall into a heap. A black high heel is kicked off. Something makes a loud ripping sound.

"You're nothin' but white trash!" Kayla yells, trying to stand up.

Rose pulls her back down and throws a punch.

Sammy reaches into the mess, but Rose and Kayla roll away.

Josh is laughing his ass off and saying, "Let 'em go!"

Amy and Jessica show up. Their faces are horrified. "You're ruinin' everything!" Jessica shouts.

Something snaps inside of me. Suddenly it matters. Us and them. It's a territory I didn't know was mine. "Oh, hell no," I hear myself scream. I grab Kayla's hair just to pull her off Rose, but I can't let go. I have her hair but not her head.

"My extensions!" She jumps to her feet and swings back at me just as I turn to Sammy for help and miss her fist.

Rose pulls Kayla's feet out from under her. I punch the air between us. Kayla falls on her butt. She's stunned.

"Bitches!" Kayla yells, struggling again to her feet. Josh is at her side, propping her up and holding down her arms. "You're gonna pay for those!" she screams.

"Trust me," Josh says, "those two ain't worth any of this." He pushes Kayla ahead of him toward the door. "Rose is an unfit mother!" he yells back over his shoulder.

"That just ain't true and you know it, asshole. You can just stay away from Bobby, ya hear?" I say. Everyone stares at our little scene, and it feels like old times. Not good times, just old times.

Rose and me hold hands and she shouts, "Get the hell out of here!" at Josh's and Kayla's backs. Then she flips them two middle fingers. "Bastard! Bastard! Bas—" I clap my hand over Rose's mouth to get her to stop repeating it.

"Nice," Sammy says, pulling us both in for a hug. "Very classy, ladies."

Rose and me run together to the bathroom.

"Rose!" I say, pressing my back to the bathroom door. "What were you thinkin'?"

"Me?" She pants. "You started it!"

"Did not!"

"Did too!"

"I was defending you!"

"Well, I'm not the one with Kayla's hair, am I?" Rose says, flicking the fake hair in my hand. I'm still holding strands of blond. "At least my extensions look better."

"They're on your head," I point out.

Rose reaches up to fluff her hair and says, "We're gonna get kicked out now, right?"

"At least we're together," I offer. It's weak but true. Rose has always had my back, even when I didn't have hers, even when I didn't deserve it. I grab a paper towel and try to wipe the sweat and beer off Rose's sparkly mess.

Unsinkable Molly Brown

Samuel Clemens isn't the only notable native Hannibalian. Molly Tobin grew up to be one of the famous survivors of the *Titanic*. She was born in a little white house on Denkler's Alley just after the Civil War. Her parents were Irish Catholic and uneducated when they immigrated to Missouri. Molly went to school for a few years, but she quit when she was thirteen and found a job working twelve hours a day, six days a week, stripping leaves to their stems at the Garth Tobacco Company. She didn't like it much, but when you grow up as a have-not in Hannibal, your options are limited. Molly left when she was eighteen and set her sights on Colorado, where she got a job in a department store.

Molly said she wanted to marry money, but she married a poor man who loved her instead. Seven years later, he struck it rich. Molly was his good-luck charm. She lived the life of the Victorian nouveau riche, but she never forgot where she came from. She fought for women's suffrage and against childhood poverty. And when the *Titanic*, on which she'd booked a last-minute trip, started sinking, Molly bossed around a whole bunch of people and helped row the boats. When they were rescued, she worked tirelessly in the relief efforts. A little thing like water doesn't scare a girl from Hannibal much. When the papers asked her how come she survived, Molly attributed it to "typical Brown luck." "We're unsinkable," she said.

After Molly died, her legend was born. She became the Unsinkable Molly Brown in books and movies. Every Saturday, for $10, tourists can have tea in the tiny white house where she grew up.

CHAPTER TEN

As soon as she can corner me, Mama quizzes me all about the reunion. Sammy. Old friends. Rose. The mean girls still being mean. I downplay the fight. Mama only needs the surface report, really. She mercifully pours me a cup of coffee to keep me talking. She'll probably hear the rest in the parking lot at Walmart. An image of Rose, Kayla, and me flailing in a heap on the dance floor pops into my head. I shut my eyes tight against it. "We just went dancin', Mama," I lie. "Rose and me and Sammy. Back at TJ's. Think we closed the place down."

"Sounds like you're glad you went?" Mama asks.

"Except for this headache. And these feet ache. My arms hurt, too."

"Yep. Sounds 'bout right. You, Laura, are officially over the hill."

"I'm not even thirty!" I object. Besides the hangover and

the identity crisis of the past few months, I'm starting to get my stride back. I almost feel like me again, recalibrated and ready.

"Lord, you make me feel old." She looks at her watch. "Don't you have to be at work today? I'll make you some eggs. Scrambled and cheesy, just like you like 'em."

My head is still pounding, but the eggs in my belly help. I pull into the parking lot at the hospital five minutes before my shift starts and sprint to the delivery floor. The floor is wet from someone's sloppy mopping and I almost fall twice. Just as I round the corner to the nurses' station, I see the familiar face I've been avoiding most since I got back to town: Josh. He's holding the mop. "What the hell are you doing here?" just slips out, before I can even try to stop it.

"Good to see you, too, Laura. Again. So soon." There's a cut above his right eye and a greenish tint under his left eye.

I lower my voice and whisper, "Why are you here?" Clearly, he's mopping, but why on my floor? In my hospital? At my feet?

"What? Rose didn't tell you? I got myself a maintenance job." Josh nods to one of the other CNAs standing to my right checking a chart. His eyes go to her backside, and I step in front to block his vision. He puts his hand on my arm and leans in, adding "That judge is gonna be so impressed that I'll have Bobby for good."

I pull my arm away. "I doubt that."

"That's because you don't know what I know about how Rose is gettin' her money."

"What?" This better not be related to the police questioning. "You don't know nothing." I nudge his bucket on wheels forward so he has to chase after it down the hall and call, "You missed a spot over by the water fountain."

"Oh, I know a lot, don't I, Laura?" he calls back.

Josh pulling stunts like this and making Rose look bad all over town doesn't surprise me. He never was any good. I should know.

A few months after I moved from St. Louis to Jacksonville, Trey called me, which he rarely does, to tell me he heard Sammy's mom was sick. Breast cancer. Stage four. They'd noticed a shadow during a routine mammogram and that was it. I wanted to reach out to Sammy but I didn't know how. We hadn't talked in almost a year. Sammy's mom had always been nice to me, but I knew I'd given up my place in their family.

On my lunch break at the hospital, I dialed Sammy. I was sitting in a corner in the cafeteria and piped in Muzak was playing Phil Collins's "Take a Look at Me Now" for the twelfth time that day. Sammy answered, and I just sat there, silent. "Laura?" he asked. It came at me in a wave, my grief, how far away I felt, how lonely I was.

"I'm sorry, Sammy," I said. "I'm sorry about your mom."

Then it was Sammy's turn to just sit there. I could hear him breathing, maybe crying. "Funeral is Friday," he said. I hung up. Like a coward. I was calling to check in about his mom and accidentally dialed him an hour after her death.

I begged for a few days off from my new job. I traded some shifts to give myself a cushion, just in case. Then I drove straight to Hannibal, stopping only for gas and pee breaks.

Mama didn't know I was coming. No one did. The funeral was the next day.

The house was a mess when I arrived, and no one was home. I started on the dishes in the sink first. Then I cleaned up all the ashtrays and vacuumed. I tossed out an entire box of cigarettes, matches, and two lighters. The washing machine was broken, so I loaded the laundry in my car and drove it to Suds on Broadway. I left a note for Mama on the counter. I knew she'd be mad at my helping, but I didn't care.

Josh was standing at a dryer when I came in. By the looks of his load, he was only washing for one. "Well, look what the cat dragged in. What are you doin' home?" he said, coming over to help me with the baskets. "That's a lot of laundry, Laura. What are you in for?"

"Sammy's mom passed away. Funeral is tomorrow. I came home for it. Washer at home's broke, so here I am." I loaded three washers full of quarters and started sorting whites, darks, and colors.

"Thought you and Sammy were over?"

"We are."

"Sounds like you still got a soft spot," Josh teased.

I paused at Mama's towels and wished I had some bleach. Josh kept talking. "I never thought you two would break up. I thought you and Sammy were for good. What happened, anyway? What'd he do? It must have been big."

The water rushed into the washer, and I slammed down the lid. The flood. That summer. I didn't want to go back over any of it. I couldn't have stopped Sammy, even if I wanted to.

"Things happen. That's what. What are you doing here, Josh?" I asked, changing the subject. "Can't you do laundry at home?"

"Rose kicked me out again. Thought you'd know that. Thought she told you everything." Josh leaned against my machine. My arm brushed his biceps as I tossed in more clothes.

"She does. I lose track of whether you're in or out, though."

"Me, too." Josh laughed. He stood watching me sort. "You're lookin' good these days. Looks like the city suits you."

I stopped my sorting and turned toward Josh. He looked just like he did the night Rose and I met him. Before he became the Bastard. Skinny with blond hair and brown eyes. There was a scar that ran a line along his chin. He was tan from working outside. His eyes were intense, and he had this way of looking at you that made you feel really heard.

"What happened to Sammy's mom?"

Something about how Josh asked was too tender for me, and I broke down. Once I started, I couldn't stop. He let me put my head on his shoulder and sob. Then he dumped in the rest of my laundry and walked me to his car. His boot tracks made crosses in the mud. "Did your boot find religion?" I asked, wiping my face.

"Nah. Those are nails. They keep the devil away. Didn't you know that? Local folks think so, anyway."

In the car, Josh flipped open his cooler, handed me a beer. It felt good to sit and talk, to not have to introduce myself to someone new and start my story all over again. I hadn't realized how lonely I'd been until then, sitting on the passenger side with someone who knew me, who knew home. I thought about my final breakup with Sammy, about how little nursing school prepared for the stress of hospitals, about Trey's recent run-in with the police, about how Sammy's mom dying made me feel farther away than ever. I never mentioned Rose. Neither did he. We both drank another beer. I asked about Bobby, and Josh told me stories about potty training him with M&M's for bribes. Bobby would only pee for a red or green one. He told me about taking him to the park and teaching him to hang from the monkey bars. "Oh, and he'll only wear Spidey underwear," Josh added, "and usually nothin' else." I pictured Bobby pretending to be a superhero.

We went back to my house for another beer in between laundry cycles. It was raining hard and the rain soaked my face. Josh grabbed my hand as we ran through the puddles together. Trey and Mama still weren't home. The trailer smelled like artificial lemons from all of my cleaning. "I've known you all these years, Laura, and I've never even been to your house," Josh said, which was funny to both of us. "Let me see your room." We were giggling by then. Josh tickled my back and held on.

When I opened the door to my bedroom, he pushed me onto the bed and kissed me. He tasted like peppermint; I knew then that he'd eaten a breath mint to cover up the beer. I didn't say no. I kissed him back; I closed my eyes. He slid his hands under my shirt. It felt good to be touched, to not think, to not worry. Josh fumbled with my bra; I reached around and undid it for him. I unzipped his pants, he let out a little moan that said he wanted me, too. Then the front door slammed. I knew it was Mama by how she tossed her keys into the bowl by the door. Josh and I froze. I opened my eyes and the first thing I saw was a picture of Rose and me marching together in the Fourth of

July parade. It was ninth grade and we were both flag girls. It was enough to make me push Josh off. He put his finger to his lips and whispered, "Shh."

"You gotta go. It's my mama," I said, which was funny because of the beers but made me panic about getting caught.

"We can be quiet," Josh said, too loud from the alcohol. He leaned in to kiss me again.

I turned my cheek away. "No. Just go."

His face was pissed. He grabbed his shirt, climbed out through my bedroom window, and spun up rocks in the driveway peeling out.

Mama opened the front door but she wouldn't have recognized the car. I got dressed and waited. "Laura?" she finally said into the silence.

THE NEXT MORNING, THERE WAS a long line waiting outside the James O'Donnell Funeral Home. I sat in my car building up my courage. It was a gorgeous early-spring day, and I'd only brought a pale-blue summer dress, not exactly funeral attire. A hearse pulled into the drive and Lance got out. He took off his cowboy hat and tossed it back into the car like someone told him he had to. A woman I didn't recognize followed him. She had short brown hair, light-brown skin, and an expensive looking black dress and three strands of pearls. With her big sunglasses, she looked like a Midwestern version of Holly Golightly in *Breakfast at Tiffany's*. Then Sammy stepped out and held her hand. She linked her arm through his and leaned on it. That's when her diamond ring caught the sunlight.

I drove back to the house and made Mama a three-egg omelet with onions, fresh peppers, and cheddar cheese, just like she liked them. I brought it to her on the couch with two forks, so we could share. She said it was the best thing she'd ever tasted. Then I ruined it by bringing up her smoking. Mama put down her fork.

"Laura, you do not get to come home and start bossin' everyone around. You think you know everything now, but you don't." Her voice was calm. It would have been easier to take if she'd yelled.

"They'll kill you, Mama—" I began. I should have said I was scared. I should have told her I loved her. "Studies have shown that—"

"You're not here for Sammy," she said, interrupting. "You're here for you." She was right. It stung. And I almost slept with Josh for me, too. I left Mama with the omelet and grabbed my keys without saying good-bye. I had the whole ride back to think about Sammy and his new girl, about his mom and how I didn't even say good-bye, and about what I'd almost done to my best friend. It's easier to run away than to stay.

Rose never even knew I was in town. Neither did Sammy.

IT'S TWO MORNINGS LATER, AND Trey knocks on my bedroom window. I worked the night shift, avoiding Josh mostly, and I've only slept three hours. I slide the window open a crack and ask, "Why don't you just come in the damn house?"

Trey's in a hurry. "Can you give me a lift out to Digger's? My bike won't start, and he needs my help."

"With what?"

"Does it matter, Laura? Can you give me a ride or not?"

I'm tired. Really tired. I want to sleep. I haven't had this much drama in my life in a while. It feels like a roller coaster and I can't believe how short the line was to get a ticket for the ride. "Sure."

I drive Trey down the dirt roads to Digger's. I haven't even had coffee, and I shouldn't be behind the wheel when I can barely keep my eyes open.

We pull into Digger's driveway and everything is wrong. Five or six people are circling outside the door like ants under attack. I don't recognize any of them. The dogs are barking and frantically running the length of their fence. Then Digger busts through the front door and comes out carrying a girl in his arms. Her head swings dangerously from side to side. Adrenaline floods me. I barely put the car in park, and Trey and I help Digger. He stumbles but manages to lay her down on the porch.

"What the hell?" Trey asks, pushing Digger aside and kneeling before the girl.

I've seen ODs in the ER plenty of times. I take her pulse and assess. Sweating. High fever. Confusion. Then she starts to have a seizure. I turn her on her side with her face pointing to the ground. It only lasts a minute, then I roll her back over with her head in my lap. Everyone else just gawks, but I'm used to it.

"She's burnin' up," I say. "You've got to call an ambulance."

"Did she smoke it, or did you stick her?" Trey asks, ignoring me.

I raise my voice: "Trey, someone's got to call 911." He shakes his head.

"In the arm. She wanted it in the arm. I don't even know her name."

"What the hell did you add, Digger? Tell me! I cooked that last batch myself with none of your goddamned fillers. Asshole. You don't even know what you're doin'. You're gonna kill someone. Look at her!" I flash back to Trey's room. Sudafed packages. Bottles in Digger's front yard. Blackout windows. How the hell did I not know it was a meth house? My brother isn't just smoking pot. He's selling drugs. I grip the girl's shoulders like I'm going to shake her. I take a deep breath through my nose and focus on exactly what's in front of me.

"Trey, she's got to get to a hospital. This ain't somethin' I can fix."

"You're a nurse!"

"She needs help!" I yell.

Suddenly the girl sits up. She chokes and vomits a pile of white bubbles. "Did she eat it, too?" I ask.

"Maybe," Digger mumbles.

"Fuck. Drive," Trey barks at me, scooping up the girl. He holds her in the backseat while I spin out in Digger's gravel driveway. I push the pedal to the floor and put both hands on the wheel. I make the twenty-minute drive back to town in twelve minutes. We pull up to the doors of Hannibal Regional Hospital. The girl has recovered enough to whisper, "I'm Crystal." Then she passes out again.

I look in the rearview mirror and say what I've been rehearsing in my mind during the drive. "Trey, I can't take her in. I could lose my job. You've got to do it."

He nods. He doesn't fight me on it.

I wait in the car and breathe in the stale heat. I wait for cop cars to arrive, but they don't. I wait for Trey to come back, but he doesn't. Clouds roll in and hang lower and lower while I wait. At some point, I doze off to the sound of the rain. Like we need more rain.

Finally, Trey opens the car door and slides in beside me. He's soaked from walking through the downpour. I'm absolutely spent, but at least he's here.

"How is she?" I ask.

"I think okay. Doctors and nurses came in and out. I was in the hallway. She's asleep now." His eyes are rimmed red. I look at the breakouts and scratches on his arms and face again. It's from the chemicals. Meth makes people stupid. It could have been much worse. If this girl hadn't OD'd, if Trey's bike hadn't broken down, if he hadn't asked for a ride, I wouldn't know any of this.

"Did they ask you questions?" I say, trying to figure out how bad this could get.

"Yeah. I didn't tell 'em anything, though. Nothin' about Digger, anyway. I told 'em I just found her that way on a bench. Gave 'em a fake name. They found her driver's license, though."

"No way they believed that story."

"I know."

"This could be big."

"I know."

The police could arrest the girl. The girl could wake up and accuse Trey of anything. She might remember Digger's house and whatever the hell happened there. If the meth house is busted, Trey could go back to jail. I don't think she'll remember me, but I am sitting here in the damn parking lot. "I'm going to find out. Wait here." I pull on an extra pair of scrubs I keep in the glove compartment. The sliding glass doors open in front of me, and I walk quickly like I know exactly where I'm going. I start reading charts in the hallway. Two nurses pass me, but they just nod. I find her in the third room, hooked up to machines, and I scan the chart by her bed. Crystal Wilkens. I know the name but can't place it. Administered haloperidol. Breathing support. Activated charcoal. Patient is stable. Fluids through an IV. Vitals are normal. She'll make it. There's a cop waiting outside her door, but he doesn't ask me any questions. I slip back out the doors, and no one seems to care.

Back in the car with Trey, I'm relieved and then really pissed.

"What the hell were you thinkin'?" I yell, just like Mama. I can't look at his face. I start the car and drive out of the hospital parking lot. I think about leaving, about just driving back to Florida and starting over there. Again.

"He said he needed my help. Digger didn't say it was an OD."

"I'm not just talkin' about the OD. You can't go out there again. You got to promise me that. Say it." We're sitting at a red light. It's almost noon, and I'm starving.

"You think I wanta be messed up in that? You're crazy."

"I'm crazy?"

"She's just a kid. I hardly know Crystal. Just seen her on our street."

Then I remember. She works at Save-a-Lot. She's underage. Practically the age I was when I left.

"Jesus, Laura. I wasn't doin' meth. I was just cookin' it. Make a little side money. Half this town is doin' it."

"Half the town doin' it doesn't mean you have to, too."

"I'm just sayin' there's money to be made. I wanted that land. A trailer. What's wrong with that? I thought you'd understand."

"Wanted?" He looks away, and I know he didn't buy the property. My money funded a meth lab, not Trey's dream.

Digger could have blown up that house. Trey could have died. We all could have died.

I drive us downtown for some food.

"We're busted now," he says as I pull into a spot in the Mark Twain Dinette parking lot. I look around for the cops, but there aren't any. He nods at the car next to me. Aunt Betty leans over her passenger seat and cranks down the window. She's wearing bib overalls and a gold Harley T-shirt. I've never seen her on a Harley, but I wouldn't put anything past her. On the back of her Chevy Impala is a bumper sticker that reads: AT MY AGE, GETTING LUCKY MEANS FINDING MY CAR IN THE PARKING LOT.

"Well, look at you two. It's my lucky day. Y'all get to buy Aunt Betty lunch," she says.

We get a booth in the back and order a round of root beers and onion rings. The mugs come out frosted, and I hold mine with both hands for the cool comfort of ice. Aunt Betty and I work on one basket of onion rings, and Trey throws down the other. There are three dipping sauces, but Aunt Betty and I fight over the chili ranch. Food has never tasted so good. Trey and I don't say much, which is probably exactly how Aunt Betty knows something's wrong. To fill the space, she tells us about her garden. She's fighting bugs that keep eating her beans. She doesn't want to spray them because she doesn't want to eat all the chemicals, too.

"Trey's good with chemicals," I say. "He could probably do it for you." He stops eating and glares at me over the last ring.

"No, no. I don't wanta mess with that stuff. I just want some beans for myself, too."

"Coffee grounds and deer pee," Trey tells her, reaching over to grab our last ring. I swat at his hand, but I'm too late. I roll my eyes. He sticks out his tongue at me and then turns back to Aunt Betty. "That's what my boss puts on his garden. He says it keeps everything out. Slugs and rabbits. Bugs and squirrels."

"Well, the fence keeps the big stuff out, but I wouldn't mind less slugs."

The waitress brings our plates. Chili with crackers for Aunt Betty. A cheeseburger for me. Pork tenderloin for Trey. I kind of want to eat it all, but then I remember my diet. "That's a lot of food," Trey teases.

"Something worked up my appetite," I say, glaring at him.

Aunt Betty slams her spoon on the table. "What the hell is wrong with you two, anyway? Y'all are actin' like a bunch of brats. I thought you'd of grown up by now." She looks straight at me, like it's all my fault. "Both of you," she emphasizes so I know I can't blame this all on my brother.

Trey and I look at each other.

"Sorry, Aunt Betty," I say. "I think we both could just use some sleep. It's been a long day so far."

"Well, whatever it is, stop blamin' each other for it, got it? That ain't gonna get either of you anywhere. Ya hear me?"

Trey and I both nod in agreement. We finish our meals with our heads hanging low. I pay the check and drive us back home. Trey and I go to our separate rooms as if we just got grounded and curl up like it's nap time.

Rising Tide

Like Tom Sawyer, Samuel Clemens also fell in love at first sight. In 1867 he was traveling as a reporter on a steamboat called the *Quaker City* when he met Charles Langdon. Langdon showed Clemens a tiny picture of his sister Olivia, and Clemens immediately swore his life to her. After the trip, Clemens called on "Livy" formally. He should have visited for the respectable fifteen minutes, but he stayed for twelve hours! Eventually, Livy fell for him, too, and they wed. There is a rich history of love in their letters throughout the marriage.

Before he met Livy, when the steamboat took the young Sam far from the Missouri shores, he celebrated the change. He loved what was new and exotic, especially in the city. He was seventeen, ripe for flight, and longing for travel beyond the sleepy river town. It took a strong dose of a woman like Livy to settle Sam down.

Later, after moving to Hartford, Connecticut, with Livy, Clemens penned, among his many books, *Life on the Mississippi*, his riverboat memoir. In chapter fourteen, he professes his desire for freedom: "I loved the profession far better than any I have followed since, and I took a measureless pride in it. The reason is plain: a pilot, in those days, was the only unfettered and entirely independent human being that lived in the earth."

Little did he know that more than one hundred years later, a riverboat would troll the shores of Hannibal bearing his very name. Or maybe he did. He was always counting on his legacy as Mark Twain to live on. He had faith that whatever came around the bend, even in marriage, he could navigate the bumps and changing tides on his own.

CHAPTER ELEVEN

BOBBY ASKS ME to chaperone the upcoming Riverboat Cruise instead of his parents. All ten Tom and Becky contestants serve dinner to local business folks and community leaders who feast on roast beef, au gratin potatoes, and biscuits slathered with butter while steaming up and down the Mississippi. The kids work for tips that are donated to the program. Bobby tells me they also perform the engagement scene. He seems nervous about it, even though he's certainly been practicing enough. Rose says he stays after school every day and rehearses in a booth at McDonald's with his Becky. I tease him that there must be more to it than just the french fries, but Bobby won't give up any details.

Bobby joins the other contestants at the dock entrance; they form a welcome line straight out of one of Twain's novels: nearly barefooted Toms and Beckys tucked into bonnets. The director, Carmen, walks up and down the line adjusting ribbons, buttoning collars, and reminding them of their manners. "Y'all are

Hannibal's ambassadors! Don't forget it! Make your hometown proud to be America's Hometown! Whatever happens, remain in character. For the next two hours, you *are* Tom or Becky. Don't forget that!" Bobby's face is earnest, and he nods along as Carmen does her pre-game pep talk.

The *Mark Twain* riverboat towers behind the contestants. Steam pours out of its pretend smokestack and a red, white, and blue banner is draped along the front deck. A faux paddle wheel churns the muddy Mississippi and the captain blows the whistle for good effect. Because of the rising waters and the installed floodwalls, we can't board at the downtown Center Street Landing. A towboat was brought in last week to move the gift shop barge upstream a ways, so we drive a few more blocks to higher, dry land.

I join the other chaperones off to the side and wait for Carmen to give us our instructions. "Who's yours?" a mom in a pearl choker leans in and whispers. She's plump and pretty in a strappy summer red dress. I'm almost sure she is a Conley but there are so many of them in town. I don't want to guess and be wrong.

"Bobby. The Tom in green. I'm his aunt."

"I'm Tanya. Michelle's mom. She's in blue. Light blue. Not the navy. She wants everyone to call her Shelly but I don't know what is wrong with the name Michelle."

"Oh," I answer and try to think of something else. "She's cute. Her braids are cute."

"Well, they should be. They cost a fortune! I had 'em custom-made in St. Louis. It took me three round-trip drives just to match Michelle's color."

I nod like I know. "I can imagine." But really, I can't. I'm just glad someone is talking to me. The guests begin arriving and take their time cooing over the contestants. Shelly is actually adorable with her dimples and wispy blond bangs. She seems ready to run for mayor if this whole Becky thing doesn't work out. Bobby shakes hands with everyone who passes, and he smiles appropriately, but he mostly watches Shelly.

"Sorry I'm late!" a tall bobbed brunette says, sneaking up next to Tanya and me. Slung over her shoulder is an overstuffed bag. Her cell phone beeps constantly but she ignores it. I get the impression it doesn't stop often. "I had a showing over on the south side. A trailer on a lot. Should sell quick." She reaches out to shake my hand. "I'm Suzanne."

"Laura. I'm with Bobby." I wonder if she means the house for sale three doors down from ours. There have been a lot of different cars in the driveway lately. It's old man Willis's place. Mama says he's been waiting for a room over at Beth Haven since he can't really take care of himself anymore.

"Oh, Bobby is the sweetest, isn't he, Tanya? We're always saying how sweet Bobby is. I've given him a ride home a few times. He is just the sweetest. So, you're his...aunt?"

"I am. Sort of. He's my best friend's son. I just moved back to town. Not permanently. Just for a while," I stammer.

"What did you say your last name is?"

"I didn't. I'm Laura Brooks. But like I said, I've been gone."

"Does your mother work over at the hardware store? Our office has an account there. I go all the time."

"She does. Uh-huh. That's her."

"And what year did you graduate? I don't remember you in school."

"In '93." Tanya and Suzanne both pause while we all add up the math that would make Rose much too young to have had a baby Bobby's age.

"Bobby shared his little book with my Michelle," Tanya says. "I mean Shelly. It was the cutest thing, really." I perk up a bit at the mention of the manual, but I doubt these mothers would be impressed with my contribution to Hannibal's history. "She's been workin' with a professional tutor mostly. So much to learn to be a good Becky!" I nod stupidly. Bobby must be such an amateur to them.

"How'd the showing go?" Tanya asks Suzanne.

"Good, I think. Those south-side ones are cheaper, but every little bit adds up."

"Don't they flood, though?" I ask. "Must be harder to sell them when the water is up like now."

"Oh, don't I know it. We had to take the long way around just to get there. So inconvenient! But if I make my quota this month, Junior and I get a night at the casino down in St. Louis!"

Carmen comes over, and we quiet down. She has a teacher power, like a bossy version of Ms. B, and I want to please her immediately. "Listen up, parents. The kids need you in supportin' roles tonight. They must stay in character. If a roll slides off a tray, grab it. If a napkin slips from a lap, hand 'em a new one. Your job tonight is to anticipate the Toms' and Beckys' every need, so they can serve the diners. Got it?" We all nod in unison. I have no idea what I'm supposed to do. I'll just stick close to Tanya and Suzanne and do what they do. While I'm calculating how to blend in, Josh walks up the platform.

"Who's that?" Suzanne asks. "He's not a parent, is he?"

Tanya shakes her head no. "Never seen him before."

"I'll be right back," I say, intercepting Josh. I grab his arm and pull him back to the parking lot. "I've got this, Josh. Bobby said they only needed a few parents to chaperone."

"Yeah, but you aren't a parent, Laura." He reeks of beer and cigarettes, and his plaid shirttails are untucked from his jeans. Something that looks like barbecue sauce is smeared above his knee. "No matter how high you think your horse is."

"You're drunk, Josh. Go home before you embarrass Bobby."

"I'm not drunk. Had a few beers after my shift is all. Why would I embarrass Bobby?" he says, much too loud. "Why would I do that? I'm here to help. My son said they needed chaperones. Here I am." Carmen joins us with her clipboard and Josh stands up straight. "Evenin,' ma'am. I'm Josh Haymaker. Bobby's dad."

"Thank you for coming, Mr. Haymaker. It appears we have all the chaperone spots filled. I'm so sorry you had to come down, but we won't need you after all. Pickup is back here at eight. Sharp."

"But I'm Bobby's dad. If anyone is leavin', it's her." Josh pokes his finger into my shoulder.

"No. No. Laura here has already signed in and been given instructions. We only have comp tickets for three extra parents."

"Well, then. I'll just go buy my own damn ticket." Josh pats his pocket for his wallet and stomps up the plank before disappearing onto the boat. It's a $25 ticket, and I wonder if he even has it. A few of the Toms and Beckys giggle as Josh storms past, but Bobby leans over to restring the line on his fishing pole like he doesn't know him at all.

For the first hour of the cruise, Josh sits at the small side bar off the dining room. He sips a watery drink and glares at me. The boat hums beneath my feet from the engines. Captain Fisher shares Mississippi River trivia over the intercom. "Folks, the mighty Mississippi ranks as the fourth-longest and tenth-largest river in the world. Her watershed encompasses thirty-one states and two Canadian provinces. But sometimes, like in the Great Flood of '93, that's just not enough space for a growing girl like her. The land to both your right and left was completely submerged then. As of this morning, our water was eighteen feet, and our fingers are crossed it won't go higher. All that river has to go somewhere!"

I duck down the narrow hall to the dining room where the ceilings are low and fans move the stifling air around. Burgundy velvet drapes frame the view of the river and its banks. The water is so high most of the shoreline is gone. In the dining room, the chairs are made of the same velvety material but their color has faded to a dull pink, and the stuffing has popped on a few. Suzanne, Tanya, and I fill iced-tea pitchers for the contestants to pour. We push the carts loaded with desserts and trays for serving along the creaky floors from the kitchen.

Outside the dining room, the weather is cloudy but dry so the guests stroll the balconies after dinner. There's a fifteen-minute break until the performance. I excuse myself, and I'm sitting in a bathroom stall when Suzanne and Tanya come in to freshen their makeup.

"Poor child doesn't have a chance," one of them says.

From the slit in the door, I watch Tanya put on another layer of lipstick. They better not be talking about Bobby.

"They shouldn't even have let her in if you ask me. You just know folks would throw a fit. A black Becky. *Please.* She doesn't even have proper braids. Why set her up for that?"

Suzanne adds mascara and fluffs her hair. "I know. I do. But times are changin'. Hannibal had better get ready for it. Her parents are big shots at the hospital."

"They ain't changin' fast enough for that." Tanya reaches into the stall for toilet paper to blot her lips.

I pull up my legs so they can't see me if they peek under the other stall door, but a part of me wants to slam open the door and tell these snobs what I really think. Another part of me knows the cost of doing so would be too high for Bobby's sake and wouldn't change their racism. Aunt Betty once told me that when she was growing up, Hannibal didn't have Jim Crow laws. She said we achieved plenty of prejudice without them.

"What are you gonna do about this Bobby-and-Shelly thing?" Suzanne asks.

"Well, what can I do? Nothing right now. They're just rehearsin'. It's kid's stuff."

"But she's tellin' everyone Bobby is her boyfriend. Nate told me Bobby tried to kiss her."

"I doubt that. Michelle wouldn't. She knows better. Did you see where he lives, for goodness' sake? The house looked like it was fallin' down around 'em. He may be her best shot to win, though. I ain't sayin' nothin' until all this is over."

"And then?"

"Michelle—I mean Shelly—will just be real busy with her

new Becky commitments and won't have time for the likes of him."

"And if she wins with my Nate, won't they be cute?"

They squeal together and grasp hands like Miss America contestants. "They'll be a true Tom and Becky!" Suzanne tells her and holds the door open for their exit.

I sit in the stall a moment longer, fuming. When I come out of the bathroom, Bobby and Shelly are beginning their engagement scene in the far corner of the dining room. There isn't really a stage because space is so tight on the boat; they're mostly filling up part of an aisle.

"Say, Becky, was you ever engaged?" Bobby-as-Tom asks Shelly-as-Becky.

She holds out both her palms in an exaggerated question. "What's that?"

"Why, engaged to be married." Bobby takes a step closer. He's a natural.

"No." Shelly leans away, awkwardly overacting.

"Would you like to?" He raises his eyebrows. His freckled cheeks are all Tom.

She cocks her head sideways and pretends to consider it. "I reckon so. I don't know. What is it like?"

Bobby puts his arm on the back of her shoulder, almost touching one of her long braids. "Like? Why it ain't like any-thing. You only just tell a boy you won't ever have anybody but him, ever ever *ever*, and then you kiss and that's all. Anybody can do it."

Shelly leans in. "Kiss? What do you kiss for?"

Bobby clears his throat. "Why, that, you know, is to—well, they always do that."

"Everybody?"

"Why yes, everybody that's in love with each other. Do you remember what I wrote on the slate?"

"Ye-Ye-Ye-Yes." Becky is supposed to be stuttering, but Shelly's sounds are more like a yodel than a stutter.

"What was it?"

"I shan't tell you."

"Shall I tell *you*?" Bobby is stealing this show. Tanya stands nearby mouthing the words as her daughter tries to act.

"Ye-Ye-Ye-Yes, but some other time."

"No, now."

"No, not now—tomorrow," Shelly whispers.

"Oh, no, *now*. Please, Becky—I'll whisper it, I'll whisper it ever so easy." Then he leans in to her neck. After a few seconds, he adds, "Now you whisper it to me—just the same."

Shelly crosses her arms over her chest and sticks out her bottom lip in a pout. "You turn your face away so you can't see, and then I will. But you musn't ever tell anybody—*will* you, Tom? Now you won't, *will* you?"

Bobby shakes his head slowly. "No, indeed, indeed I won't. Now, Becky." Then he closes his eyes.

She cups her hand over his ear and stage-whispers, "I—love—you!"

From the bar, Josh claps too loud and puts his fingers in his mouth to whistle. The dinner guests stare in the direction of the noise he's making. Josh clearly thinks the scene is done.

He doesn't know about the most important part: the kiss. He just waves back at the crowd and Carmen rushes across the room with her clipboard. She makes a cutting sign across her throat. Bobby grabs Shelly's hand and strolls off just like Tom would rescue Becky. The crowd claps at their backs because they don't even know what they missed either.

When the riverboat pulls back into the dock, Bobby and I walk down the landing together. I tell him how proud I am and how good he was as Tom with Shelly.

"We didn't get to the kiss," he says.

"I know, but you were so good, no one noticed. Really, Bobby." Someone slaps my ass from behind and I turn around with my knee raised knowing it will be Josh. I'd like to hit him in the nuts really hard but Bobby is watching. "Need some help standing up?" I whisper, returning Josh's glare.

"You don't look so good, Dad." Bobby slows at my side and reaches out for Josh's arm.

"Well, looky there. It's your mama, Bobby. I told her she didn't have to come all the way down here. Guess she don't listen too good, huh?"

Rose is by my car, pacing with her arms crossed.

"Mom," Bobby calls, "I told you Aunt Laura would give me a ride. What's up?" He's straining to be casual, maybe to buy time and let the parking lot clear.

"Can't a mom come see her son?" Rose asks.

"A good mom could, but you ain't a good mama." Josh stumbles, then laughs at himself. He hiccups loudly.

I shake my head at Rose to say he ain't worth it. "Shut up, Josh. Don't you think you've done plenty?"

"Not yet. Not until Bobby and me are livin' together, ain't that right, son?" Bobby looks between them. He's crying freely, but neither of his parents even notice.

"You're such a liar," Rose says. "You said you didn't even want him. And you sure as hell don't care what this whole Tom thing is costing me!"

"You're the liar! Why don't we just ask Bobby who he wants to live with? Let's settle this right here and now." Rose pulls her hand back like she's going to smack Josh. I reach out to grab her and miss. Then she's pulling Josh's hair. He holds up his arms to protect himself and pushes her hard to the ground. Bobby grabs at Josh's back to hold him and someone yells, "This is not appropriate! Y'all should know better!" It's Carmen, flailing her arms like she's herding ducks. I help Rose to her feet and hand Bobby my car keys. He ducks off before Carmen notices him, and she screams, "Stop making a scene, or I'm calling the police!"

"Go ahead and call 'em! Call 'em on that Bastard that just hit me!" Rose screams back.

I step between Rose and Carmen. "Ma'am, this is all just a misunderstanding. Please." Josh sways to my right. Then he's doubled over puking. A chunk of what looks like brown oatmeal lands on Carmen's red peep-toe espadrille and she jumps back. "I've got this," I say, as if I can do anything to stop this train wreck. "I'll make sure everyone goes on home. Promise."

"Well, if you say so," she answers, glancing back over her clipboard, grateful. "But I want y'all to know that if something like this happens again, Bobby will be asked to withdraw his

Tom candidacy immediately. We can't have domestic disturbances like this tainting the program's image."

Rose nods. Josh heaves again. Carmen hurries away.

Bobby is curled up on the backseat of my car like a little boy. I lean over the seat and push back his hair from his face.

"This is all bullshit," he says.

I don't correct him. He's right. I know what it's like to have parents let you down, parents who can never give you what you need. "I'm gonna quit the contest."

"Nah, Bobby. That wouldn't be right. You've worked so hard. I thought you really wanted this."

"I do. But not with them. Not if they're just gonna show up and fight at all my events. God, Shelly could of seen them. They don't even care how it looks. I can see why you left."

"Believe it or not, I can see why folks stay," I answer. "Or at least I'm beginning to. It's complicated. Family is never easy. But even when you leave, you're still you."

"But I like me," he whispers, and he sounds exactly like his toddler self.

"Me, too, Bobby." Maybe he could live with me for a while. I certainly couldn't do any worse than his parents. But Josh wouldn't let me, I'm sure. He's only one breath away from spilling everything anyway. "You were amazing tonight as Tom, kiddo. I wouldn't let them take that away from you."

He sits up in the backseat and peeks out the windows at the empty parking lot. "Really? You think I can win?"

"I know you can. And I think a lot of other good will come your way because of this."

"Think Shelly will, too?"

"Maybe. You make her look pretty good."

ROSE CALLS ME THREE TIMES the afternoon of the trial and I don't pick up. I'm sitting at the breakfast table with Mama when Rose skids into the driveway, throwing up rocks. She must have borrowed Daisy's car. It's too late to hide. Mama laughs at me and says she's going to shower. Rose doesn't knock.

"You're not doin' this to me!" she yells, crossing the living room and yanking me out of my seat. "You know what the Bastard did and you're helpin' me. Today."

"Rose, calm down," I say. "I'm comin'." She stands back on her heels with her hands on her hips. Her hair is freshly curled and she's wearing a pink button-down blouse with a long black skirt. "Didn't know you owned anything below the knee."

"Shut up and get ready," Rose says. "Bobby's in the car waitin'. We gotta drop him off at Daisy's before the trial. He don't need to watch this shit storm."

"Too late," I mumble, pulling on a blazer over my sundress.

There are two Marion County Courthouses, one in Palmyra and one in Hannibal. Josh had his lawyer request the Palmyra venue, twelve miles away, and Rose says it's just to piss her off. "Waste more gas money and have to ask for more time off of work," she says, accusing Josh of yet another plan to screw her. The courthouse is a six-story redbrick building more than a hundred years old, and it stretches over several downtown blocks. An American flag waves beside the Missouri flag. Almost nine years ago Josh and Rose were married in the same building. I was their only witness and stood beside them holding Bobby on my hip. The clerk who married them handed Rose a plastic bag of samples with the paperwork. Inside was a miniature box of Tide and a tiny bottle of Dawn dish soap. "That ain't my job," Rose said, tossing the samples in the backseat of the car as we drove away. They both probably should have known then how this would end. Who was going to do the laundry was the least of their worries.

Rose reaches for my hand as we climb together up the same stone steps. We're kids again sitting on the Ferris wheel holding on to each other so we can survive the ride.

Josh shows up late. He says Bobby got sick, and he went to check on him.

Rose yells, "Objection! I just saw him, and he was fine!"

Judge Mahan is annoyed before the trial even begins. "It's kind of you to join us, Mr. Haymaker. Please take your seat."

Mama told me Judge Mahan is a ballbuster. She said she sent Daddy up the river twice when they were first married. Both times for getting drunk in a bar and hitting somebody who was probably his best friend by morning. I'm hoping she doesn't recognize my last name or me. I'm hoping she never even hears it, but if I know Rose, I'll star in this drama.

The courtroom is boiling. A dozen metal fans are drilled to the wall, but they only circulate the humid air. There are two tables in the front that face Judge Mahan, who sits in a wooden box that's raised a few feet. She has a thick braid of black-and-gray hair and wire-rimmed glasses. Judge Mahan looks like a hippie who just climbed off a Harley in the parking lot. Her robe isn't even zipped up, and she's wearing stone-washed blue jeans. A bailiff in a green uniform rests his tattooed arms on top of his beer gut. His gun belt is unsnapped like he either just forgot to snap it this morning or is ready for some action. There are metal folding chairs on one side for the jury, but the seats are empty. We don't need a jury for this. About a dozen other folks are waiting their turn with the judge. I sit down on one of the benches in the back, as far from Rose as possible.

Because it's a divorce settlement and custody battle rolled into one, both Josh and Rose have to take the stand and see who can say worse things about the other. Rose goes first. She tells the judge that Josh is a physical threat. She has pictures of the times he's slapped her. She adds a layer of gory details about the Riverboat Cruise parking lot scene that didn't happen. Her lawyer also shows pay stubs where they've had to garnish Josh's wages for temporary child support to help with Bobby. "He quit work just so he doesn't have to pay!" Rose shouts, interrupting her lawyer.

"She's in my house, Judge. Isn't that payment?" Josh yells back. "I'll pay Bobby's bills when Bobby lives with me. I got a new job now over at the hospital and a new lease on a trailer, but I ain't payin' Rose's bar tab." The other people in the court waiting for their trials snicker.

"You'll both keep your mouths shut in my courtroom unless I ask you to speak, you hear? We'll take a fifteen-minute recess while I chat with the custody evaluator."

While everyone else leaves for the hallway, I join Rose on the bench. "The what?" she asks her lawyer.

"Apparently, the court ordered an evaluator last week to talk to Bobby, to get his preferences."

"I know his preferences. He wants to live with me."

"Now, I know, Rose, but because of the ongoing disputes between you and Josh, an outside evaluator was called in."

"And what did this outside evaluator say?"

"It's sealed. I haven't read it."

A few minutes later, the court reassembles. Judge Mahan glares over her glasses. "Are there any witnesses?"

"We'd like to call Laura Brooks to the stand, Your Honor." Rose's lawyer nods to me.

My stomach churns as I walk the aisle between Josh and Rose. I sit in the wooden chair next to the judge and the bailiff swears me in. My palms are sweating even after I wipe them on my dress. Josh smirks and blows me a kiss. Rose looks like she just won some prize, and I haven't even opened my mouth.

"Will you state the nature of your relationship to both parties, please?" Judge Mahan asks. Her pen is scribbling notes. She doesn't look up.

"Rose has been my best friend since kindergarten. I've known Josh since high school. And I'm Bobby's godmother. I'm here for him." It sounds flat when I say it, but it's probably the most honest thing I'll say all day.

The questions turn to the nature of the fights between Rose and Josh. Rose's lawyer asks how many times I saw Josh hit Rose. "I don't really know," I answer. "But I've seen the bruises." I keep my responses short. Rose is tapping her fingers on the table like she's already mad at me. Then Josh's lawyer asks if I think Josh is a threat to Bobby. "I believe it's in Bobby's best interest to be with his mom," I say. I don't think I'm helping or hurting Rose's case, and I just want to leave the stand.

"And do you know Josh Haymaker in any *other* capacity?" The question surprises Rose. She looks up to meet my eyes and I look away.

"I don't," I say, staring at Josh.

He wiggles his eyebrows like a dirty old man. "Sure you do."

Rose scrunches up her face like she's confused. Then she gets it. And, for once, she doesn't say a word.

The judge rolls her eyes and says I can take my seat. I walk back down the aisle and both Josh and Rose turn away from me.

We all watch the bench and wait. First, the judge dissolves the marriage. Then she rules in Rose's favor that the house is marital property since Josh claimed he added her to the deed years ago. She chastises Josh for falsifying paperwork but says he has to stand by it now. As a marital asset, Rose will have to pay him half of the fair-market value minus the debt he's accumulated by not covering half the mortgage since he moved out. Rose high-fives her lawyer and squeals, but the judge tells her to be quiet. "Your ex-husband will be allowed into the house for one hour to remove any premarital assets, you hear me? Namely one listed grandfather clock. Mr. Haymaker, you'll need to compile a list for the sheriff, who will supervise the removal."

"That's all I want, Your Honor," Josh says.

"Well, good. You'll only need five minutes, which should cut down significantly on the antics."

Then the judge says she's not convinced that living with either Josh or Rose is in Bobby's best interest. "So, I'm going to do something a little different here to give you both better shots at cleaning up your acts. For the next ninety days, Bobby will reside with Mr. Haymaker, and Ms. Haymaker will have weekly visitation rights. I'll leave your lawyers to work out the schedule, but it should accommodate both of your work schedules first and foremost. If I hear that either of you makes trouble during this ninety-day period, it will weigh heavily on my future custody decision. If you two want to make each other miserable, that's one thing, but your kid shouldn't have to pay for that."

Rose puts her hand over her mouth to hide her sobs. Her lawyer leans in to comfort her, but she storms down the aisle.

I follow her into the parking lot, and we circle each other. I climb in beside her in the car, and Rose still won't look at me. "I'm sorry," I say. "I wanted to help but I couldn't."

Rose doesn't answer. She just wipes her face again and again with the back of her hand. Black mascara covers her cheeks.

"Bobby didn't wanta live with me, did he?"

"I don't know. Last time we talked, he was pretty confused. That little scene in the parking lot at the riverboat didn't help."

"'Least I get the house for him. For when he's there, anyway. Don't know how I'm gonna pay the bills on it, though."

I try to tell her the rest. I try to tell her about what I almost did with Josh. "I should of told you sooner. I was ashamed," I begin, but Rose isn't listening. She's busy blaming Bobby for betraying her, too. I tell her I'm sorry. Again and again. I wouldn't want me as a friend, either. I wait for Rose to scream at me but she doesn't. Her calm defeat is worse.

"I see the way it is," she finally says. "You didn't come back to help. You just didn't know where else to go. That's all we are to you. What good are you? I wish you hadn't come at all."

I don't know if she means home or to the trial. Probably both.

AFTER ROSE DROPS ME OFF at home, I drive up to Lover's Leap. I need air, sunshine, and space. From Route 79 I take the steep grade too quickly and hit my brakes just shy of the steel guardrails. My windows are rolled all the way down. Birds are chirping as I wind my way up the bluff. I park in the gravel lot next to cars of tourists and walk to the chain-link fence that snakes the overlook. An American flag waves out over the ledge. Houses dot the opposite bluff, sneaking out behind trees. They look like they might fall and tumble down the hill at the slightest stress. There is a steamy haze covering the river; it makes Hannibal look like a mirage. Semitrucks, loaded heavy with cargo, cross the bridge below, but their sound is muted by the distance. Smokestacks on the Illinois side spew gray-brown clouds into the blue sky. The water is high on both sides, and it just keeps rising.

I sit on one of the metal benches bolted to the cement and the heat burns the back of my legs through my cotton dress. A little girl in pigtails with a crisscross suntan mark on her back picks flowers and runs to her car to present them to an old woman behind the wheel. "Here, Grandma. These are for you," she says. Her grandma smiles and I think about calling Aunt Betty. She might know what to say. I could use one of her thought grenades right about now. How do I make it up to Rose? Will she ever trust me again? Maybe I should just keep driving. Run away like always. Figure it out along the way. On my own. Then I remember I have a shift at six. At least I have that.

The Mississippi is merciless. It gives no breeze, unlike the ocean. It's stuck between its own banks. When it swells, it hurts anything in its path in order to survive.

I climb back in my car and drive to Aunt Betty's house.

"I knew it was you," she says, opening the screen door. "Always drivin' like a bat outta hell. When you goin' to slow down, Laura?"

"Don't want no one to catch me," I answer, leaning down to hug her soft layers. Her hair is still in rollers and she's wearing a pink floral housecoat. There are three white whiskers shooting out of her chin. Aunt Betty's feet are bare and her toes are painted Hooker Red. She smells like pickling juice and I squeeze a little harder.

"Uh-oh. Somethin's wrong. Aunty Betty can tell. You're goin' squeeze the life outta me, child." She pats my arm with her bony fingers. "I was makin' a salad. You want lunch? I'll make it nice."

We walk out to the garden for greens. Most of her backyard is garden and rosebushes. She tends both like spoiled children, crooning to them as she coddles and prunes. The rows are lush with tomatoes and cucumbers. There isn't a weed in sight. Three rows of corn tower over the rest. "Gotta plant enough for the deer," she says, pointing to the half-eaten cobs. "I came out and covered the tomatoes last night. Raccoons love a midnight snack. Your brother was out and sprinkled coffee grounds everywhere. Said they were yours. The fancy kind. Bugs hate 'em."

"That was good of Trey," I say. "I'm glad he stopped by."

"He's takin' me fishin' tomorrow. He borrowed some guy's boat and we're going out to Mark Twain Lake. You want to come? It'll be just like old times."

"I have to work tonight. What time you leavin' in the mornin'?"

"If I know Trey, won't be too early. We can wait for you. Want a pepper, too? Red ones are sure sweet this year. It's all the rain we've been gettin'. Grab some for your mama, too. She don't like the green ones, as I recall." I fill a plastic sack with cucumbers and peppers and a basket of greens and carrots for our lunch.

"What are you workin' on?" I ask, peeling a carrot into the big green bowl Aunt Betty uses for compost. When I was little, she'd make me take it to the pile myself. I'd dump the bowl as close to the edge as I could and race back to the house. The rotting mound stank like soured milk every time she stirred it up. "Makes the garden grow," she'd say, ignoring my pinched nose.

"Sewin'. I got a job puttin' patches on uniforms for Reliable, that pest-control place. They're good folks. Family business. Been in Hannibal for years. Didn't you go to school with one of the brothers or somethin'?"

"I think so. Gene or Mike?"

"Both. They stay, don't they?" She means that they don't leave town, like me.

"Probably," I say. "They must have to have so many kids here."

"I wish I'd had a gaggle of kids," Aunt Betty says.

I turn from the counter to watch her sew. She's suddenly hunched over more, squinting harder at the thread. Aunt Betty's always preached the idea of staying home, but maybe staying is just a fear of open spaces, of not knowing what you don't know and being too scared to find out. "Some people's fears grow like disease," she always said.

The hummingbirds chatter on the feeder outside the window above her head. They dive and dart for territory. They spend as much time making sure others don't get fed as they do feeding themselves. Seems like a waste to me.

"You? Thought you never wanted kids." I wash the salad greens and watch the dirt circle the drain. Then I pat them dry with one of Aunt Betty's faded plaid dish towels.

"'Course I wanted kids. Your mama ain't perfect, but she got you and Trey. That would be enough for me. She loved a man she couldn't hold. But you were part of the deal so it couldn't of been that bad of a deal."

Over lunch I tell her about Rose and the trial, about how I tried to stay out of it but ended up getting in so deep.

"So," Aunt Betty asks, "what are you hidin'?"

I don't answer.

"Best to stay outta other people's business."

We rock our chairs in silence a few minutes.

"I always wanted to be you when I grew up," I say, picking up our dishes and carrying them to the sink. "On my own. Don't need nobody." Aunt Betty clucks her tongue at my back.

I turn around and her face is blotchy. She wipes her mouth with her hand like she just spit.

"Don't be stupid, Laura. God gave you more brains than that. You lose your head when you're all alone."

WHILE AUNT BETTY DOES THE dishes, I call Rose. She lets it ring seven times before she answers. "I just wanta know if you did it or not? That's all," she says.

"Rose—"

"No. I just wanta know if you did it or not. You don't get to talk."

"I didn't sleep with Josh."

"Okay."

"But I almost did."

"So what? Half the town almost did. I just need to know you didn't."

"I didn't. I should have told you sooner. I thought you'd hate me."

"I don't hate you. You've stood by me more than Josh. I'm still pissed off at you, though."

"I don't blame you."

"You're supposed to be my best friend."

"I am your best friend."

"Like hell."

"I am, Rose. I shouldn't have lied. I'm not a liar."

"I know. I know you, Laura." And she does, maybe sometimes better than I know myself. I should have had more faith in her.

"Have you talked to Bobby?" I ask.

"Can't. He's at the Bastard's—I mean Josh's house. He said his stomach hurt and he didn't wanta talk. Not to me anyway."

"I'm sorry, Rose. I really am."

"I prayed hard. I spent hours with that preacher on my knees begging Jesus. And it didn't work."

"Maybe you prayed for the wrong thing."

"Yeah," she says, "maybe. Maybe it takes more than faith."

Reformation

Mostly, Huck's pap spends his time in jail and mostly, it's for drunkenness. He makes a fool of himself in town every time he gets liquor. When he's not intoxicated, Pap stalks Widow Douglas's house so he can harass Huck. He demands money and threatens the worst. He mocks Huck for learning to read and puts him down for acting civilized. A new judge in town doesn't know about Pap's ways and decides he can be saved after all. The judge takes Pap home with him, dresses him in proper gentleman's clothes, and lectures him on temperance. The men weep together at the glory of his rebirth from scoundrel to citizen. Pap is a reformed man until midnight when he gets a little thirsty and trades his new clothes for whiskey.

But it's money Pap really wants; his drink isn't cheap, and he's not much of a working man, so he sues Judge Thatcher for Huck's side of the fortune he and Tom discovered in the caves. Justice isn't swift to Pap's cause, though, so he kidnaps Huck and locks him in a cabin in the woods. But neither Nature nor man can hold a boy like Huck.

Widow Douglas also tries her hand at reformation. She grooms Huck and sends him to school. She lectures him and locks him up. At first, Huck hates the restrictions of the desk, the bells, and the books, but then he gets used to it. And when he gets ornery and full of the devil again, he has his own plans for salvation. "Whenever I got uncommon tired I played hookey, and the hiding I got next day done me good and cheered me up," he says.

CHAPTER TWELVE

BOTH JOSH AND ROSE are working, so Bobby and I drive out to meet Trey and Aunt Betty at the marina dock on Mark Twain Lake. Trey waves from the water and pulls the boat up beside us. "Did ya bring minnows?" he asks. I swing the Styrofoam bucket toward him, and the water overflows and splashes his feet. "Easy, Laura. Let's feed the minnows to the fish, not my feet." He reaches out his hand to help me into the boat. Bobby jumps in and rocks the boat from side to side before he sprawls out on the front seat with one hand over the side in the water. I settle down in the seat next to Aunt Betty, who is wearing a floral headscarf to keep her hair in place from the breeze. I turn my face toward the sun and soak it up. Coconut sunscreen and a waft of fried fish drift from the dock bar. The lake is so lush in the middle of summer that the trees reach out into the water and provide welcome shade. The rains are flooding the river but the lake loves it. I get sleepy from the sound of water lapping at the side of the boat. Trey snakes the boat down a narrow finger of the lake by trolling motor. Aunt Betty pats my knee and says, "Your mama would of liked this." I nod in agreement. She would have, it's true, but she's hosting a training program today for new Jalaxy! ambassadors. She now has seven folks selling for her and almost thirty of her own clients. It may be a scheme, but she's scaling the side of the pyramid fast. I've never seen her so happy, and the pounds just keep falling off of me.

We spend a few hours fishing the banks without much luck. On minnows, Trey pulls in one bass and a few crappies, but they're too small to keep. Bobby fishes with worms and catches three catfish. He puts them in the live well and checks on them every minute or two. Trey warns him not to stare the fish to death. Aunt Betty and I haven't had a single bite, but we're pretty content nonetheless, sitting on the back of the boat while Trey schools Bobby on girls.

Or at least I am until I check my phone. I turned my ringer off for the day, but Rose has left six messages. She sounds desperate, and I don't recognize the number she's calling from. I dial the number back.

"Hannibal Police Department, how can I help you?" Rose is at work. Why would she be calling from the police station?

"I'm lookin' for Rose Haymaker," I say. The officer puts me on hold while she looks up her records. Then she says she'll transfer me, and I wait. The line clicks several times and then it's Rose.

"Jesus, Laura. I was just about to have to call the Bastard—Josh. Why haven't you been answerin'?"

"I'm out on Mark Twain Lake in the middle of nowhere. What the hell is going on?"

"I need you to come pick me up. It's a mistake. A misunderstandin' with my boss. Just come get me. And don't bring Bobby."

"What happened?" I crank in my line and hand my pole to Trey, mouthing *Rose*. He shrugs at another developing Rose drama. As if he should talk.

"Nothin'. My boss is just being a jerk, that's all. He can't figure out how to do his goddamned books and is blamin' it on me. Just because money is missin' I must have stolen it."

I know better than to ask Rose if she did it. I have to help her either way.

"It's going to take me at least thirty minutes to get there." Trey tells Aunt Betty and Bobby to pull in their lines. He says we're going back to the dock for more bait and a bathroom break. He's reading my signals, and I'm grateful.

"I'll wait. I ain't goin' nowhere."

I cup my hand over the speaker, so I can talk without Bobby hearing. "Rose, did they actually arrest you?"

"Not yet. He's waitin' to press charges. I'm here on questionin'. Got me a fancy ride in a police car. Guess he thought that might scare me."

"What does he want?"

"He wants his money back. That's it. He'll let me go if I pay him. But I didn't take his damn money, Laura." She delivers this last line clearly for her audience at the jail and not just for me.

"How much?"

"Why does that matter?"

"Damn it, Rose. Just tell me, how much?"

"Eight hundred dollars. A little less."

"Sit tight. I'll be right there."

I ask Aunt Betty if she can take Bobby home with her. He seems perfectly happy to keep fishing and finish all the homemade Rice Krispies treats. Trey drives me back to the dock where my car is parked. He gives me a salute as I climb out of the boat. I tell him to behave himself. I don't need another thing to worry about today.

On my drive back to town, I call Sammy and ask him to go down to the station and wait with Rose. He doesn't even question it. He's only a few blocks away and happy to help. And if I know Sammy, he probably knows all the cops in the department, and they all adore him. Most of them probably even owe him a favor or two. For once I'm grateful that everyone knows everybody.

Rose is on a bench in the front room when I arrive. Sammy is beside her telling a story to the whole waiting room. He gets to the punch line just as I walk through the door and everyone cracks up. Two cops walk past and slap Sammy on the back. "Ah, that was a good one!" one of them says. "Wait until the wife hears it!" Rose sees me and sits up straight in her chair.

"Excuse me, ladies. I'm gonna go find the little boys' room." Sammy ducks out and leaves us alone.

Rose grabs my hand and pulls me down to the bench with her. "Sammy talked 'em into lettin' me go tonight. There's no charges if I pay the money back."

"Good to have friends in the right places."

"In this town? It means everything. No one would of given *me* a break, that's for sure."

"Did you take the money, Rose?"

"Josh is probably the one who made up this whole story. The Bastard. He and my boss are drinkin' buddies down at Scoville's. They're both complete assholes."

"You didn't answer my question," I say.

"The thing is, it doesn't really matter."

"Of course it matters."

"The only thing that matters is him gettin' his money back and leavin' me alone."

"Then that's what we'll do, Rose. We'll pay him back."

"We?" Rose shakes her head and washes her tired face with her hands.

Sammy comes back into the waiting room, which saves Rose from a real answer. I thank him for his help. He says it's nothing, like going to the police station is akin to picking up milk on your drive home, and pulls me into a hug. "I'm grateful, Sammy. I really am," I say into his neck.

"Happy to help," he says. "I really am."

"You need anything?" His divorce must be finalized by now. It's a tough time for him, and here he is helping me out.

Sammy gives me a sideways grin and plays with the bill of his hat. "Maybe," he says. "Lance's wedding is Friday night. Don't suppose you're free, are ya?"

I actually am. It's my night off and I was planning on spending it with Bobby and Rose. "Are you asking me to be your date?"

"I think so."

Rose pokes me in the pit. "Would you just say yes so we can the hell get out of here already?"

"Yes."

Sammy's face is beaming like he just won the Powerball. I must be blushing from head to toe to be his prize. He tips his hat and thanks all the officers at the front desk like the local celebrity he is.

Rose and I leave the station and drive through the ATM. She doesn't say anything when I make the withdrawal. The account is near zero. I've been mostly living off my savings and the hospital doesn't pay much. We pull up at Deter's, and I tell her she should stay in the car. "Let me do this, okay?"

Her face is furrowed, years past her age. I've seen her defeated over the years, but she usually puts up a fight. "I did it for Bobby," she says, looking out my window. "For his Tom stuff." The tears come and her pretty face is grim. Rose not behaving isn't a surprise, but Rose being a criminal is. The whole town will know about this. She probably just blew any chance Bobby had to be Tom, too.

"I know, Rose." And I do. I get what it feels like to lose your way and to make mistakes you don't know how to fix. Rose was just trying to get Bobby to the other side; life looks easier there.

"I've made such a mess," she whispers. "The judge can't know about this."

"She won't. There wasn't an arrest. We can thank Sammy for that."

"You're wrong about him. You always have been."

"Let's stick to your problems, Rose."

She nods. "You know Lance is marrying a girl from St. Louis, right?"

"Yeah. So?"

"You know it's an out-of-town wedding, right? Fancy one, I heard."

"I think I can manage myself, Rose."

"At a hotel. Overnight. You knew that, right?"

"Of course I know. It's no big deal." But I didn't know and it is a big deal. I leave Rose in the car and go inside to pay her bill with the very last of my safety net.

BOBBY IS IN THE FRONT yard playing with Lulubelle when we pull up to Aunt Betty's house. He throws a stick and Lulubelle retrieves it. Then she darts to the backyard, looking over her shoulder to make sure Bobby is chasing her. Inside, the dirty dishes are still on the table from a supper of corn on the cob and turkey sandwiches. Rose and I make plates and finish off the leftovers. We don't tell Aunt Betty about the police department and she doesn't ask. She gives plenty of straight talk but she doesn't pry.

"Is Trey around?" I ask, drawing a sink of soapy water. Aunt Betty watches me and picks at her cuticles.

"Your brother finished all those beers. Passed out in the backseat, and I had to drive us home. He's in the back room sleepin' it off." I scrub the plates too hard and fish around in the water for the forks.

"He had a little run-in that should of scared him straight," I tell her. "He promised he wouldn't get messed up again."

"Looks like he didn't keep that promise," Aunt Betty says, reaching for a towel to dry. "He's actin' just like your daddy."

I don't want to hear any of this, even if it's true.

Aunt Betty squints her eyes like she's reading me for signs. "You seem awful cheerful all of a sudden. What's up?"

"Nothing, really. We ran into Sammy. He asked me to his brother's wedding."

"Is that so?"

"Yep. And I said yes."

"Huh."

"We're just friends, Aunt Betty. Don't look at me like that."

"Like what? I'm just dryin' dishes."

Out the kitchen window, I watch Bobby wrestling with Lulubelle over the stick. "Thanks for takin' care of him."

"He's a good kid, that one. Don't know how with all the bad stuff swirlin' around him, though." She stacks the dishes back in the cabinet and hangs up the towel to dry.

"Well, I always had you in my corner."

"You give me more credit than I deserve. You're tough and smart. That's it."

"Thanks for gettin' him supper. Rose is grateful, too." We both turn and watch Rose join Bobby in the garden. Aunt Betty sent her out with plastic bags and told her to take some of the tomatoes off her hands. Soon we can just see their heads as they weave in and out of the corn rows.

"She okay?" she asks, nodding toward Rose.

I watch Rose pretend to steal Bobby's basket. They're fighting over a huge pepper. "She will be."

"There's been a lot of drama since you hit town, kiddo." Just as she says it, Mama drives up. The shit is going to hit the fan if she finds Trey in his condition. Maybe I'll say he's just napping.

"Think it's me?" I ask. Aunt Betty turns on the oven and

pulls out the ingredients for corn bread even though we just cleaned up the kitchen. When in doubt, she feeds people.

"Nah. I think you're a good friend. You wanta help people," she says, cracking three eggs and beating them up. "Can't save everybody, though, Laura. Sometimes you gotta just save yourself."

I BEG MAMA TO GO shopping with me for a dress to wear to Lance's wedding. We drive over to the dress shop on Fifth Avenue in Quincy. It's a boutique in the downtown that specializes in formal and semiformal wear. Rose and I came here once for prom dresses our junior year. The store kept track of who bought what dress in which color so that no two girls would show up at prom in the same dress. We wanted to be like the other girls. One look at the prices let us know we weren't.

I'm down fifteen pounds, too, and a whole dress size. My body is starting to feel like me again. Jalaxy! I have more energy. I got a small raise at the hospital, and they've offered me a one-year contract. I haven't told anyone yet. One step at a time. It's almost Fourth of July, my deadline, and I've had to refine my to-do list:

- ✓ Wedding (look amazing)
- ✓ Tom and Becky (help Bobby win)
- ✓ Get new life

Mama says I should wear pink because it makes me look younger. "I'm not even thirty," I protest.

"Girls grow up faster these days," she adds. "Need all the help you can get."

We search the racks of satin dresses looking for something less formal than a bridesmaid's dress and nicer than your Sunday best. It's a wedding, not a prom. I want to look good, but I don't want to look like I'm trying too hard. Mama keeps talking loudly about how overpriced the dresses are. "This one's only half a dress, too. Who'd pay that for half a dress? Costs a fortune!" Mama holds up a green dress cut way above the knee. "You bend over, everyone'd see your business!" I try to hush up Mama, but she's making me giggle, and that encourages her more.

I make my way quickly through a rack of black lacy numbers. They'd be hot as heck. Low-cut would be good. Show off my assets. Then I notice the wedding gowns. I can't help it. I touch a few, fingering their satin-covered buttons and tight waists.

"Don't play with him if you don't want him, honey. That's all I'm gonna say."

"Oh, please, Mama. Can't a girl look? I don't mean it."

"Nope. Not at weddin' dresses. Not you. Not with one foot always out the door you can't. You gonna break his heart again, Laura? Is that your plan?"

"We're just friends. He *just* got divorced. And maybe he broke my heart. Did that ever occur to you?" She always assumes I'm in the wrong. Sammy broke everything. Not me. I'm the one who came back to fix it.

"I know a good man when I see one. Sammy's good stock." She squints her eyes to let me know she means business.

"Yeah, well, even good stock does wrong sometimes, Mama."

She stands with her hands on her hips. "Well," she says, "I only came shoppin' to help you. This ain't for me."

"I'll just borrow somethin' from Rose or Daisy," I say and head for the door. "There's nothin' I want here." I don't look back to see if Mama is following me.

We're quiet on the ride back to Hannibal. Mama keeps changing the radio station. She hates the new country they play these days. She'll take a Dolly Parton over a Dixie Chick any day. We turn onto our street, and there are spilled boxes, stained mattresses, and broken shelves piled on the lawn of the Wilkenses' trailer. Crystal and her brother are picking their way through their own evicted possessions. I pull down the sun visor to hide my face. That could have been me if I'd stayed.

Just as we pull into our driveway, Mama says, "Let's stop by Betty's instead. She said she had more tomatoes than she knew what to do with." I don't have a better idea, and I don't want to watch these kids get kicked out of their home, so I drive past the city limits and take the dirt road. I drive slowly so Mama can keep her window down without getting all choked up by the dust. I pull into the driveway, and Mama bolts from the car. "Hello," she calls, opening Aunt Betty's door without knocking. She grew up in this house, too. "Thought we'd take some tomatoes off your hands."

"Sure you did," Aunt Betty says, looking up from her sewing machine. She's got pins between her lips that make her mumble. "Tomatoes in the garden. Dress is right here." She shakes out a simple sheath of pink satin with buttons up the back. It's elegant and understated. It's perfect. She holds it out to me like it's no big deal. "You'll have to get your own shoes, but this should do.

Hope it fits. Don't know why you had to get all skinny. It's tough sewin' for someone who keeps changin' sizes every time you see 'em. I tried to make it nice, though. Next time you might give me more than twenty-four hours' notice."

"Jalaxy! works, don't it?"

"I doubt it," Aunt Betty answers. "Looks like nothin' but chemicals, if you ask me."

"Well, I didn't," Mama says, her voice tight. Sisters.

I take the dress in my hands and I'm five years old again. I want to curl up in Aunt Betty's lap where I can feel all this grown-up stuff will turn out all right. This is what it means to be home. Family that drives you crazy and you can't live without them.

"Told you she'd like it," Aunty Betty says, nodding at Mama.

"You're crazy, you old woman," Mama says, throwing her arm around her sister. "I told *you*." Aunt Betty leans her head on Mama's shoulder. They watch me through the same mud-colored eyes.

"Ain't you gonna give us a show? Seems the least you could do," Mama says. She crosses the room and pours three glasses of iced tea. She scoops in an extra serving of sugar for her sister. "You done good, Betty. Only Mother could stitch a seam tighter than that."

A minute later Mama and Aunt Betty are sitting on the front porch, sipping tea and watching the road. I twirl out and do a curtsy for them. "Now *that*," Aunt Betty says, "is good stock."

JUDY, LANCE'S BRIDE, IS IN air transport for the National Guard stationed at Scott Air Force Base. Sammy tells me that she and Lance met online and only dated a few months. Lance was spending weekends at her apartment on the base until the floodwaters started to rise and he was needed back home. This is the first time Sammy's even met her. "What's their plan after the wedding?" I ask on our drive, scooting closer on the truck's bench. I shade my eyes from the bright sunshine; there isn't a single cloud in the pale-blue sky.

"She'll stay reserves and go down on the weekends," Sammy explains, resting his arm on the back of the seat. "She's moving to the farm next month. It all happened kind of quick, if ya know what I mean."

"Oh," and I do. If I'd gotten pregnant with Sammy, we'd have gotten married quick, too. There would be kids between us on this seat. His hand brushes my shoulder, and I don't pull away. "How'd the online thing happen?"

"Lance has to do everything the hard way. He said Hannibal girls did him wrong. He'd leave if it weren't for the farm and Dad." Their farm is the only land left. Corporate bought up all the families around them for pennies after '93. The pact not to sell couldn't hold when people were hungry. If they didn't have the gas station, Sammy's family would have gone under, too.

"Would you? Ever thought about gettin' out?"

Sammy takes his eyes off the road and glances my way. "Haven't had a reason to go, really." Then he pops open the glove compartment and pulls out sunglasses for both of us.

Aunt Betty always says weddings are slices of false hope. Love is contagious when you're watching a bride and a groom happily commit to whatever may come. And everyone is beautiful and suspended in the flashbulb moments: at the altar, holding hands, walking the aisle separately, then together. "Weddings make you believe," she once told me, "in stuff sane people shouldn't believe in."

On the bench beside me are two cowboy hats. The black velour that Sammy always wears and a white one with pink trim. "Who's the other hat for?" I ask.

"Didn't I tell ya? It's a hoedown. That's your hat, partner."

"A what?"

"A hoedown. Square dancin'. With a caller and everything."

"I'm a little overdressed." I study Aunt Betty's tight stitches and fancywork. I do have my boots and jeans in my bag, but I'd rather show off this dress.

"You're just right, Laura. I'll have the prettiest date there."

I put the cowboy hat on and lean over to look at myself in the rearview mirror. It suits me. Sammy slides his hand up the back of my bare neck and tips the hat forward a bit from behind. My grin meets his but his hand remains warm on my naked neck. I put the hat back on the bench beside me, lace my hand through his free arm, and he rests it on my thigh like ten years hasn't passed. Sammy sings along to the radio while he drives, and I'm exactly where I want to be, even if I didn't know I wanted to be here.

THERE ARE ABOUT TWO DOZEN people at the ceremony, including Judy's three older brothers, all dressed in Air Force uniforms. We fill the front rows of the small base chapel. Sammy stands up by Lance and I sit next to their dad. He doesn't look ten years older since I last saw him. He looks twenty. Farm life in a floodplain wrinkles you fast.

"Is that a power suit?" I tease Mr. McGuire.

"It's my only suit." He pats his brown lapels with his bony hands and smiles.

I cock my eyebrow in a flirt. "Looks pretty powerful to me."

At the altar, Lance is gripping the shoulder of his suit and whispering in Sammy's ear. They leave together through the side chapel quickly and it's clear something is wrong.

"Uh-oh," Mr. McGuire says, "looks like cold feet." He laughs at himself, and I wonder if he might have already snuck some booze.

Sammy comes back through the door and motions me over. "Don't suppose you got a needle and thread with ya, huh?"

"Sure I do. What's wrong?" I grab my purse. Tucked inside is the tiny sewing kit Aunt Betty gave me for my tenth birthday. Over the years, I've restocked it plenty.

"Lance ripped his jacket. Maybe he bought it too small. He can't stand up there lookin' like he does."

Sammy leads me to the dressing room, and Lance hands me his coat without a word. Sammy shoots him a dirty look. I turn the sleeve inside out and thread my needle. "I can fix it but it'll have to be white thread. It won't show, though." Lance mumbles thanks, walks over to the window, and watches the parking lot while I sew.

The ceremony takes less than ten minutes. Lance fumbles over his words and keeps touching his sleeve, like he's making sure my stitches hold. Sammy smiles in his easy way and slaps his brother on the back when he hands him the ring. He winks at me and waves at his dad. Judy's family seems misty watching it all. I hear Aunt Betty in my ear, but I can't help but believe, too, just for a minute in happily-ever-after.

Lance and Judy walk down the aisle to Dolly Parton's "I Will Always Love You" and I wonder if Sammy is thinking what I'm thinking, about that song, about how we both ended up here, in this chapel, together, of all places, and what might happen next.

The reception is held in the cramped basement of the chapel. It smells like mildew and grease. Five picnic benches are covered in red-checked cloths and spread out to fill the space. We eat family-style: plates of fried chicken, buttery mashed potatoes, and green-bean casserole smothered in French's fried onions. Sammy and I sit with two of Judy's cousins, Bryan and Stephanie, who are from O'Fallon. Stephanie is a hairdresser, and she tells us how long it took her to convince Judy to let her give her fancy curls for the wedding. "I'm tellin' you, she wanted to wear a ponytail." Bryan works in real estate and Sammy asks a lot of questions about price per square footage and flipping houses like it's the most fascinating thing he's ever heard.

In the corner, the caller, wearing a name tag that says BILLY, props up his legs on the karaoke machine and eats from a paper plate of fried chicken he rests on his balloon of a belly. He has a red napkin tucked into his silky black cowboy shirt. His boots are steel tipped and he taps them along to an instrumental version of Mary Chapin Carpenter's "Saturday Night at the Twist and Shout." He wipes the crumbs from his lap and then starts calling into his microphone, "Line up, folks! We're about to begin. Our first one's gonna be real easy. Even you can do it, Grandpa! Line up!"

Mr. McGuire shuffles out to the small dance floor and grabs the arm of Judy's aunt. "Now promenade! Travel halfway around. Walk into the middle and spin her around. Spin that top!" Sammy holds my hand, and we watch couples stumble and laugh over the dance moves.

After a few more songs, Billy announces the wedding couple's first stroll. Lance and Judy do a slow two-step to Garth Brooks's "The Dance." After a few minutes, other couples trickle onto the dance floor.

"Would you like to dance?" Sammy asks, leaning into my ear. "With me?" His breath on my neck is hot. He slides his arm around my waist.

"With you? Yes. I would like to dance with you."

Sammy holds me tight and leads confidently. I'm light-headed from my beer. His moves are smooth, and I float following his feet.

"Have you taken lessons, Sammy?"

"Maybe I learned a few things in ten years."

BY THE SECOND SLOW DANCE, we both knew we'd end up right here.

This time it isn't urgent, and it isn't rushed.

We aren't eighteen, and we don't have to sneak around.

We're both a little broken and injured holding on to each other in this bed.

Sammy trails a finger over every inch of me, like he's drawing my body, to make sure I'm real. Then he kisses the lines, and I watch his head move.

I try not to think about what comes next or how the world will work outside this hotel room or how much of the past I can't forgive.

Maybe Aunt Betty is wrong for once.

Maybe a little faith and false hope are exactly what I need right now.

My pink dress is draped over a desk chair, where Sammy carefully laid it after peeling it off. When I said I was starving, he broke into the mini bar for almonds and a three-dollar Pepsi.

He keeps pulling the sheet back up to cover me from the hotel room air-conditioning.

I'd rather be exposed and uncertain and happy.

ON THE DRIVE BACK TO Hannibal the next morning, I curl up next to Sammy on the truck bench and listen to the radio. Every time a thought about what's next creeps up, I turn up the music louder and try to stay in this content bubble. It doesn't last, though. The news comes on to burst it.

"Residents should be advised that floodwaters are overtopping levees between Hannibal, Missouri, and Quincy, Illinois. The city well used by Palmyra is in danger as are the Burlington-Northern Railroad tracks. A levee protecting four thousand acres of farmland has been breached. Residents in low-lying areas should seek higher ground immediately. Repeat: A levee in the rural area on the Missouri side has been breached. A suspect is in custody. Residents in these areas should evacuate immediately."

Sammy keeps one hand on the wheel and calls home with

the other. He's talking to cousins about whether the levee will hold. It's not the worst-case scenario yet, but the pressure is building and more rain is on its way. Machines make Corporate levees, not men. Because the big levees will hold, Sammy's family's levee probably won't.

Everything from that summer ten years ago rushes back in, and I scoot a few inches away. I keep my hand on the door, ready to run again. I'm falling back in love with the man I swore I'd never forgive.

Jackson's Island

Pirates called it Pete's Island. It's a narrow, wooded strip of land, no more than three miles, just beyond Lover's Leap. Erosion and floods have turned it from one landmass into three separate pieces. When the Mississippi is really angry, like when it ran backward, Jackson's Island disappears completely.

Mark Twain made it famous in *Adventures of Huckleberry Finn*, when Huck fakes his own death and escapes to the island. He spends his days eating berries and fish, smoking tobacco, and watching the stars. Then a ferryboat, carrying Tom, Becky, and other prominent villagers, passes. Huck hears them discussing his murder and realizes their boat is on a rescue mission to recover his body. As was the custom, they float loaves of bread filled with mercury to make the body rise. Huck catches one of the loaves to eat and is touched that they're using bread of such high quality for his cause. On the third day of his island escape, his friend Jim, a runaway slave, arrives, and Jackson's Island becomes a symbol of equality.

Mark Twain biographers claim that it was his early life on his uncle's farm among slaves that framed the stories he told through characters like Jim. In Clemens's autobiography, he writes that Daniel Quarles, or Uncle Dan'l, as he called him, was the real inspiration for Jim. Slaves taught the young Sam how to tell stories. They were some of the most influential voices of his upbringing. He once saw a slave beaten to death on the same Hannibal streets he roamed. Slave auctions were held just a few blocks from the Clemens house. Their mistreatment shaped his humanitarian roots. It's a history most of Hannibal is only beginning to be brave enough to share.

No one lives on Jackson's Island today, that we know of anyway. It's a happy paradise for muskrats, turtles, snakes, beavers, and birds. If you take a ride on the *Mark Twain* riverboat, they'll drive you right by Jackson's Island, so you can see it for yourself. But if a visit to the island is what you're after, Clemens himself just might meet you there at his favorite hour: midnight.

CHAPTER THIRTEEN

IT'S MY NAME over the intercom, and I don't recognize it. "Laura Brooks, please come to the ER stat." I don't work the ER. It's three floors below the classical music we blare on the maternity ward. Sometimes the strings and piano make me grit my teeth. It's like Schubert is yelling "*Calm down*," which someone like Schubert would never do. "Paging Laura Brooks. Laura Brooks, you're wanted in the ER." I duck into the nearest ladies' room and run directly into Sonya, my supervisor.

"Laura, they're paging you. Didn't you hear?"

"Can't be me," I say, pushing past her to pee. "I don't work ER."

"It's you," a voice behind me says. I turn around. It's Cindy, the floor manager. "There's been an accident. Your brother's in the ER. Motorcycle."

I don't see either of them. I take the stairs. My feet are loud on the concrete.

I lose track of the floors on the way down. I hit the basement and have to turn back around and climb one flight up.

They don't play classical music in the ER. Voices argue, machines beep, scrubs rush to the left, to the right. There are lines of people waiting, and the place smells like it's had a bath in hydrogen peroxide. I'm dizzy from the panic and input.

It can't be Trey. It can't be Trey. So why do they want me?

I'm not supposed to be here. I was never supposed to come back home.

Trey wouldn't be on this side of the river. I stop at a desk, but there's no one behind it. As a nurse, I blend in. I'm nobody's sister. I go behind the counter and flip through the clipboards. Trey Brooks. He's in Operating. Theater 3. Head trauma. Bleeding on the brain. Punctured lung. Cracked ribs. Multiple lacerations. Needle tracks. It's not Trey. Not my brother. Why would he be in Quincy? Why would he be in my hospital's ER? It's another Trey Brooks.

But it isn't. It's my brother. I call Mama. She doesn't answer.

My next instinct is to call Trey. That's my emergency phone tree.

I call Rose. Now it's her turn to help me. "Rose, I'm in the ER."

"Of course you are. You work in a hospital," Rose says. Loud country music plays in the background, and her voice is prissy.

"It's Trey. There's been an accident. He was on his bike." *Please come, Rose. I need you now.*

"Sit tight. I'm on my way. Where's your mama?"

"I don't know. She didn't answer."

"I'll swing by the house. I'll be there in fifteen minutes."

"They're operatin'. It's bad, Rose. I'm here alone."

"Sweet Jesus, Laura. Trey's tough. Start prayin'. I'm on my way."

Trey isn't tough enough. He didn't have a helmet. His bike slid sideways under an SUV. I tell Mama and Rose the little I know when they come bursting through the doors together. The doctors say there may be brain damage. I can't catch my breath. My knees buckle. Rose slips her arm through mine and holds me up. Me, the nurse. I have no equipment for this. Mama is stone. Her makeup is caked on heavy. I don't know what she's thinking. She nods her head when the doctors speak. She pats her purse like she has a secret in there.

"The MRI is inconclusive. We'll wait a bit. Let the swelling go down. Try again," the doctor says.

"Anything else?" Mama asks. She wants them to say if he was high. It's tough to even ask.

"Traces of methamphetamine. Does he have a history of drug abuse?"

We all nod.

"Does he have a living will?" the doctor asks.

"A what?" Mama says, turning to me.

I can't. I can't explain this to Mama. Her eyes plead, and I fail.

"Would Trey wanta live or die if somethin' like this happened?" Rose says.

"How the hell would I know? I'm his mama," she snaps. The doctor is quiet. Rose reaches for Mama's hand. I swallow hard.

"Let's just wait," I offer. It's the first reasonable thing I've managed to say since I saw Trey's jacket, shredded and bloody, through the window on the operating floor. "We don't know anything. Let's just wait."

"Trey's gonna be just fine," Rose adds. "He's tough." Mama and I both look blankly at her.

"God, I need a smoke," Mama says with a tiny crack in her voice.

THE NEXT FEW DAYS RUN together. They keep Trey in a coma so his brain can rest. The doctors say he's better. The doctors say he's worse. The doctors say we won't know for a while. I work my shifts just so I can have something to do in between checking on him. The nurses on his floor keep the extra bed in his room empty. I sleep at the hospital and live on cafeteria food. Josh seems to be cleaning our floor more than usual. One time he touches my arm and whispers, "Sorry about your brother." It angers me that his familiar face is comforting. I look away when other families huddle together crying, as if their bad news might be contagious.

I convince Mama to go home and wait, and I promise to call her every few hours. On the phone with Aunt Betty, I just cry and she doesn't ask questions. Mama comes over in the mornings and sits in the rocking chair by Trey's bed, but his progress is slow. The MRI shows more activity each day. Rose says everyone at her church is praying for him. It's something, I suppose. She has Bobby bring me a DQ sundae one afternoon with a whole bowl of nuts on the side. He doesn't know what to say, so he tells me about his busy schedule leading up to the Fourth of July. I'm missing his Tom events, but he forgives me. I don't even have to ask. He's a better kid than the adult I'll ever be.

In the afternoon, Sammy stops by and brings me KFC with baked beans and unpacks a picnic for both of us. He hands me a melting iced tea with two packets of sugar. "You used to like it sweetened," he says. "Don't know if you still do, though."

I take the iced tea from Sammy and fold myself into his arms. We hold each other and neither of us says a word. Then Sammy kisses the top of my forehead, just like he used to. I run my hands up his back, and it feels so known. Maybe love always leaves familiar scars. Maybe it wasn't him that night. Maybe he didn't and I've been blaming him all this time. But it was him. I saw him. How could *this* Sammy have done *that*?

On the third day, Trey's eyes flutter a little when I'm talking to him. He squeezes Mama's hand back. I watch like it's a movie.

Trey's friends come and go. Digger doesn't show his face, though, which is good. Hannibal's gearing up for Tom Sawyer Days and Trey's mud volleyball team stops by. They make small talk about the weather in the hallway with Mama and me. It's what people do when they don't know what else to say. We talk about the rain and the floods. "Water's comin' up anyway," one of them says.

"Oh, yeah?" Mama says, like this is news to her. "What's the crest?"

"Twenty, I think."

"Huge levee broke in Rock Island last night."

"That'll relieve some pressure, for sure."

"Huh. Too bad we're on the wrong side," she says. "I don't wanta get stuck on the Illinois banks." That makes the boys laugh. The only thing we loathe more than a flood is Illinois.

"We'll probably lose without 'im. 'Least Trey won't have to watch," another adds. It's the first time in twelve years that he won't be playing.

"I'll tell him you were here," I say in my comforting nurse voice. Their faces flash relief. They've done their duty. They can go now. Trey's busy fighting just to breathe.

Rose stops by one afternoon, Trey's fourth full day in a coma. She brings me a little distraction: *People*, a deck of cards, and pudding snacks, like we're kids at summer camp. She's working at Walmart now in the Beauty Department stocking perms and arranging makeup displays. She doesn't hate it. She needed a job quick or it would look bad in front of the judge, and Walmart is always hiring. "It's fun to talk to customers," she tells me. "I give 'em beauty tips for free. They certainly could use 'em. Geez. Walmart brings in some ugly bitches."

Seeing Rose is exactly what I need to break up my day between the shifts I'm keeping, sleeping, and worrying. She tells me she stopped by to visit her preacher first. A special prayer session for Trey. She's sitting on the side of the bed with her eyes closed, pleading with Jesus under her breath for my brother to wake up, when Martha walks in. I haven't run into her much since she hired me.

"Just thought I'd check on our special patient," Martha says. "How are you holding up, Laura?" Then she sees Rose and stops. I look from Martha to Rose but I don't get what's wrong.

"Martha, this is my friend Rose," I begin.

"Oh, we know each other," Rose says, reapplying her lip gloss. She's propped up her makeup mirror on Trey's thigh. Even I know that's tacky. "Martha is an elder at River Passage, ain't that right?"

"My son is the preacher." Martha closes her eyes like she's hoping when she opens them again Rose and I will be gone.

"I appreciate you checkin' on me. Trey's doing better every day—" I offer.

"I already know that," she says, cutting me off. "What I didn't know was the company you keep." Rose laughs at this and swings her legs from the side of Trey's bed.

"I was just prayin'." Rose smiles. "Would you like to join me?"

It's clear she wouldn't. Martha looks like she just sucked on a lemon. "We've decided for the sake of our patients' health to end visiting hours early today. You'll both need to go now." I've never seen anyone in this hospital enforce visiting hours.

Rose hops off the bed. "Happy to. I was gonna stop by church again anyway."

"You'll do *no* such thing, you little hussy!" Martha's jaw flinches. "If you come near my son again, I'll…I'll…"

"What?" Rose asks, crossing her arms over her chest. "Tell everyone their favorite preacher gives out prayer favorites?" *Aw, Rose. You didn't.* But clearly she did.

"You are *no* Christian woman. Get out of this hospital now. Both of you."

"Me?" I ask.

"Yes, you. Both of you. Now."

"Martha, this is clearly a mix-up. Rose was just leaving."

"Well, go with her. You don't work here anymore, Laura. I need to be able to trust my nurses and their assistants. Several of your colleagues have been complaining that you've been slacking."

"That's not true!" I'd done my job and done it well. Better than most of these townies.

"You can leave now or I can make it true. With documentation that will make sure you never nurse again. Got that?"

I don't want to work for the likes of Martha anyway. Someone who uses their power to pay a grudge. I can hardly blame Rose.

My brother is the only thing on my mind as I clean out my locker. A few weeks on the job isn't enough time to accumulate much. It'll be better anyway to be more available for Trey, I tell myself. Trauma has a way of boiling things down to the basics.

Rose is waiting for me in the parking lot. "I'll bring you back first thing in the morning," she promises, as if a ride will make it all better. "To visit Trey, I mean."

"It's probably best I come alone," I say and she nods.

"I didn't mean for that to happen, Laura. Jesus can do good things."

"Not the way you're tryin' to make them happen, friend."

Jesus didn't do any of this. The same people who know you enough to give you a break take it away just as fast. I'm always going to be someone's daughter, sister, or friend here. And their baggage is mine, for better or worse.

THE NEXT MORNING I'M READING a day-old *Hannibal Courier Post* when Trey finally wakes up. I look up from the paper, and he's looking straight at me. "Don't move," I say, "just take it easy."

Trey squirms around in the bed and then lifts a hand to scratch his watery eyes.

"Shit," he says.

"You're alive. You're lucky." I push the call button to let one of the floor nurses know. The doctor will want to check up. They'll run all the tests again. He'll get something stronger for the pain. I hold up a cup of water with a straw. Trey takes a sip. The water dribbles down his chin, and I wipe it off with my hand.

"Goddamn. It hurts. How long I been out?"

"Almost a week." Maggie, an ER nurse I know from the cafeteria, comes in and nods at me. She pages the doctor from the side of Trey's bed. Then she starts taking vitals. I watch her record blood pressure, pulse, and temperature. She moves the flowers that Aunt Betty brought over to a shelf to make room for the equipment. In the corner, GET WELL SOON helium balloons float from a sand sack wrapped in foil; the nurses on my floor sent them down.

"My bike?"

"Dead. You ain't, though." It's a good sign that he remembers it right away.

"Mama?" Trey asks.

"She's on her way."

"I remember a truck. What else happened?"

I move closer and sit gently on the side of the bed. "Think you tried to kill yourself on your bike," I joke, offering him another sip of water.

The corners of his bruised mouth turn up a little.

"I'm gonna live?"

I let out a loud sigh and take his hand in mine. "Looks like it," I say. I put my palm on his cheek, and I swear I feel my own face.

THE LAST THING I DID in the summer of '93, just hours before I pointed my car south out of town and left for school, was go on a flood ride with Trey. When the levees start busting and the waters keep rising there's not much else to do but drive around and look at the mess. Trey drove, and we took turns taking pictures of each other with the flood behind us. Places we'd visited our whole lives were half underwater; some were entirely flooded.

There's a shot of Trey standing next to the ROAD CLOSED sign on Lindell Avenue where there is a little bridge we call the Humpty. If you could get Mama going real fast, when we went over the bridge, you'd get a little flop in your belly from the dip. Trey always made us hold up our arms and touch the cloth ceiling in the car.

There's a picture of me pretending to fish in the muddy water next to the giant Sawyer's Creek billboard where a twenty-foot cutout of Tom casts his line into the water. The Mississippi rose high enough to make it look like Tom might actually catch something.

Several of the pictures are blurred from my thumb, but you can make out Trey doing cartwheels on the levee. Except for one where he's looking out over the water and smoking. His profile looks exactly like Daddy's. Right after I took the picture, Trey tried to push me into the water. He was joking at first but then my shoe slipped and I almost did go over the side into the fast-moving current. Trey grabbed my arm so hard it left a bruise.

Then there's one of us together at Riverview Park. We're standing on a stone wall that boosts us up high enough for the mile-wide view of the Mississippi over our shoulders. Behind us looms a bronze statue of Mark Twain; he's the lookout for Jackson's Island, but the floodwaters have completely submerged it. There is water for miles, water where it's not supposed to be. Trey has his arm slung over my shoulder and our heads are tilted together, like we have a secret that only the two of us know about.

Fault Line

The seismic shifts that occurred along the New Madrid Fault Line in 1812 were a long time coming. The people of the Missouri Territory knew that the ground beneath them was unreliable. They'd heard tales from the natives and pioneers of the past. Still, because of the proximity to the river, it was home.

The Muskogee people, who lived near Hannibal, saw the Mississippi running backward as a sign that a river god, known as Tie Snake, was thrashing about under the riverbed. Tie Snake preserved the line between the upper and lower realms of Earth. His writhing indicated that the balance of order and chaos had been upset, which the Muskogee blamed on invading Europeans. Tie Snake was telling them to return to their native roots. The Muskogee decided that the river running backward was their signal to fight back, which led to the Trail of Tears.

The earthquakes also caused numerous fissures that covered hundreds of acres. Deep, angry pits in perfectly good earth cracked open, swallowed the neighboring contents, spit out sand, water, and rock, and rumbled violently closed. When the water went right again, fish littered the banks. They couldn't swim fast enough to save themselves. A thick blanket of wet sand covered boats, houses, and bodies. The sand was specked with a type of impure coal, not much different from what was mined nearby but unexpected from the depths of the Mississippi. The earth also coughed up a sulfurous gas that choked the Muskogees and blackened the air.

The riverbanks receded from their water source ten to twenty feet in some places, looking more like a desert than lush Missouri farmland. The earthquakes changed even the landscape of drought by depositing water in places it had never been. A new lake, more than one hundred miles long and several miles wide, was discovered in Indian country. The Mississippi fed this new water source on both ends and threatened to gulp it up just as quickly as it had given birth to it.

CHAPTER FOURTEEN

S AMMY SHOWS UP with a backpack the afternoon after Trey wakes up. The boys smile at each other like they're conspiring against me. Mama slips into the room behind Sammy and says she'll take a shift. "You could use some airing out, ya know."

Trey shuffles to the bathroom. He seems steadier today. "Where am I goin'?" I ask.

"On a date. The skies are blue. No rain in the forecast." Sammy smiles. "Here's a preview." He pulls a bottle of wine from his backpack. On the label is a black-and-white photo of a dapper man and woman from the 1800s who are bowing to each other beneath the script AN INNOCENT BROAD.

"Hannibal makes its own wine now?"

"We're decent, kid," Mama says. "Times have changed."

"Naming everything after Mark Twain hasn't."

"Folks gotta make a livin'," Sammy says. "Can you blame 'em? Tastes good. It sells."

"I'm sold. I could use a drink. Let me check with Trey's doctor first."

Mama stops me at the door. "I already did. Trey's restin' today. They'll run some more tests tomorrow. Then maybe let him come home. Go on and go. Take a break." She cocks her head back toward Sammy and lowers her voice. "That's a good man and he's packed a picnic. I wouldn't keep him waitin' if I were you. Not any more than you already have."

THE CAR LINE LEADING UP to the Mark Twain Cave campgrounds is crawling. It's almost the holiday weekend and families are streaming into town for the Fourth. Nearly every campsite has a car parked beside it, a tent, or a pop-up trailer. Dogs are straining on their chains. Some roam freely, sniffing the base of grills for scraps. Coolers dot the grass like baseball bases. The whole campground reeks with the acrid smell of charred meat. A kid with a Kool-Aid mustache runs in front of our truck, and Sammy hits the brakes. "I'm guessin' you've got it all planned and I'm just along for the ride, is that right?" I ask.

"You could use someone else in charge for a while. Just relax. Our tent is already pitched. One of my cousins did us a favor and got us a spot away from the noise."

"Tent? You said wine." The RV in front of us inches over the rock entrance to the campgrounds. It sways and the kids tucked inside scream with delight. A hound hangs his head out the window and howls.

"Well, you gotta have someplace to fall down after all those drinks." Sammy holds my hand and brings it up to his lips and I do know. He's put the camper shell on the bed of his truck, and I'm guessing if I looked back there, there'd be a mattress made up with sheets.

"I haven't been campin' in years. Rose, Bobby, and me pitched a tent on the beach when they visited me in Jacksonville. We didn't put it far enough back and the tides flowed in the next mornin' and woke us up."

"Bet that was cold."

"Freezing. But I don't remember minding. It was Bobby's favorite part of the whole trip. Next to Disney, of course."

"Never been. I'd like to go, though."

"It's more fun with kids," I say and we're both quiet for a minute with the weight of what I just implied. Did I mean to bring up kids? It's hard to casually date with this much history. It's even harder to think of what might have been. I seem to be going backward rather than forward. Almost losing Trey puts the future in a different perspective.

"Here we are," Sammy says, pulling into a spot on the edge of the campground. He's set up a small green tent on the side near a campfire. He's built up the logs, and they're just waiting to be lit. There's also an outdoor zippered room with mesh sides. Inside are two plastic chairs and a small table. "I borrowed some Christmas lights. Hope it's not too much."

"It's perfect."

"Picnic or wine or walk?"

"Yes," I say, lacing up my sneakers.

We spend the afternoon hiking the trails behind the caves.

Sammy makes us both walking sticks out of branches. We stop at each view of the river for water, for a kiss. Over a ridge we run into a deer and her two fawns. Sammy and I stop and so does she, each waiting for the other to make the next move.

Back at the campsite, we devour the picnic. Ham sandwiches, deviled eggs, dill potato salad, and sweet slices of watermelon. Just as we're debating the brownies Judy baked, a little boy pushes his face against the mesh walls and sniffs. "Hey, little man," Sammy greets him. "You all alone?" The boy shakes his head no. He looks just like Bobby at that age.

"Where's your mama?" I ask. He shrugs. Then wipes his eyes and sniffs again. "You want a brownie?" I peel back the aluminum foil. "They're chocolate chip fudge. You should probably ask your parents first, though. Where are they?"

He stares at the brownie and sucks on one of his fingers. "I was chasing fireflies," he whispers. His bottom lip starts quivering.

Sammy pulls back the side of our outdoor room and ties it up. He squats down to the boy's level and wipes out his tea jar with his shirttail. "I'll tell you what. You hold this lid and I'll hold the jar. We'll catch fireflies back in the direction you came. Got it?"

The boy nods and takes the lid. Then he looks to me. "Oh, I'll bring the brownies along," I say.

Sammy and the boy catch three fireflies before a woman comes screaming toward them. She's barefoot and flushed. "Tyler! I told you to stay close! You scared me to death!" Her fingernails dig into the boy's pale arms.

"I'm sorry," Tyler cries. "I was chasing the fireflies."

"Everyone is out looking for you! Don't do that again, okay? You hear me?" Tyler's mama starts crying, too. Then she hugs him tight, and Tyler wraps his arms around her and drops the lid. She nods at Sammy and me. "Thank you. I was so scared," she whimpers. Her panic is laced with love.

"These are for y'all," I say, holding out the brownie package to Tyler and his mama. "We have plenty."

"Brownies!" Tyler squeals, reaching out to me.

"No, we couldn't. Thank you for keeping him safe. That's enough."

"Really," Sammy says. "My sister-in-law packed a dozen. There's just the two of us. Take 'em off our hands, please. Tyler looks like he could use a treat."

Tyler blinks several times and nods fast. "Please! Pretty please!"

"Thank you again," she says, accepting the brownies in one hand and holding tight to Tyler with the other. "We come here every year, and people are just so nice."

Sammy pulls me into a hug, and we watch them walk away together. "We are nice, aren't we?"

"Most of us, yes."

"I want that," Sammy says, nodding toward their backs.

"Looks painful." Loving means losing. It's always a risk. They'll disappoint you. Who can you trust? Sometimes, not even myself. I used to see in black and white. Now there are confusing shades of gray. I slip my hands into Sammy's back pockets and squeeze.

"What isn't painful? What's worth it that don't hurt?"

"I guess."

"Don't you want a family?" Sammy kisses the side of my neck, behind my ear, my cheek. "I'm serious."

"I do. Someday."

"That's good enough for me," he says, stepping me closer to the truck bed. "You got plans for the fireworks? I'd be happy to take you. It'd be like old times." The problem in my gut isn't the present; it's the past. The same fireworks on the Fourth of July ten years ago broke everything between us.

SAMMY'S FAMILY FARM SURVIVED MOST of the rising water that summer, but his daddy's gas station, which sat low on the south side, had three feet of water. We spent our spring break moving inventory while a crew from St. Louis emptied the underground gas tanks. We boarded up the windows with plywood, and by morning somebody had spray-painted *There's No Place Like Home* in red, white, and blue. Sammy missed another week of school adding five more feet to a sandbag-and-rock levee around the farmhouse; the wall made them an island. The basement of the farmhouse took on water, and because of contamination, they couldn't drink from the well anymore. Even though the rains kept coming, they ignored the evacuation orders.

As the waters rose, we didn't go to after-school jobs anymore; we went to the levees to add more layers. We carried mattresses, dressers stuffed with clothes, family Bibles, and dishes piled in boxes through the sloshing waters and passed them up a human chain to flatbed trucks backed up as far as they dared. We helped wherever we heard word to go, mostly low-lying land, where the water bled and seeped from the river's main vein. Afterward, Rose and I walked the floodwalls that kept the downtown dry as a bone, while the angry brown water of the Mississippi carried trees and furniture downstream. The river was miles and miles across; I'd never seen it in such a hurry.

The morning of the Fourth I'd been downtown with Mama walking through the arts-and-crafts tent and visiting with cousins and friends. It was what we'd done every Fourth in my memory. Each conversation turned back to the rising waters and what-ifs. We were standing on Broadway during the morning parade as the Hannibal Pirates marching band passed by playing "The Star-Spangled Banner." Daisy waved me over and asked, "How's Sammy's family farm holdin' up?" Daisy had dropped out of school and the time since had worn her hard; dark eyeliner was smeared in triangles under her eyes like she'd rubbed them too much, and an inch of black roots crept through coarse, bleached hair. She had a snotty-nosed toddler, a fat baby on one hip, and another on the way.

"Water's pretty high," I told her. "They've built levees around the house, but it's still comin' in anyway."

"Suppose that'll be your house one day, huh, Laura?" she said.

"I'm leavin' for St. Louis next month, Daisy. Didn't Mama tell you that?" I knew she hadn't.

Daisy didn't say anything about my plans. She wiped her kid's nose with the bottom of her shirt and brushed back her baby's mullet. I handed her what was left of my lemonade. Daisy patted her pregnant belly and said, "Sure you are."

It hadn't rained that Fourth of July, but the gray clouds crowded each other and built at my back. Every ripple of thunder was a tease. The sky seemed to be holding just for the fireworks, but the waiting and watching for more flooding was exhausting. Sammy spent most of the day moving equipment and bulldozing to build up the levee with Lance. Even after their daddy said it wouldn't make a difference, they got up every morning and went out to assess the new damage. Then they loaded more sandbags, piled them on top of their levee, and the water seeped in at their feet.

Sammy picked me up about seven o'clock that night. I'd curled my hair twice waiting for him, but it just hung limp under the weight of the water the sky promised to dump. We took blankets and lawn chairs to Kiwanis Park to set up our spot for the show.

Usually on the Fourth folks lined the banks of the river, filled the grass at Nipper Park, or took out their boats to float on the Mississippi with the fireworks bursting above their heads, but the river kept pushing us back. Roads were closed and the boat launch was on the other side of the floodwall so you couldn't get to it. The boats had been moved weeks ago, and the water was too dangerous to be out on. The crowds were smaller that night, so Sammy and I had most of the parking lot to ourselves. I'd brought a cooler of Pepsis and ham sandwiches. "You hungry?" I asked, pulling the plastic off a sandwich with pickles and mustard, Sammy's favorite.

"I guess so," he said, reaching over into the ice and popping open a soda. He drained it in a few gulps and took the sandwich. He smelled like Dial soap, but there were still flecks of mud on his neck. I wondered if he'd checked the levee one last time before he came to get me.

"Everyone out workin' on the levee?" I asked, scooting closer.

"Yep. Cousins too. It's not gonna do any good, though." It wasn't like Sammy to be defeated. He always thought he could win, even when it hurt him. He never minded the odds being stacked against him. Months before when I told him I probably wouldn't get in to nursing school, he said they'd be fools not to take me. When Mama slapped me for talking back at our graduation, Sammy said I didn't deserve to be hit. I could always count on Sammy. At least I thought so then.

"Levee's holdin' so far," I said. "That's something, ain't it?"

"Laura, look up at the sky. Can't you see it's about to rain?" The flood wasn't anybody's fault, but Sammy needed someone to blame and somewhere to direct his anger. "Crops are ruined. The well water is poisoned. We moved everything we could. There's nothin' else to do but wait. Nothin's gonna save it anyway." His voice was resigned.

The first firework cracked into the black clouds and drowned the end of Sammy's words. The blue sparks lit up the sky and I felt a fat raindrop on my cheek, like someone had spit at me. I reached over for Sammy's hand, but he lay back on the blanket too far away to reach. A burst of red, white, and blue came in a circle with silver stars surrounding it. Then a purple sparkling dud fizzled out. There was a pause as the smoke cleared. Folks in the distance clapped and laughed at the dud. Lee Greenwood's "Proud to Be an American" blared from a car stereo. I curled up next to Sammy and tried to put my arm around him.

He sniffed a bit in the dark and wiped his face from the drizzle. We watched the rest of the fireworks and didn't talk. It was the first time I'd felt really alone with Sammy, and it scared me to think he was so far away.

Sammy tried to take me home after the fireworks. He said he was tired and just wanted to sleep, but I insisted on staying. "Nobody goes home on the Fourth!" I complained, as if Sammy was ruining my fun, as if his whole life wasn't about to be a lot worse. "I'm gonna call Rose to find out where there's a party. She knows where there's fun, even if she can't join it. That'll cheer you up."

"I'm tired, Laura."

"Then take a nap. I'll drive."

"I'm gonna go out and check on the levee. Lance'll be there. Can't do much, I'm sure, but still. I'll drop you off wherever you want."

"I don't want you to drop me off, Sammy. You're the only reason I even stayed for the summer. I'm only here because of you, because of us. Doesn't that mean anything to you?" It was almost true. My scholarship covered a summer session. Mr. Eggleston wanted me to start earlier because I hadn't earned any credits yet like most students who came from high schools with honors programs. Hannibal didn't have those kinds of things then; there wasn't much demand. At the beginning of summer, I wasn't ready yet to leave. I'd spent so much time planning to go; my duffel bags were packed, but I just kept pushing back my move-in date. If I'd left before Sammy did what he did, things might have turned out different.

He drove me home but didn't say a word. In front of my

house, he parked, slid across the seat, and kissed me hard. He cupped his big hands around the back of my head and I climbed over into his lap. I looked out through the window to make sure Mama hadn't left the porch light on. I knew if she saw us she'd come out running and yelling about putting the cart before the horse. As if she hadn't done it, too. The trailer was dark and she wasn't home yet. My brother was probably inside sleeping off his shift. "Let's drive up to Lover's Leap," I whispered.

"Can't," Sammy said. "Road's flooded." He kissed me again behind my ear and arched my back to get closer.

"Your truck'll make it. Come on."

"What's wrong with here?"

"It's gotta be Lover's Leap," I said.

He pulled back to look at me, to make sure he understood. He did. A roadblock and rising water wasn't going to stop us.

After Lover's Leap, we ate the rest of the sandwiches and drove out to the farm. I kept my leg laced over his and my head in his neck wanting to be close, to have our bodies tangled up again. The rain pelted the window in rhythm, and I almost dozed off curled next to him like that. When the rain slowed, the tires gripped the gravel as we slid a bit. Sammy over-corrected the wheel and his elbow caught my cheek. It bruised but he didn't notice.

It was past midnight when we pulled up, but the lights were still on inside the house. Sammy's daddy was probably up listening to the radio, hoping someone else's levee would break to save his own. We sat in the driveway and waited. Sammy rubbed his chin like he was thinking. He flipped on the radio, but there was only static. We waited, but I wasn't sure what for.

Then we drove twelve miles south on the dirt road as far as we could without getting the truck in water. The numbers on the odometer clicked away and a wind rattled the truck.

I kept asking where we were going but he wouldn't answer. The water roared around us as the rain stirred it up. "Just stay in the truck, Laura," he'd told me when he pulled up to the levee and turned off the lights. He didn't sound like Sammy at all, but I'd already decided to trust him, to trust our future together. "Just in case," he said, shoving a life jacket into my lap.

His ghostly figure was lit up every time the moon peeked out of a cloud. He was checking the water level on the other side. He leaned so far over the edge of the sandbag pile that I could only see his white socks. But when he sprinted back to the truck, I knew something was wrong.

He was soaked all the way up to his waist. He grinded the gears and drove us away from the creeping waters. Finally, the tires hit gravel again. He was trying to catch his breath. I kept asking what had happened, but he wouldn't tell me. His face was wet. There was no difference between tears and rain and sweat. We drove a few miles. Then he whispered, "Their levee's breached. We're safe."

Water always runs to the lowest point, which was to the south, away from Sammy's farm. Eight sandbags were pulled from the weakest spot and Mother Nature did the rest.

When I saw him breach the levee, I wanted to get as far away from him as possible. Only lowlifes sabotaged levees. The rest of us fought against the water by building our walls up. Tearing down someone else's was cheating. He didn't deny it, mostly because I hadn't really asked, and I was the only one who knew we'd been there. He'd risked everything, including our future together, to save his own. I'd read the morning paper over Mama's shoulder for days worried that they'd mention sabotage. They never did.

There were pictures in the paper of the family whose property had flooded. They were a farm family, like Sammy's. They'd barely had time to grab their dogs as they drove away from the rising water. Two years after the flood, that same farmer hanged himself from the rafters in his own barn. He had a wife and two kids, a boy and a girl. He'd never recovered from the ruin. The Army Corps of Engineers had investigated, but they hadn't been able to prove anything.

I changed that Fourth of July. When Sammy got back in the truck I heard the water coming, and my faith was shattered. He'd breached a levee, and it was the final push I needed to run.

Innocents Abroad

Scores of Samuel Clemens impersonators roam Hannibal's historic district. Before the tour at the Mark Twain Cave, visitors are treated to a ten-minute one-man show. In a remodeled barn on Main Street, Sam comes to life. Even Twain's legendary impersonator, Hal Holbrook, makes it to town once in a while. They conjure up a time when steamboats polluted the air downtown and ladies strolled the bricked sidewalks hitching up their dresses to keep them out of horse manure.

In 1853, when boredom struck, Sam left his hometown. He accepted a position as a typesetter in St. Louis, a few hours south on the Mississippi, but his wandering spirit took him quickly beyond the Missouri state line. A decade later he penned his name as Mark Twain for the first time in a piece of journalism. It stuck. Six years later he published his first book, *The Innocents Abroad*, a satirical observation of world travels far from Hannibal. But leaving was never easy. Neither was being away. After he had enough fun and found his beloved Livy, he sought a quieter life: raising kids and writing books. His debt as a result of the Panic of 1893 and his newfound celebrity demanded otherwise. He continued on the lecture circuit and gave his publishers what they wanted: books that would sell. Even with a foundation firmly under his feet, Clemens ran off no fewer than twenty-two summers, to Quarry Farm in Elmira, New York, where he could write in peace and escape fame.

Clemens had to leave Hannibal to find a place he could finally call home; he had to retreat in order to write about the place he'd left.

CHAPTER FIFTEEN

Mama could use a reason to get out of the house. I was over late last night at Sammy's, and she waited up for me. She's been talking to her chickens for company. Trey is home from the hospital, and he sleeps most of the time. It's the painkillers. The doctors said the recovery and physical therapy will take months, but it could have been much worse. He's lucky, too, that the other driver wasn't hurt and won't press charges. His license is suspended for at least a year. And he's agreed to drug counseling to avoid jail time. Watching him rest doesn't do either of us any good.

I peek into Trey's room. His eyes are closed, so I back out the door.

"I'm awake," he mumbles. I go back in and sit on the side of his bed. His face is still puffy, but it looks a lot better now that the bruises are fading. He has an arm still in a cast and a brace around his waist to help him breathe better. I check his other bandages. He moves to one side to alleviate the ache from his cracked ribs.

"You're still banged up pretty good," I say, giving him a sip of water. "When did you last take a Tylenol?" Trey isn't a good patient. He takes his meds in a double dose when he feels like it. He waits until the hurt gets worse rather than taking Tylenol on a schedule that would prevent the pain. I've tried explaining it to him. I've warned him and Mama that the codeine makes addicts. I've watched a lot of patients survive accidents only to become druggies. A life without grief is a hard thing to turn down.

"I'm all right. Got me some time off of work, didn't I?" Trey lights a cigarette, takes a long inhale, then puts it out. "Looks like you did, too," he teases.

"I thought I'd mind a lot more. Who loses two jobs in two months? Me. That's who." I feel free, though, not defeated. Like I can do anything I want now. Get another job and stay. Apply somewhere else and go. Either way, I'll be fine. The question now is what to do about Sammy. I take out two pills and hand them to Trey. He puts them on his tongue and takes the water. "I'm going to write down that I gave you this dose at eight, okay? You need to take it again at twelve. Then write that one down, okay?"

"'Least I'll get disability." He makes it sound like he's won a prize.

"You need anything before I go?" I ask. "Want that heat sock?" I glance around Trey's room and my eyes land on one of the pictures of our flood drive. It's the one from Riverview Park. He looks like he's about to put me in a headlock, but my grin is huge.

"Stop fussin'. I'll live."

"I'm nervous as heck about what's happenin' with Sammy."

"Good." Trey smiles again with his eyes closed. He leans over and punches me in the arm. "Y'all been spendin' a lot of time together, huh?"

"You could say that."

"Well, then I'm sure everyone in town already is sayin' it, Laura."

In the kitchen, I ask Mama if she wants to come with me to the Fourth of July events.

"Nah, I got stuff to do. Two more ambassadors signed up this week. I have more deliveries comin' in and orders to fill. This town is goin' crazy for Jalaxy! You go on ahead."

"Trey's gettin' better every day," I reassure her in my nurse voice.

"It's easier to have him stuck in that bed than worryin' about what he's out doin'. 'Least I know he's safe when I can see him."

"He'll be okay, Mama."

"Okay as ever, I suppose. Scared us pretty good. I'm hopin' it scared him good enough, too. Trey's gotta make his own decisions. Same as you."

"What time is it, anyway?"

"Almost nine. You got some place to be?"

"Parade starts at ten. Bobby's Tom thing is after the parade. I told him I'd stop by and check if he needed help. With his costume and whatnot." I sip the hot coffee and stretch.

"I'll swing by the park after the parade to see him. Think he could win?" Mama picks up the shoes I left by the door. She pairs them up and puts them in my closet.

"Why not? He's pretty damn cute. He's been practicin' the engagement scene with one of the Beckys every single night for weeks. Rose says that all he wants to do is practice."

"Well, folks are comin' over to barbecue later. Aunt Betty, too. I think it'll cheer your brother up."

"If he's up for it."

"Oh, and I invited Rose and Daisy. Ran into 'em last week at Walmart. I'm headin' out to get some groceries. Need anything?"

"Nope. Not a thing," I say. Mama walks to the door and starts to pull it closed behind her.

"Love you, Mama," I call. She stands still on the other side. She lets out a sigh. It's a sad sound, and I'm not sure why.

"You stayin', Laura?" she asks shyly. Her face is hidden.

I don't have an answer. I know she's not asking about the barbecue. "Maybe. Maybe not."

Then I hear her keys in the front door, and she's gone.

BOBBY'S WAITING ON JOSH'S BACK stoop when I pull up. I'm fifteen minutes late. He climbs in and doesn't say a word. "Sorry I'm late, kiddo."

"It's okay," Bobby mumbles.

"You by yourself?"

"Dad had to work his shift early at the hospital this morning. He asked for the day off, but they said he hadn't been on the job long enough to get it. He won't be downtown. Hope Mom is, though."

"Hungry?"

He shakes his head. He's mad, but I'm not sure it's at me.

"How's Trey?" he asks, studying me.

"Better. At least he's home," I say. "I'm glad I'm going to watch you win today, Tom Sawyer."

Bobby cracks a smile. He's added a slingshot to his Tom Sawyer costume and he plays with the elastic band. Then he pours out a glossy rock from his bag like he's getting ready to load his weapon. "I've got a bad case of the fantods," he says.

"The fan what?"

"Fantods! It's what Huck calls it when he's all nervous and stuff."

"I'd be nervous, too, kiddo. I'd of been nervous long before I got to where you are. Aren't you supposed to be in the parade?" I look at the clock on my dashboard. The Fourth of July parade unofficially kicks off Hannibal's National Tom Sawyer Days. The parade marches straight toward the Mississippi, but they take a sharp left to downtown just before they hit the water. The police close off Broadway for about ten blocks and the high school's Pirate Pride marching band leads the way. Normally the marching pirates don red, white, and black pirate-themed costumes, but for the parade, the girls dress like Tom Sawyer in cut-off pants and suspenders, and the boys put on dresses and braids like Becky Thatcher. The entire drum line wears Aunt Polly spectacles and wigs. We're making fun of our mythology and ourselves and laughing along.

"Nope. They want us in the crowd this year. Toms and Beckys are supposed to mingle, then meet at the gazebo at noon for the announcement."

"What's that for?" I nod toward the plastic bag of bulk candy in his lap.

"I guess we're supposed to give out candy to kids as we pass through the crowd. I don't know. Shelly's mom gave it to me."

"Shelly, huh?"

"She's kind of my girlfriend."

"Your *what*?"

Bobby ducks his head and looks out the window. "You heard me," he mumbles.

"Well, now I've got a case of the fantods. We'll get you there on time," I say. "Promise." I run a yellow light and swerve around some orange cones. Flatbed trailers of floats are already lined up. After the band comes a line of convertibles carrying our local royalty: Little Miss Hannibal, Little Tot Hannibal, Cutest Hannibal Baby, and the actual Miss Hannibal, too. They wave and sweat from the leather seats. Then come the service organizations, handing out candy, and the politicians, shaking hands and passing out flyers. Reliable, the family-owned pest-control company that Aunt Betty sews for, puts enormous mouse ears and tails on their cars and "poop" out big plastic turds. Their uniformed exterminators follow close behind and scoop up the mess. Other local businesses sponsor floats, too, and show off their new equipment. Boys in Hannibal dream of driving those huge green Caterpillar combines and operating the controls inside a cement-truck cab. There's always a bit of a hush when a company rolls out a new toy and proudly drives it down Broadway to a grateful crowd. When Bobby was little, the farm equipment was his favorite part.

"I'm supposed to be back at Dad's by five," he says as I'm

pulling into a parking spot three blocks off Broadway. The streets are packed with people wearing patriotic T-shirts and carrying lawn chairs. A couple walks in front of my car lugging a huge cooler between them. The dial on my dashboard reads ninety-one degrees, and it's going to get hotter. Thunder rumbles from somewhere, but it's not close enough yet to be a threat.

"Okay. I can do that," I say. "That gives us enough time for the parade, the announcement, and the cookout at my mama's." Technically, Rose doesn't have visitation until this weekend, but the judge left it up to Josh and his lawyers, who, thankfully, don't count the time Bobby spends with me.

The parade is almost over when the sky cracks open and the rain begins. I grab Bobby's hand, and we race to the car just as the first heavy drops splatter. My sleeveless shirt is plastered to my body from sweat and rain. I start the engine to get the air flowing and Bobby offers his open candy bag to me. "You sure?" I ask, digging through the sugary stash for Tootsie Rolls.

"Just don't take the good stuff," he says. Red syrup pools in the corner of his mouth as he chews a FireBall. I hand him a tissue so he doesn't look like a clown for the Tom-and-Becky announcement.

"You nervous?"

Bobby nods. "'Least we'll be under the gazebo and not on the flatbed truck, where we'd get soaked."

I drive us as close as I can to Central Park where they'll announce the official Tom and Becky at noon. The park is tucked between two city blocks and surrounded by historic churches. It's packed with vendors for the annual Kiwanis Samuel L. Clemens

Arts & Crafts Festival. Tom Sawyer might not have wanted hand-made doll clothes, customized footstools, or crocheted tea cozies, but Aunt Polly would have appreciated them.

Bobby bolts from the car in the rain toward the crowd huddled together. "I'll meet you there!" I yell after him and look around for parking.

There's a brief break in the clouds, and I make it to the stage just as the announcer asks us to stand for the national anthem. Rose and I see each other at the same time. I move closer and duck under her umbrella. "Did Bobby see you?" I ask.

"He walked right past me." Rose rubs her temples.

"Ladies and Gentlemen, it's my honor to present to you the President of the Hannibal Chamber of Commerce, who will say a few words about this year's Tom and Becky Program."

"Where'd you end up last night?" I whisper.

"Palmyra. Kayla, that girl Josh brought to the reunion, was prankin' me, so some of us went lookin' for her. She's been sayin' shit all over town. Then I stayed over at Johnny and Seth's apartment." Rose slides her big sunglasses back on even though the clouds are still heavy. "Beats being home alone. It's too quiet without Bobby around. 'Least it's only temporary."

"We're so proud of each and every Tom and Becky this year. They've worked so hard these past few months learning to be the best ambassadors for Hannibal. They are true representatives of America's hometown! Mark Twain would be proud of these youngsters, too, who help us keep our history alive. Thank you, Toms and Beckys, for your service. Let's have a round of applause for all of them."

"How about you?" Rose asks.

"Went out with Sammy again. Had dinner at the farm. Then we watched a late movie." There wasn't much movie watching, actually, but Rose doesn't need to know everything.

"And none of this would be possible without the parents. Let's hear it for the moms and dads."

"It's a regular thing, huh? You and Sammy, I mean."

"I've got some time on my hands now that you got me fired, Rose," I remind her. "It's no big deal really with Sammy." That's not the whole truth, either. Since the wedding and the accident, I've spent a lot of time with Sammy. It feels urgent. Like we might expire any minute.

"Before our big announcement, let's hear from some of the outgoing Toms and Beckys."

Suzanne and Tanya walk right in front of us without saying hello. Maybe they don't remember me. Or maybe they saw the whole Josh-and-Rose fight in the parking lot after the Riverboat Cruise and want nothing to do with us. Can't say that I blame them. And the feeling is mutual.

"As you come up to the microphone, tell us your favorite moment from your year of service to this great program."

Bobby looks around the crowd and stops when he sees us. We both wave. *The fantods*, I think. I certainly wouldn't have had the courage at Bobby's age to do what he's doing. I'll bet every other person on that stage has been going to school together on the same side of town since birth, but I'll also bet they don't know what the fantods are.

There is a couple in front of me holding hands, two among the few African American faces in this white crowd. They're both wearing expensive suits like they each just came from important meetings. "Who are they?" I whisper to Rose.

"Dr. and Dr. Cooper. From the hospital. Moved here about a year ago. That's their daughter." She nods toward the stage.

One by one, outgoing Toms and Beckys say their little speeches about the past year. One Tom cracks the crowd up when he mentions how much he enjoyed kissing all the Beckys. A Becky talks about "goin' strollin'" and links arms with a Tom to demonstrate.

"Now, the moment you've been waiting for."

A lady in a raincoat in the front row turns around to shush us. Rose shushes her back.

Onstage, last year's official Tom Sawyer weaves his way through a row of seated Becky contestants. He teases them, leaning in for a kiss and pulling back just before contact. The crowd oohs and aahs. At one point Tom's fishing pole wraps around one of the Becky's knees. There's a moment of confusion as the fishing line is untangled.

Finally, after a few more laps, Tom stops before a Becky with blond braids and braces. Her cheeks turn red. Then Tom plants a quick peck on her neighbor Shelly's cheek and the crowd explodes. That single kiss means Hannibal's next official Becky Thatcher has been announced. Tears stream down the face of a mom to my right, whose daughter wasn't the one.

"Ladies and Gentlemen, please help me in congratulating our new Becky Thatcher, Michelle Conley."

Bobby beams, but the rest of the Toms are anxious as they wait for their fates.

"Ain't that Tanya and Dave's daughter?" Rose asks. "That's the Becky Bobby's been practicin' with."

I don't tell her that Bobby called Shelly his girlfriend. Rose might have a fit, and this is not a moment about Rose.

"And now, who will be our next Tom Sawyer? I'd like to invite Emma Dawson, our reigning Becky, to pass along her slate."

Emma skips up to the row of Toms. She carries a small slate with the words *I love Tom* painted on it in white. Bobby sits in the middle. Emma stops and whispers something in the ear of the boy next to him. Then she skips to the end of the row.

"Who's the boy next to Bobby? He looks familiar," I whisper to Rose.

"Brandon Hanson. You know him. Remember Heather Hanson? It's her nephew. She's been coaching him through the whole pageant."

I look around the crowd until I find her face. There she is in her country club tennis jacket. Lots of gold. She's definitely had a nose job. My high school bitterness bubbles up again. "I hope she, I mean he, loses."

"He will. Because Bobby's gonna win!" Bobby will win either way, I think. He's better than the Heather Hansons of this town.

Onstage, Emma twirls a braid and assesses Bobby. Then she links her arm in his and passes the slate to Nate, the boy on the other side of him. Suzanne screams, "That's *my* baby!" She and Tanya are hopping up and down together. Onstage, Bobby shrugs. The crowd claps and whistles. All the Toms and Beckys stand to congratulate each other. Bobby crosses the stage quickly, twirls Shelly out of a conciliatory hug with a losing Becky, and puts his arm around her shoulder. She kisses him on the cheek.

"At least he doesn't look too disappointed," I say.

"Oh, who cares? That stuff is so rigged," Rose sneers loudly. A few people around us stop and stare. Tanya and Suzanne are busy celebrating. The Coopers turn around to make eye contact that says, *If you think it's rigged for you...*

"I guess I care," I say, realizing it's true. We probably all wanted to be Becky once. She was ideal: beautiful, demure, and well mannered. It didn't hurt that her daddy was a respected judge in town, too. But, more importantly, I just didn't want to be who I was. It's hard to move forward in a town stuck in time. I always thought I had to run away to be someone different, but plenty of these parents love this place and what it stands for. And they want things for their kids just as much as Rose, and probably Josh, too, want for Bobby. Maybe their lives aren't easy either. They've just got different problems. "Didn't you want to be Becky?" I ask Rose.

She snorts and puts on her big black sunglasses. "Not if it meant bein' like them." Rose nods at the stage, where cameras are snapping away.

"I always wanted things to be different," I admit.

"And I always thought things were good enough." Rose reaches for my hand and puts her head on my shoulder. "Or at least I wasn't really willin' to change 'em. You changed plenty for both of us, Laura."

"Think so?" I ask, wondering if it's true. It's not a sore spot when Rose points it out.

"Yep. For the better. And you came back."

"He looks pretty happy up there," I say "'Least he tried. That's more than I ever did."

"He did. That's for sure." Rose watches the stage where Bobby is high-fiving the Toms. She looks up to the darkening sky. "Guess we'll need a ride home."

As we drive, with Bobby tucked in the seat between us, more rain rolls in. Bobby chatters on and on about how much fun it was to watch Shelly win. He even says that Nate, the official Tom, is one of his friends. As one of the ten finalists, Bobby still gets to represent Hannibal and travel. He chatters about an upcoming trip to Florida, Missouri, to visit where Mark Twain was born. Ms. Keller is going to chaperone. He doesn't seem to mind losing at all.

"You looked pretty brave up there, boy," Rose says. She squeezes Bobby's shoulder and lets her hand linger. He doesn't shrug it off.

Lightning cracks from the clouds in front of us, and my thoughts turn to Sammy. He's probably out working on the levee with his brother. Last night he said that another storm might do them in. Flood levels mean a lot when you're already underwater.

MAMA IS SERVING GRILLED hot dogs with all the fixings. She's set out canned chili, bottled relish, and chopped raw onion. A can of Easy Cheese stands beside the packages of buns and open bags of Ruffles chips. A supersized white tub of French's dip has two plastic spoons sticking out of it. I take a knife and slice through the charcoaled skin of my dog. Then I plunge the Easy Cheese nozzle into the cavity and squeeze. It's creamy and orange, and the can burps like it's empty. Trey grabs the can and shakes it. "Stop stealin' the good stuff," he says, elbowing me out of the way.

"You know I could knock you off them crutches." I cut a slit in both the hot dogs on his plate, and he hands me back the can. "You want relish, too?"

"Yes, please. And a Pepsi. With ice."

"You're pushin' it."

Trey smiles. He needs to shave and shower. The accident has aged him. He looks grubby and tired like Daddy did before he left.

"Aunt Laura, will you make me a plate, too?" Bobby asks, nudging Trey. Bobby is still wearing his Tom costume, straw hat and all. He doesn't want to take it off.

"Happily," I say.

"Oh, I see how it is," Trey teases. "Where'd Rose run off to?"

"Said she had to run errands. She'll be back." I get them both settled with plates and tuck a napkin into each of their shirts like a bib. I leave them together in lawn chairs and pat them both on the head before making a plate of my own. Pamela and the girls cluck noisily at their feet hoping for scraps.

Daisy's littlest kids are splashing in a plastic pool Mama filled up in the side yard away from her patio. It's generous of her to even let us sit in her favorite spot. The pool sits on uneven ground so water keeps pouring out and snaking its way through the gravel. The sun is back out, momentarily, and the water dries in minutes. It's hard to breathe in the humidity. It feels like we're all covered in a hot, wet blanket. The kids call for a refill and Daisy stands with the hose in one hand and a Pepsi in the other. The cold water makes them squeal, and she splashes it on their baby bellies. "They ain't always this cute," she says to me, pulling a cigarette from her back pocket and lighting it, "especially my older ones."

"You're smokin'?" I ask. My face is shock and judgment. It doesn't take a nursing degree to know you don't smoke when you're pregnant.

"Just one a day. For my nerves. You had kids like this, you'd need 'em, too." Daisy complains some more, but all I see is how simple and happy her kids are. A plastic pool and a hose is enough to make their summer day perfect.

"I wouldn't mind kids like that," I admit. "You look pretty lucky to me." Daisy puts out her cigarette beneath her sandal and turns toward me. She smiles and she's still pretty and much calmer with the smoke. I always thought kids would get in the way of what I wanted. I thought it was a matter of self-preservation, but underneath the gruff, Daisy looks like a proud mama. Maybe kids just make the things you want more, or maybe they change the things you want in a good way. I wouldn't mind finding out. Every time I've handed over a baby to its mama in the past few weeks, it's been more like an ache than a relief.

Aunt Betty and Mama are on the front porch rocking together on a bench swing. Pamela clucks in Mama's lap pecking grain from her hand. I bought the swing for Mama last week when they were on sale at Walmart. It's still got the price tag hanging from the metal frame. Mama said not to cut it off until we knew if it was a good one, but I know better. She wants everyone to know how much it cost. Like everyone in town doesn't know that bench swings were on sale last week at Walmart.

The TV blares the news inside the house, but nobody's watching it:

Quoted in an article from the *New York Times*, "Fundamentally, we've changed the landscape of the Mississippi River Basin," said Andrew Fahlund, senior vice president of conservation for the advocacy group American Rivers. "We've basically developed all the way up to the edge, and, really, the water has no place to go but to run off and create these massive floods." Fahlund concedes that floodplains that could be realistically reclaimed are "limited" but said that should not deter the government from attempting to purchase certain low-lying farmlands, to contract farmers to allow their land to be flooded during wet seasons, or to relocate outright some small, rural communities built in flood-prone areas. "We need a combined approach," said Fahlund. "Levees need to be our last line of defense, not our only line of defense."

I grab the pitcher from the fridge and refill Aunt Betty's tea. "So, what's your plan, missy?" she asks.

"Don't have one," I say, sinking into the space beside her on the bench.

"Sure you do. You can't stop smilin', so I know you're cookin' up somethin'. And you're bein' all nice." She fans herself with a paper plate and studies me. Her housedress is soaked through with sweat. I don't answer.

"Sammy?" she tries. Ice clinks on the side of her iced-tea glass. It's melting fast.

"Don't know. He said it was up to me. To stay. Or to go. He won't get in my way." I grab another paper plate and fan her, too. She looks momentarily relieved. "It's easier to be with someone else when you know yourself a little more, know what I mean?" It doesn't just feel good, it feels right, and I kind of hate him for making me fall for him all over again, especially when I still can't forgive him. He said he probably wouldn't make it downtown tonight. He and Lance are going to try to reinforce the levee one last time.

"You kind of wish he would get in your way?"

"Might make things easier," I say. I watch Daisy drying off the kids with a beach towel. Before she can catch them, they dive back into the kiddie pool and soak themselves all over again.

"You'd hate him for it, Laura. That ain't how you hold on to people."

There's a pit in my stomach. "Don't know that Sammy wants to hold on." Coming home was right, but I don't fit anymore than I ever did.

We both turn to watch Bobby and Trey play cards. Trey's

taken to keeping a deck tucked in his back pocket at all times. Bruises still line his jaw and arms, but he looks like he's put some weight back on. His eyes are clear again and his spirits are up.

"He lost the Tom thing, huh? Seems okay to me," Aunt Betty says, nodding toward Bobby in his full costume.

"Bobby's tough. Rose said he could come stay with me a few weeks over the summer. If I go again."

"Well. That'll make it nice, won't it?"

"It will. He was amazing on that stage today, so gracious about losing. He knew exactly who he was. Those other kids with more don't bother him at all. He's certainly been through plenty with his parents, but he was so confident today and mature. I'm so proud of him."

"I remember that feeling. Makes me remember how scared you were to leave for nursing school and how proud I was."

"Scared? I wasn't scared. I was ready to go. Couldn't wait to get out of town."

"Huh," she says. "That's not how I remember it." She shakes her head at me and cracks up. I stop fanning her and stare.

"Really?" I ask. Her memory must be fading.

"Oh, you put on a brave front, sugar. Sure. But you forget your people know you pretty well."

"I was certainly scared when I got there. That I remember clearly. All the other girls were so prepared. I didn't know a thing."

"But you worked hard. It paid off."

"I should have worked harder."

"What d'ya mean?"

"I should of stayed in school. I was so anxious to get my first job, to make some money and support myself. I took the first offer for a CNA and left. I wish I'd stayed in to get my RN degree. It would of only taken another couple of years."

"Is it too late? You act like you're way over the hill. Don't let your mama put you down. She's always been scared you'll want too much and lose. From where I'm sittin' seems like you could do anything you want. Go back to school. Just stop bellyachin' about it. Do it."

"What 'bout Trey and Mama and you?" I ask.

"Kiddo, we were all fine before you came back and we'll be fine when you're out there livin' again. Folks think there's a right or a wrong choice in life. There ain't. You just choose and make it work. Bloom where you're planted, I say." I refill her tea glass and she wipes her face with a handkerchief. Then she stuffs it back into her bra. "That's what I told your mama about your daddy, too."

"You mean after he left?"

She puts her iced tea to her forehead to cool it. "Your daddy would be sittin' on this porch right now if your mama hadn't put her foot down. He never left y'all. She made him leave. Kicked him out. And it weren't easy. She loved that man. But she couldn't change him. And she didn't want a drunk raisin' her kids."

I stop swinging our bench and hold very still while the news sinks in. Would things have turned out differently with Daddy around? Probably for the worse. That's a hell of a choice Mama had to make.

"Your mama left, too, ya know? You probably don't even

remember. You were just a little thing. She packed your bags, dropped you off at my house, and rode away on the back of your daddy's motorcycle. I never thought we'd see her again. But she came back. Alone."

"I never knew that."

"There's a lot you don't know. A lot you assume. A lot you're wrong about, sugar." Aunt Betty pats my knee and looks at me with her watery eyes. "She did the best she could. Go easy on your mama, okay?"

I nod and wipe away some tears. My daddy never left me. Aunt Betty and I rock in silence and watch Bobby beat Trey at another round of poker. His straw hat hangs loosely on his back, but his red suspenders are still tight.

"He still thinks he's Tom," I say with a chuckle.

"Maybe he is." Aunt Betty's right again. About a lot of things.

After the cookout, I help Mama do the dishes, and Aunt Betty takes a nap under the window air-conditioning unit. Bobby and Trey are sitting at the kitchen table playing poker and betting with pennies. Another storm is swirling up outside, so we turn on the radio for updates. I'm praying they don't cancel the fireworks; it's the first time I can remember all of us planning to go together since that Fourth of July when everything broke.

In the kitchen, Mama turns up the radio and the announcer says the fireworks are delayed by at least an hour. She asks Bobby if he wants to watch the fireworks in New York City on the TV with her. He rubs his eyes, nods yes. Mama, Bobby, and Trey settle themselves on the couch. Bobby's taken his hat off but he's still wearing the rest of his Tom costume. Thunder rumbles so loud that the trailer shakes a little and stirs Aunt Betty from her nap. Mama looks up at the ceiling like she's waiting for something. Then the rain comes.

A loud knock on the screen door tells me Rose is back and probably a little tipsy. She wouldn't normally knock, certainly not loudly. "Some errands, Rose," I say, holding open the door. She's soaked from the rain. "You walked?"

"Couldn't get a ride. None of 'em wanted to leave the party." She takes the towel I offer and leans against the kitchen counter while she dries her hair. "Wanta have some fun?"

"What kind of fun?"

"The kind we used to have before you got all square and in love again. Come on, Sammy is busy anyway. You might as well settle for a night with your best friend."

Mama turns up the volume on the TV and tells us to keep it down. "Is this going to be fun for you or fun for me?" I say in a low voice.

"Let's slash Josh's tires," Rose whispers like we're kids at a slumber party again.

"No way. What would that prove?"

"It'd prove he shouldn't mess with us."

"Us?"

"Come on. Just drive me. That's what friends do." Rose's face is fresh and flushed from the rain, like when we were kids and ran down to the river to jump in. Rose called it baptism by Mississippi. I grab my car keys and Rose reaches for my hand.

We leave Bobby with Mama and drive over to Josh's trailer. Kayla's car is there, too. The house is dark but a TV flickers inside and lights up the room. Shadows move about. The rain is coming down in sheets, and I'm not getting out of the car.

"This is stupid, Rose. Josh won't even know it's you who did his tires."

"Oh, he'll know."

"I ain't doin' it. You're on your own."

"You owe me, Laura. You know you do."

It's a gut punch. It's a guilt trip. It almost works. "And what about Bobby?" I ask.

"He ain't here, is he?" Rose turns around like she's looking for Bobby in the backseat, like maybe I think she's such a bad mom that she just forgot him back there.

"This isn't a game. It's your life. It's Bobby's life. You could get arrested. You could lose Bobby for good if the judge finds out."

"Oh, you're one to give life advice. Coming back home with your tail between your legs."

"My life fell apart, Rose. I didn't destroy it."

Rose squints out through the window, like she's trying to decide what to do. She leans over and turns my wipers on full blast as if she just needs a clear view.

"This could all blow up in your face. Josh could haul you back to court. He could tell the judge about the shit you've pulled. You've bragged about gettin' revenge all over town. Everyone knows you call him the Bastard."

"Well, he is one. Even you know that." Rose puts her pocket-knife back in her purse. It doesn't look big enough to do the job anyway. "He told me you slept with him. He had a very different story than yours."

"He what? He's a liar."

"The problem with liars is they like to talk."

"I didn't sleep with him. I told you that."

"What would Sammy say?"

"We were broke up. Sammy doesn't need to know nothing. You are just stirrin' the pot, Rose. We should go. Josh could call the police. Then look where you'd be. They've already questioned you twice. I'll bet they'd like nothin' more than to arrest you for trespassing."

"Don't you think he'd have called 'em by now if he was plannin' to? Clearly, he ain't." She thinks this is all a joke. She and Josh might be enjoying their cat-and-mouse game with Bobby as the bait and the rest of us just don't know it.

"And what about Bobby?"

"What about me?" Rose whines.

"You have Bobby. That's more than a lot. More than me."

"For God's sake, Laura. For the thousandth time, *This is not about Bobby*!"

"When you're his mama, it's all about Bobby. When you going to grow up?"

"Grow up and run away, you mean?"

"That's not what I mean."

"It's exactly what you mean." Rose puts her hand to the window as I start the car and pull away, like she's trying to feel the rain from the inside.

Village Pariah

Mark Twain rewrote the opening lines of *Adventures of Huckleberry Finn* many times before he got it right. The content of Huck's introduction didn't change, but the revisions reshaped the dialect until it sounded authentic. Twain knew these people. He was one of them. Wherever he traveled, his tribe was with him. And he left a part of himself behind. But that ain't no matter.

In his autobiography, Twain shared that Huck's character was based on Tom Blankenship, the son of Hannibal's town drunkard, who lived in a ramshackle house a few doors down from Samuel Clemens's boyhood home. His family was so poor they couldn't afford school, so Tom Blankenship got to do whatever he pleased with his days. His freedom must have been irksome to the young Sam. In *The Adventures of Tom Sawyer*, he describes Huck affectionately as "idle, and lawless, and vulgar, and bad," which made the town children love him even more. Even with the aforementioned warning, readers fall for Huck. Just like Tom Sawyer. Just like Mark Twain.

The house where Tom Blankenship's family lived was torn down more than one hundred years ago, but the land remains. It was donated to the Mark Twain Home Foundation and a new house, based on photos from 1911, was built on the site. Out back, there's a plentiful vegetable garden that Tom's family would have appreciated.

Adventures of Huckleberry Finn was first published in 1884 in England and it came out the following year in the U.S. It didn't immediately cause controversy, though some objected to its "coarse" language, like *sweating* instead of *perspiring*. Mark Twain took on weighty topics such as slavery and racism, topics that critics didn't attend to until the mid-twentieth century. The book continues to cause trouble today and is sometimes banned from classrooms. The distinction would probably make Mark Twain excessively proud.

CHAPTER SIXTEEN

BACK AT MAMA'S, Bobby's curled up asleep on the couch. Mama's sitting beside him watching TV. She scoots over to make room for Rose, who settles into her place with a sigh. I check on Trey to see if he took his pain medicine, but he's already snoring. Aunt Betty decides she doesn't want to wait for the fireworks anymore and asks me to give her a lift home. I drive through sheets of rain, gripping my steering wheel. The weather just won't let up. Mama said they announced on the news that most of the Fourth's evening activities were rained out. The creeks under both bridges are overflowing and the main road is impassable.

"Take Route O," Aunt Betty says from behind closed eyes. The cookout wore her down. "Honey, I've lived through a few floods. This ain't nothin'. Most problems look better in the mornin'." She pats my cheek and I reach over to hold her hand.

At the house, I grab my umbrella in the backseat and walk

her to the door. "Think on it before you do whatever you're about to do," she says, kissing me on the cheek. "You'll make it nice." She pats my face again, this time a little harder. Then she lets the screen door slam shut behind her.

Thunder rolls at my back. I dial Josh, but there's no service. The rain has stopped; the roads have mostly cleared. I drive right by Josh's place on my way home, so I decide to confront him in person without Rose as an audience.

Kayla's gone, and Josh is sitting on the metal stairs of his trailer, smoking, when I pull up. His shirt is off; his arms are covered in snake tattoos. There's a rebel flag on his right pectoral. He used to crack Rose and me up by flexing and making the flag ripple. The red, white, and blue have faded. It looks cheap now.

I roll down my window on the passenger side. "Rose told me you told her," I call through the window. "Nothin' happened between us, Josh."

Josh shakes his head at me. He takes his time putting out his cigarette, then walks over to my car and leans down through the window. He tries the door but it's locked. Permanently. I'm glad I never had it fixed. "Door don't work. Sorry."

"Least you could do is come inside and talk like you're civilized," Josh says. "Known each other a long time, haven't we?"

"I'm on my way home. Can't really stop." I inch my car forward so he knows that I haven't even taken my foot off the gas. "I just want to make sure you didn't have any ideas about telling anyone else."

Josh grins. "About us?"

"There is no 'us.'"

"What kind of manners are those?" He shakes his head like he's disappointed in me. "What would your boyfriend say about the way you're actin'?"

"I ain't actin' like nothing, Josh. This doesn't involve me. You and Rose want to keep fightin'? Fine. Least you could do is be straight for Bobby's sake."

"Well, that's what I wanta talk about. Bobby. I'm worried 'bout him." Josh pulls two longnecks from a cooler on the porch, pops off their tops with his hand on the bench, offers one through the window to me.

I shake my head. "No thanks." I put the car in park. "Why are you worried about Bobby?"

"I don't think all this fightin's good for him." He takes a long swig off the beer. "Said he wants to come live with me. For good." He leans half of his body in the car.

"He wouldn't do that to his mama."

"There's things you don't know, Laura." Josh finishes one beer, tosses the bottle in the yard, and starts on the second. "I'm worried about Rose, too. Can't you come inside for a minute?" He steps back from the car, disarmed. He shoves his hands in his pockets just like Bobby does. "I'll make you a deal. I won't tell Sammy if you'll come inside."

Josh's trailer is tidy. The dishes are washed and stacked up in the strainer to dry. His kitchen table is clear except for one blue plastic cup with *Bobby* written in red marker on the side. There's a basketball and a pair of kids' sneakers in one corner.

Pictures of Bobby and Josh together are framed on top of the TV and the gun case.

"Make yourself comfortable," Josh says. "I'll get us some beers."

I stand and look at the photos. There's one of them playing Putt-Putt golf at Sawyer's Creek. There's one of them at a St. Louis Cardinals game and Bobby is waving a huge foam finger that says GO CARDS! There's another picture where it looks like the side was ripped off. Rose, I assume.

"He means everything to me, Laura. You gotta know that." He stands close, looks at the photos with me. Then he crosses to the couch, puts his hands over his face like he's crying or something. He sniffs a little.

"Me too," I say.

Josh pats the space on the sofa beside him. "You're his favorite by far. You know how much the kid talks about you? It's Aunt Laura this and Aunt Laura that. You'd think you walked on water."

"Did he tell you he'd like to spend the summer with me? Wherever I end up?" I take the beer from Josh and sit down next to him. He smells like sweat and Old Spice.

"That'd be great," Josh says, clinking his beer bottle with mine. "Maybe I'll even drive him down."

"He's the one thing that might make me stay, though. Maybe put down some roots."

"He'd like that," Josh says, leaning toward me. "I might, too." His hand slides up my thigh. "It's good to set things right, don't ya think?" I push his hand away. He reaches for the back of my neck, pulls me to him, and unzips his pants.

"What the hell do you think you're doin'?" I say, slapping at arms that are suddenly around my backside.

"Making things right." His teeth are clenched; his face is hard. "You owe me some fun for all the times I've kept my mouth shut." His grin is mean; his hands close around my hair.

"I don't owe you shit," I say, spitting into his face. Josh lets go, wipes my spit out of his eye.

"You're just a bitch, too!" he yells at my back as I run out the door. I throw my beer bottle, and it hits the side of the table and shatters before it lands on the floor. Glass and foam splatter the carpet. "I'll let Bobby know you were here. He'll know everything! And your boyfriend, too!" Josh screams. I slam the door shut behind me and get into my car. I'm halfway down the block when Bobby's slingshot slides out from under the passenger seat. I put the car in park, open the door, and grab the biggest rock I can find. I retrace my steps in the dark. Then I use the slingshot to shoot it at Josh's truck. I can't see it land, but I hear glass shatter. I wish Rose could hear it, too. Josh'll never believe a girl could aim like that. The Bastard.

I'M DRIVING FASTER THAN I should when I hit the gravel road that leads to Sammy's family's farm. Tears are leaking down my face, and I don't really remember making the turns. I park behind a tractor on the side of the house and walk around to the porch that faces the pasture. Sammy's daddy is rocking in a chair. His dog, Everett, walks over and sniffs my feet. It's not the same Everett I knew ten years ago. Sammy told me his dad just keeps naming the replacement dogs the same name. This must be at least Everett III. "Well, looky here," Mr. McGuire says, clearing his throat. "We've got company." Then he spits tobacco off the side of the porch. His aim is just right.

"Evenin', Mr. McGuire. Sammy around?" I ask.

"Out with his brother at the levee. Don't know why, though. Think they can fight Mother Nature, I suppose. Can't fight the big guy, that's for sure. Wanta have a seat?" He waves a bony finger toward an empty rocking chair. The chair creaks against the floorboards when I sit down. I wipe my eyes and smear away the mascara from my cheeks. I feel calmer just being here on this porch. Everett lets out a moan and flops himself sideways. I reach over and scratch his belly, and he kicks a leg spastically in gratitude.

"Did you know that just pettin' a dog lowers your blood pressure? That's a proven fact."

"I didn't," I tell him. "At work, sometimes they bring in therapy dogs for the patients. It makes the whole floor happy."

I keep scratching and look out over the cow pasture, which is mostly a sloppy mess of mud. The cows have been moved to higher ground. To my right is row upon row of corn, brown and rotting at the stalk from all the water. The soybeans in front are making it, though. "The water'll come straight through there," Mr. McGuire says, nodding toward the soybeans. "Always does. I'm too old to stop it." He spits again, aiming at the exact same spot.

"Levee might hold," I say. It sounds stupid even as it comes out of my mouth.

"Won't hold. Won't be as bad as '93, but we'll still get wet."

"How's your neighbor?"

"Low and dry. Every time. Corporate. Fancy levees and all."

"Don't seem fair," I say.

"Who ever told you life was fair?" He chuckles and reaches down to pat Everett.

We watch the land together. In Hannibal people sit on porches and watch nothing. For hours. Dirt roads. Crops. Kids playing. Weather. But maybe it's something after all. Maybe the difference is whether we wait and see what comes up the road or reach out and grab it before it gets us.

"Why don't you take the four-wheeler out and give those boys a drink?" he says, pointing his finger at the barn. "They're probably parched. Keys are in it. Cooler's packed. Go on and take it."

Everett follows me out to the barn and sniffs at me while I climb on the four-wheeler. He wags his tail and it's encouraging. I strap the cooler on with bungee cords, turn the key, and feel the engine beneath me. It takes a few starts to remember how to ride one, but then I let loose and fly. I stick to the path between the fields and head straight for the levee. It feels good to have the wind on my face, to be going somewhere fast. Ten minutes later I see Lance's truck and people moving about on top of the hill. One of them must be Sammy. I stop about a hundred yards back because the water is so high. It's seeping through the sides; the levee looks like an igloo melting into itself.

Just as I'm climbing off the four-wheeler, I hear an engine coming up from behind. Lance comes over the hill on a bulldozer and pulls up beside me. "You lost?" he calls over the sound of the motor. Then he smiles and cuts the engine. His face and hair are speckled in mud. He's wearing black waders up to his thighs and mud is caked on them, too.

"Just came by to visit Sammy," I say. "Anything I can do to help?"

Lance looks at the levee and back at me. Then he climbs down from the bulldozer cab in one swift jump, walks to where I'm still straddling the four-wheeler, and leans over the handlebars real close. "Well," he begins, "the only thing you could probably do to help is stay away." It stuns me. I came here for some kindness, and it's just another slap. Lance has always been quiet, but I thought he liked me. "The way I see it," Lance continues, "is you've got my brother all tied up in knots again. I don't really know what game you're playin', but I have a feelin' it ain't gonna end well." I got the impression he wasn't thrilled about Sammy bringing me as a date to his wedding, but I thought it was because the divorce was so fresh. "We've got work here. Real work. It may be a losin' battle but we're fightin' it anyway. You gonna help with that?"

"I will if I can," I say. "I'm not here to hurt Sammy."

"Then why are you here, Laura?" Lance keeps his grip tight on the handlebars. This is his territory. I'm an intruder. An unwelcome one.

"I'm tryin' to make things right," I sputter. Tears sting my eyes. I wonder if what I just said is true. Who am I trying to make things right for? Me? Sammy? Bobby? Trey? And who am I to say what right really is? After what I've done, who am I to judge anyone?

"Here's what I think," he says, reaching into the cooler for a bottle of water. He drains it and wipes his mouth before he continues. "You're still tryin' to figure out why in the world you let go of a guy like my brother ten years ago. I think you made a big ol' mistake, and you regret it. I think that you saw something, made yourself a snap judgment, and ran away, like a coward."

A coward? I'm the coward? Lance doesn't know what I know. He wasn't there the night Sammy sabotaged the neighbor's levee to save their own. "What mistake is that, Lance?"

"Sammy didn't do it. He doesn't play that way. He's honest until the end, and you're a fool for not knowin' that. I breached the goddamned levee. And I'd do it again. And you can judge the likes of me all you want, Laura."

"You?" I sputter. "You ruined a family. They lost their farm. Their father killed himself. He had kids."

"The Wilkenses? That ain't all my fault."

"Wait. They were the Wilkenses?"

"Crystal and her brother live on your street. They're fine. Somebody had to lose. Us or them. And they're fine."

"I've seen 'em. They got evicted last week."

"That ain't on me. There's a few things you just don't get," Lance says. "Sammy was tryin' to fix it. He told me. That's what you saw, and I figured when you left him like that I knew why, what you thought. But I didn't tell him, 'cause he was better off without you. And I was right. You aren't from here any-more." He twists the four-wheeler's handlebars away, pointing me back in the direction that I came. "Go on. Get outta here."

I'm paralyzed. Stunned. Lance climbs back on the bull-dozer and drives it to the base of the levee. Sammy notices me and waves. If Sammy didn't do it, then I've been blaming him all these years for nothing.

Sammy climbs down from the top of the levee and takes off his gloves as he crosses the path between us. He nods at Lance, who grinds past him without a word. Then Sammy swings his legs wide and climbs on the four-wheeler behind me. It feels right. To be this close. To have him around me. I lean back into his arms, and he wraps them around my chest and squeezes.

"Didn't think I'd run into you here," Sammy says.

"Didn't think I'd be here," I answer, closing my eyes. At least that part is true.

"It's gonna rain again," he says, looking up at the sky. "Nothin' we can do now."

"Doesn't sound like you to give up." I turn around on the four-wheeler and put my legs over his in a straddle so I can see his face. There's mud in his hair, and it's crusted on his ears. I scrape some of it off and brush his hair from his face. His brown eyes are rimmed red. He feels solid to me, like a wall. He smells like sand and earth; the familiarity catches in my throat.

"I've been out here all day. Lance was still workin' when I got home last night. Not that it's done any good."

"Sorry I kept you up so late," I say, running my hands up and down his arms.

"I kept me up so late, Laura. Had a good time. You?"

I nod. "Anything I can do to help?"

"Stay."

"Not sure what good that'll do, but I'll hang out. I do know my way around a sandbag."

"No. I mean stay. I'm not offerin' much, but we could make another go of it."

"You and me?"

"Why not?"

"Here? In Hannibal?"

A light rain starts to fall. I wait too long to answer. He turns away.

"You don't know everything, Sammy."

"You'd be surprised by what I know. You'd be surprised what I can forgive." He leans forward and buries his head in my hair. Then he looks me straight in the eye. "I'm just sorry you didn't get to say good-bye to Mother, that you drove all that way and didn't come in to give your regards."

"Who told you?"

"Does it matter?" It doesn't.

"I'm sorry," I say, holding out my hand to him. He hesitates. "I'm sorry for so many things. I thought it was you. I thought you breached the levee that night."

"Me? Why would I do that?"

"I don't know. You came runnin' back to the truck. You were soaked. There wasn't anyone else around. I thought I couldn't trust you. And if you could do that, you could do worse. I was wrong." Then he takes my hand and kisses it. His lips are gentle, and I don't deserve them. He doesn't tell me it was Lance, but we both know.

"Was it really all that different, all that better somewhere else?" he asks.

I don't answer. I don't have an answer. Sammy's good enough. He always was. Tears are falling down my face unchecked. Thunder cracks over the water.

"I had this notion all these dumb years that you cheated. I decided this one thing you did when we were kids was the reason we couldn't be together. There were rules. You broke them. I thought it meant that you'd always be on your family's side and never on mine." It's hard but I have to say this. "Turns out you didn't. Turns out I did. And now it doesn't matter at all. I left. And not just because of you. I left because of me."

"And now?"

"I want a place. Something that's mine. Someone I belong to. I do, Sammy. But it isn't here."

"But it could be with me," Sammy says. I look up to meet his eyes, to see how much he means what he just said. A new round of tears well up and spill, but this time I'm smiling, too.

"Maybe I'll come visit you, Laura. Wherever your tide takes you."

"Maybe you should."

"Maybe I should of a long time ago."

I bite my bottom lip and nod my head yes. I don't want to run backward. I can't change any of that. Rose was right. But I can move forward, even if the path is winding and uncertain. "Maybe you should of." I smile and tuck myself back into his arms.

"I gotta go. Lance needs my help," he says, squeezing me tight before he climbs off the back.

"I'll call you, Sammy. I will." He nods and leans over to kiss me.

"Be sure you leave the four-wheeler inside the barn," he calls, scrambling back up the levee. "Rain's gonna get heavy. We're all gettin' soaked."

I drive the four-wheeler back the way I came but faster, spinning up mud behind my tires as I go. There's a chance I'll get stuck. The speed can sometimes make the tires dig in deeper, but I don't care. I just want to be moving.

I park the four-wheeler in the barn and wave to Mr. McGuire, who doesn't wave back. Everett lifts his head off the porch floor, but he doesn't come out to meet me, either. They both just watch and wait.

I drive my car down the road that snakes the levee twelve miles south to a fence that marks Sammy's family's property.

The storm clouds are at my back. They're close, but they haven't reached me yet.

I leave my car and cross under the barbed-wire fence. Below Sammy's farm the land is mostly dry. Green soybeans sprout in the breeze. Miles of healthy corn plants sway. The levee is holding, and it makes me angry. There's no one else around, no bodies frantically stacking sandbags in hopes of a miracle. The levee is tight and packed, clearly done by machinery, not hands.

I jog a mile down to the spot I think Sammy parked a decade before. Nothing's changed. It looks the same. Two enormous maples frame the curve in the grass wall. A yellow sign declares the mile marker. Sandbags have been stacked on top in a neat row to reinforce the barrier.

I stand on top of the levee and stomp my feet like a child, kicking at the grass and the dirt. My face is wet again, and it's a relief. Something explodes in the sky toward Hannibal. Lightning, I assume, but then white and blue flashes. Green showers of sparkles. They light up the darkness. The fireworks. They set them off, after all. It's the Fourth of July in my hometown, and I'm standing on a wall trying to hold back the Mississippi. The water is so high it laps at the levee, licking the barrier. I wonder if Aunt Betty can hear the boom from the fireworks all the way out at her house. I hope Mama is curled up with a sleeping Bobby on the couch watching the show in New York City. Maybe Rose will even stay put and enjoy the peace. But what I want most is for them to know that they're my tribe, that everything I feel and wish for them is real, and that I'm grateful to have a place to call home. Huckleberry Finn whispers in my ear, *"All right, then, I'll go to hell,"* and I know exactly what to do.

I reach for a sandbag in the middle and tug, but it's wedged tight.

I grab one off the top and roll it down to my feet.

Then I grab another. And two more. As many as I can manage.

Water pours over the side and soaks my ankles.

It's cold. The rain has begun. It's freezing. It numbs my face.

People think a flood is a gush of roaring water, but the truth is a levee breaks down slowly. The water trickles in at first. The liberation builds momentum until there's nothing left to hold it back. The river's to blame. When you grow up on the banks of the Mississippi, you need an escape route, a safe passage. You never know when the water is going to rise and you have to run. You can leave and hold on. You can stay and dig in. A flood makes fertile ground on both banks.

Acknowledgments

Hannibal, Missouri, is and always will be my hometown. I love its people, especially those who raised me and cheered me on. You are my roots, friends and family, and I owe you everything.

I'm grateful to the MFA students and faculty at Southern Illinois University for their kindness and support. To Allison Joseph and Jon Tribble for sharing their *Crab Orchard Review* office wisdom. Thanks to Jacinda Townsend, who showed me that writing and mothering are compatible. And bouquets of homage to Beth Lordan, the toughest and kindest mentor when I needed it the most.

Lovely friends have endured early drafts and embraced me anyway. Cheers to Kristen Beracha, Caron Martinez, Rachel Maizes, Stina Oakes, Heather McDonald, Blake Sanz, and Catherine McGrady. Thanks to book clubs and readers along the way, especially Kate Kile, the classiest book lover I know.

This book wouldn't exist without Wendy Besel Hahn's friendship. Thanks for always being a Skype call away and for picking me up and helping me put these pages back together so many times.

Huge hugs to my Bread Loaf community, especially the king of the mountain, Luis Alberto Urrea. Thanks to the amazing artists who shared my view of the Mediterranean while I wrote a book about the Mississippi through the Bread Loaf Bakeless Camargo Residency Fellowship. Cassis is always calling.

Thanks to my colleagues at American University in Washington, D.C., and champagne toasts to all D.C. Women Writers.

Light and love to my dear students who have taught me more than I could ever teach them. I adore you.

My agent, Claire Anderson-Wheeler, believed in this voice before it was really a book. My editor, Christina Boys, nodded along with her Twain bobblehead and took a chance on me. Thank you to the wonderful Center Street/Hachette Book Group team for pretending I was never high maintenance.

I'm grateful for my family, especially my parents and parents in-law, who left me alone in my rooms and managed my life with love and grace while I was writing. Thank you to my brothers, my sister-in-law, and their spouses and all my nieces and nephews for putting up with me.

To the sunshine of my life, Isabelle and Piper. You matter more to me than words, and that's saying a lot.

Mostly to Joe, for falling for a small-town girl with big plans. Thank you for taking the seat beside me on this roller-coaster ride, white knuckles and all.

Notes

This book is a nod and a nudge to so much of Mark Twain's work. *Flood* is a work of fiction, but I am in debt to many sources and Twainiacs along my writing path.

Thanks to Dr. Cindy Lovell, executive director of the Mark Twain House & Museum in Hartford, Connecticut, for her generous feedback and friendship. I'm also grateful for the work of Henry Sweets, executive director of the Mark Twain Boyhood Home & Museum; and Faye Dant, executive director of Jim's Journey: The Huck Finn Freedom Center.

The following are books I consulted and learned from and websites of places I visited and can't wait to return to:

Clemens, Samuel L. Edited by Michael Kiskis. *Mark Twain's Own Autobiography: The Chapters from the 'North American Review.'* Madison: University of Wisconsin Press, 1990.

Fishkin, Shelley Fisher. *Was Huck Black? Mark Twain and African American Voices.* New York: Oxford University Press, 1995.

Hoffman, Andrew. *Inventing Mark Twain: The Lives of Samuel Langhorne Clemens.* New York: William Morrow, 1997.

Kaplan, Fred. *The Singular Mark Twain: A Biography*. New York: Doubleday, 2003.

Kaplan, Justin. *Mr. Clemens and Mark Twain: A Biography*. New York: Simon & Schuster, 1966.

Loving, Jerome. *Mark Twain: The Adventures of Samuel L. Clemens*. Berkeley: University of California Press, 2010.

Meltzer, Milton. *Mark Twain Himself: A Pictorial Biography*. New York: Wings Books, 1960.

Morris, Roy, Jr. *Lighting Out for the Territory: How Samuel Clemens Headed West and Became Mark Twain*. New York: Simon & Schuster, 2010.

Neider, Charles, editor. *The Autobiography of Mark Twain*. New York: Harper Perennial Modern Classics, 2000.

Powers, Ron. *Mark Twain: A Life*. New York: Free Press, 2005.

———. *White Town Drowsing*. Boston: Atlantic Monthly Press, 1986.

Shelden, Michael: *Mark Twain, Man in White: The Grand Adventure of His Final Years*. New York: Random House, 2010.

Steinbrink, Jeffrey. *Getting to Be Mark Twain*. Berkeley: University of California Press, 1991.

Varble, Rachel M. *Jane Clemens: The Story of Mark Twain's Mother*. New York: Doubleday, 1964.

Willis, Resa. *Mark & Livy: The Love Story of Mark Twain and the Woman Who Almost Tamed Him*. New York: Atheneum, 1992.

Center for Mark Twain Studies, Elmira College. http://www.elmira.edu/academics/programs/Center_Twain/index.html.

Jim's Journey, the Huck Finn Freedom Center, Hannibal, MO. http://www.jimsjourney.org.

Mark Twain Birthplace, Florida, MO. https://mostateparks .com/park/mark-twain-birthplace-state-historic-site.

Mark Twain Boyhood Home & Museum, Hannibal, MO. http://www.marktwainmuseum.org.

Mark Twain House & Museum, Hartford, CT. https://www .marktwainhouse.org/index.php.

Mark Twain Papers & Project. University of California, Berkeley. http://www.lib.berkeley.edu/libraries/bancroft-library /mark-twain-papers.

Reading Group Guide

1. Why is it so hard for Laura to return to Hannibal? Can you ever really go home again?

2. What role does Ms. B, Laura's high school teacher and the writer of the Tom & Becky manual, play in the larger narrative? Why is she important to Laura's journey?

3. What does *Flood* illustrate about the issue of class in rural America?

4. How does Samuel Clemens's leaving Hannibal parallel Laura's story? How does distance shift perspective?

5. How did you react to the reunion with Sammy?

6. Does the Tom & Becky Program represent opportunity for the young residents of Hannibal or does it reinforce socio-economic, class, and racial barriers?

7. Why is Mark Twain's literature and social criticism still relevant?

8. Have you ever had an *"All right then, I'll go to hell!"* Huckleberry Finn moment that was morally right but socially wrong? Do you agree or disagree with Laura's final decision?

Copyright © 2018 by Hachette Book Group, Inc.

About the Author

Melissa Scholes Young was born and raised in Hannibal, Missouri, and proudly claims it as her hometown. Her writing has appeared in the *Atlantic*, *Washington Post*, *Narrative*, *Ploughshares*, and *Poets & Writers*. She's a Contributing Editor for *Fiction Writers Review* and a Bread Loaf Bakeless Camargo Fellow. She teaches at American University in Washington, D.C., and lives in Maryland with her family and a chocolate Labrador named Huckleberry Finn. *Flood* is her first novel. You can visit her at www.melissascholesyoung.com.